The PIG SCROLLS

About the author:

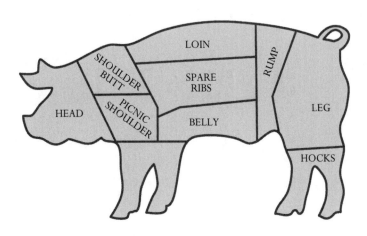

About the translator:

Working on *The Pig Scrolls* allowed Paul Shipton to pursue his interests in ancient mythology, even more ancient jokes, and crispy bacon.

Other books by Paul Shipton

BUG MULDOON: THE GARDEN OF FEAR
THE MIGHTY SKINK

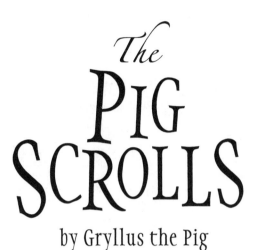

The PIG SCROLLS

by Gryllus the Pig

PAUL SHIPTON

CANDLEWICK PRESS
CAMBRIDGE, MASSACHUSETTS

Copyright © 2004 by Paul Shipton

First U.S. paperback edition 2007

The Library of Congress has cataloged the hardcover edition as follows:
Shipton, Paul, date.
The Pig Scrolls / by Gryllus the Pig ; [as translated by] Paul Shipton. — 1st U.S. ed.
p.   cm.
Includes glossary.
Summary: A translation of an ancient Greek manuscript written by Gryllus,
a talking pig who was once a man, which describes the many adventures
that he and his companions—a junior prophetess named Sibyl and
a bumbling goatherd—experience while traveling to Delphi
to try to prevent the universe from coming to an end.
ISBN 978-0-7636-2702-7 (hardcover)
[1. Pigs—Fiction. 2. Mythology, Greek—Fiction. 3. Courage—Fiction.
4. Humorous stories—Fiction.]   I. Title.
PZ7.S55765Pig 2005
[Fic]—dc22   2005050177

ISBN 978-0-7636-3302-8 (paperback)

2 4 6 8 10 9 7 5 3 1

Printed in the United States of America

This book was typeset in Perpetua.

Candlewick Press
2067 Massachusetts Avenue
Cambridge, Massachusetts 02140

visit us at www.candlewick.com

For Megan and Emma

INVOCATION

Tell us, O Muse, of the fall of Troy
And the one named Gryllus, a crafty boy.
For many years he did not see home —
I'll tell you more in this er . . . epic poem.
Dee dum, dee dum, dee dum, di DAH
Er . . . something, something . . . very far.
Um . . .

Hello, Calliope, silver-tongued Muse of Epic Poetry? Gryllus calling. Are you there or what? Because if I'm going to tell this whole thing in verse, I'm going to need a bit of help.

Hello-oo?

. . .

. . .

Oh, stuff this for a game of Homeric heroes. I'm just going to rattle off what happened—no frills and no fancy poetic meter. And if the Muses don't like it, they can lump it.

All right, then—settle down and clean out your earholes. . . .

BOOK I

A mighty hero is brought down in the woods by a bunch of nitwits.

I woke up nice and slow, just checking off the many chores that *weren't* on the cards for me this fine, sunny day. So much time, so little to do.

"You know how to live high on the hog, Gryllus, my old son," I grunted to myself. Did even the immortal gods of Olympus have it sweeter? Well yes, probably, but things weren't half bad for me either.

I was out in the woods. You know, trees and bushes and grass and all that. Birds chirping merrily all over the place—just chirp-chirp-chirping from dawn onward, without a single thought in their little featherbrains that other occupants of the woods might actually want to sleep in. No, every day they're up and about, just chirping and chirping and ch—

Hold on! There *were* no birds chirping today. The woods were silent.

Some folks might have bothered trying to work out why. Me, I just enjoyed the chirp-free peace and quiet while I had a leisurely breakfast of acorns and roots—the woodland platter.

The only other creature I spotted was a little, fluffy-tailed squirrel, gripping an acorn in its tiny front paws.

That squirrel had life figured out, I can tell you. There it was, managing just fine without a name or a job or an informed opinion on why the sun is driven around the earth. It had never fretted about money or time or new trends in rodent fashion. It never had to sort through the thoughts in its brain, all squabbling to be the one to reach its mouth. Right then, I bet only one thought was rattling around its little squirrel skull: "Nuts!"

That was all. NUTS! It was beautiful in its simplicity.

Yes, well, it was time old nutbrain received a lesson in Natural Law. I charged forward and burst through the thicket, aiming myself at the stash of nuts with a fearsome grunt. The squirrel spiraled up the nearest tree and chittered angrily from the lower branches.

It was only then that a gasp let me know someone else was there. It was a teenage lad—the first person I'd seen in ages—over on the other side of the clearing. Puzzlement crossed the big lad's face, like a cloud across the moon on a night when the moon is looking especially puzzled.

He stepped forward and called, "Soooo-ey!" It was the sort of call they do out on the old farmstead to herd the pigs. A bit rude, you reckon? Well, yes, but technically he was on the right track. I *am* something of a pig. It's not just that I stink to high Olympus or that when I eat I make noises such as might be heard in the general vicinity of an ox's rear end. No, I would say the snout, hooves, and little pink curly tail also have something to do with my overall porcine quality.

I *am* a pig, okay? A wallow-in-the-mud, stick-your-snout-in-the-trough, real-life, big fat pig.

Oinky oink oink.

But there are pigs and then there are *pigs*. See, I'm clearly not a wild boar of the kind most sensible folks would prefer not to encounter out here in the woods. The boy's thoughts were as obvious as if they had been written across his forehead (assuming you could read, which I couldn't) and they were, *What's a farm pig like this doing out in the woods?*

"Here piggy-pig! Sooo-ey!" the lad continued. It left something to be desired as introductions go.

In an attempt to raise the tone, I burped and said, "What you looking at, sonny boy?"

Obviously, talking pigs were in short supply in these parts of rural Thessaly. The kid's eyes went as wide and round as two Athenian saucers (the extrawide and round kind). His lips flapped but produced only an astonished squawk.

"Go on," I said. "Beat it." Then I went back to my grub.

This lad wasn't the brightest—clearly several Spartans short of the full three hundred—but I'll say this for him. He took my advice and ran away without even a fare-thee-well. *What has become of the youth of today?* I thought sadly as I gobbled some more acorns.

Still, this little social encounter had broken up the interlude between my morning snack and my late-morning snooze nicely. I didn't think anything more about it . . . until I heard the shouting and the pounding of feet through the forest.

Something about the noise reminded me of how my crewmates used to carry on, back when I was one of you lot (which is to say, human). It wasn't a pleasant memory.

They were always charging all over the place and shouting and waving spears and stuff. That sort of thing can give you a tense, nervous headache.

Suddenly four or five men crashed into the clearing. They were dressed up in rugged outdoor gear and, yes, they were all carrying spears. There was lots of gruff shouting. The bearded man at the front of the hunting party pointed his spear in my direction and yelled, "There it be!"

Under other circumstances I would have shot him down with one of my more sarcastic comments. But the only thing that sprang to mind on this occasion was *EEEK!*, and this didn't quite have the cutting razor edge I was after.

So I turned and ran.

You must have seen a thoroughbred horse gallop—the way all those muscles and sinews and whatnot work together in perfect harmony? Yes, well, I'm not a racehorse. I'm a pig, and I took off through those woods like a barrel on four legs. Still, I was a *fast* barrel on legs. I scuttled as fast as my hooves could take me, crashing heroically through several bushes, as if it didn't hurt one bit (though in fact I picked up a couple of scratches and a nasty rash on my haunches from a patch of nettles).

When the hunters' shouts were far enough behind me, I doubled back and veered off the path. Then I wedged myself deep into a bush of something or other. I lay as still as I could to prevent the telltale rustle of leaves.

Cunning, eh?

A couple of minutes later I could see the hunters on the path. They were still doing a lot of yelling as they swept

4

right on past my ingenious hiding place. *Dumb hicks!* I thought triumphantly. *Half-wits! Quarter-wits!* (I would have gone on but, surprisingly enough, fractions aren't one of my strong points.) With a smirk, I thought, *Guess you picked the wrong pig to tangle with today, didn't you, my friends? Just strike up another victory for brains over brawn.*

But then brawn picked itself up off the mat and made an unexpected comeback. It did so in the form of a spearhead, which was suddenly pressing into the back of my neck.

"That kid brother o' mine reckons you speaks the Greek good as us, pig." On present evidence, I spoke "the Greek" considerably better, but before I had a chance to point this out, the man went on: "Betwixt you and me, he ain't the brightest button on the tunic. But . . . if you does speak and you wants to save that pigskin o' yours, speak now, eh." I couldn't help noticing that this voice lacked the warmth that is the hallmark of most successful first meetings. I knew it belonged to the man with the beard. He must have detached himself from the rest of the group and sneakily tiptoed up behind me in a completely unsporting, dirty, low-down manner.

The spear pressed harder, and I found my tongue. "Ow!" I said.

This wasn't good enough. "I says, speak, pig!" Beardy demanded. *Prod! Prod!* went the spear in the quietly persuasive way of all pointy weaponry.

"Okay, okay, keep your undies on. I'm THINKING, aren't I?"

The man gasped and said a quick prayer to Artemis,

Goddess of the Hunt. (Now, why wasn't I surprised that he didn't offer up a prayer to Athena, Goddess of Wisdom? I'd hazard a guess that she didn't have too many followers out in this part of the country.)

The other hunters had stomped up to us. They looked every bit as amazed as their hairy-faced chum. The lad I'd seen first was busy gulping "I told you it were a talker" to anyone who would listen.

My feelings toward the slope-shouldered lad weren't the warmest, but perhaps right now wasn't the ideal time to share this. First I had to talk myself out of this little fix.

No problem. When you've been through the things I've been through, dealing with a few simple-minded hunting folk is a cinch. I slowly unleashed my most winning smile on the spear-carrying nitwits. The dazzle of that smile had never failed me, as man or pig.

"So, lads," I began warmly, "nice day for it."

As if we were all old buddies, see? Of course, old buddies like us *often* have differences of opinion. For example, in *my* opinion, it was a nice day for strolling through the woods, having a relaxed chitchat about this and that, and then putting your head down for a quick snooze before lunch. Whereas, in *their* opinion, it was a nice day for grabbing the miraculous talking pig, flipping it onto its back, tying both pairs of legs to a long pole, and carrying it upside down out of the woods.

Trouble is, there were more of them and they all had spears, so I was outvoted. It can be a real pain, this newfangled democracy thing, can't it?

6

BOOK II

A noble hero is treated no better than a sack of spuds.

It took ages to get out of those woods. The hunters took turns carrying the pole on their shoulders, two at a time. There was lots of unnecessary (and frankly hurtful) grumbling about how much I weighed. After several hours and a good deal of chafing on my hocks, the woods began to thin out. Finally we passed a small building—well, more of a shack, really. It was followed by a few other buildings, any of which would have been proud of the name *hovel*.

On Beardy's order, I was set on the ground and my feet cut free. Now that I was right side up, I could see a cluster of other ramshackle buildings ahead of us. We were on the outskirts of a small town.

I shook out my legs one by one. "Well, thank you for a delightful journey," I said. "Next time, why don't I just drag myself along on my belly through a briar patch for five hours? It'd be more fun, I can assure you."

"What do it say?" asked Beardy's younger brother with a look of intense confusion.

"Abomniation of nature like this can't say nothin' what makes sense," answered Beardy.

He tied a length of rope into a loop and tightened it around my neck. Then he knelt down and held something to my throat. It turned out to be a rather well-sharpened dagger.

Beardy's eyes met mine. They were hunter's eyes—which is to say steady, piercing, and altogether a bit too close to each other. "Listen to I, pig, and listen right careful," he murmured. "If folk here learns you do speak the Greek, they'll have you in that temple and be lookin' at them entrails o' yours quicker'n you can say Jack Robinios . . . and we won't get us a single obol* for our troubles, neither." He leaned in even closer. "Today be market day. If you wants to live and see sundown, you'll be keepin' that big snout of yours shut. Only chance you've got is if folks don't realize they's seein' an abomniation of nature like what you are."

"I think the word you're looking for is *abomination*," I offered.

Beardy grimaced. "See, that's just the kind o' yack what I AIN'T looking for. Be you clear on that, pig?"

I sighed heavily. "I've been meaning to mention: it really ought to be '*Are* you clear on that?' I know we have a duty to preserve regional accents, et cetera. But what if you decide on a change of profession? With your language skills, you won't just waltz into any old job, you know. You'll—"

The dagger pressed closer, so close that it would soon be on the wrong side of my skin, which is to say the *inside*.

*Obol: iron coin used in much of Ancient Greece. First written usage in Hesiod's *Works and Days*: "An obol for your thoughts?" Several obols made a drachma.

"Yes, I be perfectly clear on that," I squeaked.

Beardy hopped up and gave the rope a tug. Preferring not to be throttled, I followed at a steady trot, and we all headed into town.

As far as I could tell, it was a dinky market town, typical of this corner of the country—that is, a dilapidated dump populated by backwoods bumpkins. The whole place was little more than one square, with just a few dirt roads running away from it.

The hunters led me past a small, ragged crowd of (small, ragged) people who jostled outside the doors of a little temple. I couldn't see who it was dedicated to—probably the king of Olympus, Zeus himself.

It didn't really matter, because the doors were barred. A skittish-looking priest was trying to calm the crowd.

"We'll be reopening soon," he called nervously. "No, no, the gods aren't angry. They're just . . . they're taking a bit of a break! Probably off on vacation. . . ."

I would have stuck around to see more, but Beardy tugged me into the square. It was agora day—that's market day to you. On one side of the square, a handful of shoppers wandered from stall to stall, scrutinizing the pathetic displays of sad and shriveled produce. Clearly starved for entertainment, a knot of children searched for amusingly shaped vegetables. I didn't want to go—call me agoraphobic—but I had no choice.

In the middle of the square, a dozen or so yokels lurked around a rickety enclosure in which a bored-looking cow flicked its tail idly. It was a livestock auction. A man holding a rooster to his chest waited his turn outside the enclosure.

Beardy pulled me along with a final hiss of "Remember, 'bomniation. I'll stick you good an' proper if you speaks a word." Beardy led me to the weasely man who was running things. The auctioneer appeared to have slicked his hair back with half a bottle of olive oil in a doomed attempt at big-city style. He gave me a look that was as beady as a hungry bird spotting a beetle with a limp.

"What have we got here?" he murmured with a thoughtful rub of his underdeveloped chin.

A grisly thought slipped into my mind as his eyes took a walk over me. *I am a pig, true, but I am also a slab of bacon-to-be. Or ham, or chops, or pork sausages, or gammon steaks with one of those pineapple rings and an unnaturally red cherry on top.*

I am a walking lump of potential pork-based foodstuffs.

That may be, but the auctioneer didn't look impressed. "Well, it's got a big potbelly, I'll grant you," he told the hunters. "But there isn't much muscle on the hams or the hocks. Wouldn't get much lean meat off this'un, lads."

He walked all the way around me, though he didn't linger long at the back end. Up at the front again, he gripped my snout and squeezed to have a good look at the old choppers. He shook his head in disapproval. (The nerve of it! It's not as if you can brush three times a day and floss out in the wild. Anyway, *his* teeth weren't exactly gleaming like the pearly choppers of Adonis.)

The auctioneer gave a reverse whistle in an attempted display of deep thought. "Well, he's not the finest specimen

I've laid eyes on, lads," he told the hunters. "He's fat enough, but there's still the look of the runt about him. Tell you what . . . times are as hard as *Euclidean Geometry Made Easy,* but I'll see what I can do. If we manage to sell it, I'll give you . . . thirty percent?"

The bearded hunter's chin jutted out like yet another edged weapon. "Eighty per-sint," he snarled.

"Okay, okay, we'll split the difference," said the auctioneer. "Forty percent."

Beardy smirked. His fellow hunters slapped him vigorously on the back, in admiration of his negotiating skills. They prodded me into the enclosure and swung the gate shut.

"What am I bid for this . . . er . . . fine figure of a hog?" called the auctioneer.

I looked around as several sets of un-wowed eyes fell on me.

"I'll give you three eggs and a pair of socks," called out a stocky farm woman with a laugh. She bent down to pull a sock off one of her boatlike feet.

Thankfully, the auctioneer responded quickly: "Bartering day is Wednesday, madam," he said. "Cash offers only today, ladies and gents."

The woman's foot was once again sheathed, and the universe breathed a cosmic sigh of relief.

"Do I hear fifty drachmas?" called the auctioneer.

The rabble fell silent again. A mix of feelings swirled in my brain like a badly made moussaka. I was not hugely enjoying this whole experience. I mean, let's get one thing straight—I AM NOT A PIECE OF MEAT to be paraded and sold off like this. I AM NOT AN ANIMAL. Well, okay, I *am* an animal, if you want to split bristles, but in addition I am a thinking, feeling creature with firm opinions on a broad range of topics such as world peace and vegetarianism. (For the record, I'm *for* both of them, especially the vegetarianism.)

But then again, I *was* a trifle put out that no bids came in. After all, wasn't I a splendidly fine, fat pig? Why, then, wasn't anyone bidding for me? I took a deep breath and held it, trying to look as boarish as I could.

"Come on," the auctioneer cajoled. "Can't you hear it now—the sizzle of bacon in the pan?"

One man at the fence struck me as different from the rest of the onlookers, who all looked (and smelled) fresh from the farm. This bloke seemed less of your country type. He was a solid sort with lamb-chop sideburns on his big red face. Next to him was a pale-faced boy of about thirteen or fourteen. They looked as different as fish and feta.

Slowly the man raised one fist.

"Fifty drachmas to the man with the unfortunate sideburns," declared the auctioneer. "Do I hear fifty-five? . . . Pig like this would make a perfect sacrifice to your favorite god, and there'd still be some left over for pork scratchings and a bacon sandwich. . . . Anyone? Fifty-three?" He shook his head sadly. "Fifty drachmas it is, then. Going once . . ."

A flap of black in the distance caught my attention. Someone had detached himself from the crowd outside the temple across the square. He was wearing long black robes with one of those hoods that hides pretty much all of your face. It wasn't the kind of outfit that lends itself to the hundred-yard dash, but that didn't stop this guy. He had hitched up his robes and was charging over in a highly undignified manner.

"Going twice . . ."

Flapping along like a flightless crow, the mysterious figure was kicking up a trail of dust across the market square. The pack of kids scattered out of the way.

"Go—"

"Two hundred drachmas!" shouted the hooded figure in a high, breathless voice. A pale hand held aloft a leather bag that was emitting the sweetest sound known to mankind— the merry jingle of loads of cash. The red-faced man's mouth fell open in shock. It was clear that he couldn't match this bid.

Knowing when he was on to a good thing, the auctioneer didn't waste time with any of that "Going, going, gone" business this time. "Sold!" he yelled. "Sold to the . . . er . . . mysterious gentleman in the cowl."

The hooded figure went to pay the auctioneer, and the hunters waited impatiently for their cut of the takings. Meanwhile, a couple of the market slaves began driving me out of the pen by the unpleasant method of poking sharp sticks into my flanks. The language they spoke suggested that they were Trojans, no doubt taken prisoner during the lengthy siege of that city.

I'd never really given much thought to slavery before. It

was always just a fact of life, like the sun rising in the east and lint collecting in your belly button. But it's funny when you think about it—I mean, there you are, living free, quite possibly a pillar of the community in your barbarian city-state. And then you go and get captured in battle. Next thing you know, you're in a far-off land, toiling as someone's slave, and you don't even count as a human being anymore. All a bit weird, frankly.

It's only when you spend a while on the outside of a species that you come to see how odd it can be. Of course, there were slaves everywhere, and yet, and yet . . . I felt a Very Important Thought rise in my mind like a suspicious air bubble in a mud bath. Wasn't there a better, fairer way? I mean, what if humans simply realized that they were all just the sa—

"WAAARGH!"

The rope yanked on my neck and the Very Important Thought popped and was lost to the ether, as I was forced to concentrate on more immediate concerns (like, for example, making sure I could still breathe).

The person on the other end of the rope was the hooded figure. The face remained dramatically hidden in shadow.

"Come on, pig," said a steely voice from beneath the hood—a female voice.

As we moved away from the enclosure, I saw the auctioneer counting out coins for the hunting party.

"Okay, gentlemen, forty percent of two hundred is . . . thirty drachmas." He doled out the coins. "There you go. Don't spend it all in the first shop."

The hunters were grinning away at the money in a way that suggested they weren't planning on investing it wisely for their retirement. Only the mountainous lad who'd first encountered me watched as I was led away.

When we were out of earshot, the hooded figure on the other end of the rope leaned over and hissed something else—something that set my heart pounding like a hyperactive Cyclops playing the bongos.

"You're the one, aren't you? You're the talking pig."

BOOK III

The Fates show mercy to a weary traveler on the rocky road of life.

You know those three-headed monsters you hear about? Ever wondered what they do when one head wants to find a victim for supper, one head wants to rampage through the countryside terrorizing the locals, and one head just wants to stay in and flick through a magazine?

Well, that's how torn I felt. On one hand I could just make a run for it. I'd probably be able to pull the rope free of this woman's hands—but then what? How long before I got caught and dragged back to the agora? My second option was, I could simply come clean with her and see what she wanted.

And yet . . . something about this hooded figure set the bristles on the back of my neck on end. I went with option three—playing dumb. I gave a little piggy grunt and ran my snout along the ground as if looking for something yummy.

We turned off the agora square into an alley. With no one around now, my new owner threw back the black hood. She was younger than I'd expected—no more than fifteen or sixteen. Freckles dotted her snub nose. Her face looked tired, but it had a determined set to it.

"There's no need for the pig act," she said. "You're the talking pig, all right. Admit it." The girl looked at me levelly. "My name's Sibyl and you're . . . ?" The sentence dangled. "You may as well save us both some time and get talking."

I let out a heavy sigh. "Maybe it's some *other* talking pig you're looking for," I said at last. "It doesn't pay to jump to conclusions."

Not for the first time, I marveled at how the Fates had turned the thread of my life into a tangle that made the Gordian Knot look like the bow on a child's shoelace. I mean, just about this time of day I ought to be settling into a nice leisurely mud bath.

A relieved grin flashed across the girl's face. "I knew it! I've been on your trail for weeks, you know."

I made a point of not asking why. In my experience, mysterious hooded strangers who have spent weeks searching for you don't come bearing good news.

We turned onto a small, muddy street. Sibyl fell silent until a couple of passersby had passed . . . er, by.

"This is where I'm staying," she said. We had stopped outside another grotty little hovel.

"'Mrs. Skaleris's Bed and Breakfast Emporium'," Sibyl read aloud, and she pointed apologetically to a handwritten sign on the gate.

"Why don't you just read it out?" I said.

The girl raised an eyebrow and read the sign to me:

NO GOATS.
NO PIGS.
NO SANDALS,
NO SERVICE.

"I don't think they had intelligent, talking pigs in mind," she added, "but Mrs. Skaleris is a bit of a stickler for the rules."

She led me down a narrow path along the side of the house. Around the back was a tatty little shed lined with straw. The front was open, and it had a rail to tie animals to. There was a trough of water that provided the habitat for a thriving ecosystem of pond life.

"I think this place is for donkeys," explained Sibyl, "but you can sleep here tonight. We've got a long way to go tomorrow."

As she spoke, she busied herself about the shed, trying to fluff up the straw and generally spruce the place up.

"First I really ought to give you some idea of what this is all about," Sibyl was saying. "It's the least I can do." She hesitated. "It's a bit hard to explain . . . but here goes."

Her voice took on a more official tone.

"I have been sent to find you by the great god Apollo."

Uh-oh. This sounded like a turn for the worse. Over the years I had developed my own belief system concerning the gods. It came down to this: keep your head down, don't do anything to offend the immortals on high, and if a booming voice from behind a cloud addresses you, run like your butt's on fire.

"Ah," I answered. (You're always better off humoring zealots like this.) "So . . . the gods talk to you a lot then, do they?"

"Only Apollo," she said with a curt shake of the head. "I work at Delphi, you see."

I'd heard about Delphi, of course. Apollo's temple there housed the biggest oracle in all of civilization. A lot of day-trippers visited from Athens, but supplicants traveled there from all over Greece, looking for a glimpse into the future. If the god looked upon their request kindly, he sent a message to them via the pythia—the priestess who ran the whole show.

"So are *you* the pythia?" I asked.

"Not exactly." The girl's lips tightened. "I'm the Junior Assistant Assistant Pythia-in-Training," she said stiffly. "But that's not the point. The point is that Apollo sent me to find you."

"Er . . . why?"

I kept my voice good and calm, just as you're supposed to when dealing with potentially dangerous nutcases, especially ones who are holding the in-charge end of a rope while the business end is tied around your neck in a slipknot.

Sibyl glanced around for eavesdroppers. "A few weeks ago, the Delphic oracle stopped working. Apollo just fell silent . . . which isn't like him, I can tell you. We tried to find out what the problem was, but all our offerings were ignored."

I nodded in what I hoped was a sympathetic way.

"That's not all," she continued. "The word from other temples is that *all* the gods have fallen silent. You saw what was going on at the temple of Zeus even out here, didn't you? It's the same story everywhere. In the central plains they've had the worst wheat crop anyone can remember, and the nighttime constellations are all messed up, too. I'm sure you've noticed that the birds are migrating way too early."

I gave a noncommittal nod (although, amazingly enough, I count neither astronomy nor zoology among my strong points).

The girl's eyes were big, serious. "You know those hunters who brought you in?" I nodded slowly. "You were the first thing they'd caught in ages. Something has spooked the wild animals, or worse than spooked. . . . There've been sightings of monsters on the loose."

"Monsters, eh?" I said.

"Oh, yeah. . . . Something bad is going on," she continued. "Something terrible."

"Fascinating," I murmured. "Do go on."

The girl broke into a shy smile. "Listen, I know this all sounds unbelievable. . . ."

"Not at all," I reassured her in a voice as smooth as butter, or maybe silk, or perhaps butter wearing a silk jacket. "Don't be so hard on yourself."

"You see, Apollo got a message to me in a dream. He said that I had to find you, the talking pig. He said that this was the only way we'd be able to do it."

"Do what?" I asked (foolishly).

Sibyl had the good grace to throw in an embarrassed shrug. "Save the world, I suppose."

"I see."

The fixed grin on my snout was starting to ache, but my mind was racing as fast as winged Hermes. The way I saw it, there were only two possible explanations. Number one: the poor misguided child had somehow convinced herself that one of the gods was communicating with her. If so, I had to play this very carefully, as you could never tell what a nervy type like that might do next.

Explanation number two was even less appealing: the kid's story was true, and for some reason the god Apollo really *had* ordered her to come and find me. After all, the gods didn't have any qualms about mucking about in mortals' lives. I also knew that, when it came to the Olympians, it didn't pay to go looking for Reason or Justice or any other fancy-schmancy word beginning with a capital letter. The gods just did whatever popped into their immortal skulls. And if you kicked up a fuss, you just might find yourself turned into a small shrub or perhaps chained to a rock with one of your internal organs on the Menu of the Day for passing eagles.

But what would a god want with me? One thing's for sure—this porker didn't want to stick around and find out.

Sibyl furrowed her brow. "You mean . . . you believe me?" she asked incredulously.

"Why wouldn't I believe you? Of course I believe you," I purred.

"I . . . I just never thought it would be this easy," she said. "You know, persuading you to help. . . . I've been so worried that you'd think I was spouting a load of old hogwash, if you'll pardon the expression."

I shook my head in amused sympathy. But here's the thing . . . I was acting! Please, please, no applause. It was all part of the brilliant master plan that had landed in my brain like a chariot of the gods.

And now it was time to make my move.

"It sounds as if we've got a lot to do," I said with appropriate resolve. "I must admit, though, I *am* getting a bit on the hungry side. Have you got any grub in your room?"

"Oh, yes, of course. Sorry, I should have thought."

Now that I was apparently going along with her crackpot scheme, Sibyl seemed as relieved as Atlas just after he'd put the heavens down and snuck out for a cappucino with some of those little chocolate sprinkles on top. She started toward the B&B.

"One more thing," I said quickly. "You couldn't just loosen this rope around my neck first, could you? Seeing as

2 1

how it's for show only? I do have very sensitive skin, and it's giving me a bit of a rash."

"Of course." Sibyl smiled, and she began to tug at the knot. "There, how's that?" she asked.

I rolled my neck experimentally. "Much better."

"Great! Well, I'll be back in a few minutes, okay?"

"You said it."

She hesitated. "Have you got something in your eye?"

"No, I was winking. It's a friendly gesture where I come from."

Sibyl considered this for a moment. "Right . . . Well, see you in a sec, then."

She scurried inside, where I heard muffled voices ("I hope you aren't planning on bringing that pig inside; I've just done the floors." "Don't worry, Mrs. S.").

There was no time to spare. I tugged my head backward. The loop around my neck was much looser, but it still wasn't easy getting my head free. (The head of the pig is a wonderful design, with its splendid big ears, but the designer clearly hadn't taken a scenario like this into account.)

I gave a final yank, and I was free. Now all I had to do was get the Hades out of this place.

I charged back along the narrow passage to the front of Mrs. S.'s shanty-style B&B. I knew I couldn't turn back toward the agora square. But would I have time to make it out of town and back to the safety of the woods?

Then I saw it . . . my one-way ticket to freedom. Parked

on the dirt road ahead was an empty covered wagon, already harnessed to two horses. OK, the horses weren't the finest stallions going, but they could be encouraged to work up some speed by a master horseman such as I (OK, a master horsepig). It was all a matter of showing them who was boss. I was going to leave this dump in grand style. The Fates must have been smiling on me!

I scrambled up onto the front seat and swept up the reins in my teeth. Then I tugged as hard as I could and shouted, "Yee-argh!"

One of the horses let out a bored whinny and rolled its marblelike eyes.

"Go on then! Giddy-up! . . . Yee-haw! Yar! Yar! Mush!"

The other horse lifted a lazy tail and dropped a load of grade-A rose fertilizer, which steamed nonchalantly in the late-afternoon sun.

"Go, you stupid nags! Get moving!"

Nothing. Not a glimmer of solidarity with a fellow beast of the fields.

"Please? . . . It'll be carrots all around at the other end."

No luck. Nothing would persuade them to budge. A volcano of panic erupted inside me like a nasty bout of indigestion.

So the Fates *weren't* smiling on me, after all. No, the three old hags were probably all sitting on the couch, having a good old cackle at my expense.

Suddenly I heard footsteps from within the B&B. Someone was coming! I had time only to swing around and dive back into the wagon. There were a few sacks of grain there and a couple of blankets. I began to burrow into the blankets, but I was too late to hide.

What could I tell Sibyl?

"Oh, I'm sorry," I began innocently. "I was just——"

But it wasn't Sibyl. It was the pale-faced boy, the one who had been accompanying the red-faced man (and his sideburns) at the auction.

"Never mind," I grunted. "Thought you were someone else."

The boy's mouth moved silently. He didn't appear to be coping well with the shock of encountering an urbane, talking pig.

I seized my opportunity. "Listen, you seem like a nice lad. You'll help a pig in distress, won't you?"

The boy's head trembled in a forward-and-backward motion that might have been a nod.

"Someone's looking for me," I said. "She's a bit touched by the gods, if you catch my meaning. Don't give me away!"

Another tremble and/or nod from the callow youth. I would have to take it for a yes. I finished off the job of hiding myself under the blanket.

Just in time, too. A moment later there came another voice—and not a very happy-sounding one.

"You there, boy," Sibyl called imperiously. The anger in her voice blazed like the lighthouse at Pharos. "Have you seen a pig come by this way? A big, fat, *shifty,* downright *untrustworthy* pig?"

I peeked out from under the blankets. The boy's shoulders gave a little shudder that might have been open to interpretation as a shrug.

"Probably ran off into the woods," Sibyl said in disgust.

I heard rapid footsteps fading as she raced off up the road.

"Listen, kid," I breathed with relief. "I'll just hitch a ride with you a short distance and then I'll be on my merry way."

The boy didn't say anything or even look around.

He was still sitting that way, all wide-eyed and amazed, when the bulky red-faced man joined him on the front seat. I slid farther back under the covers.

The man took the reins and started the horses with an outrageously easy "YAH!" The wagon rumbled forward. I figured I'd bide my time until we were well away from town, then I'd make my exit. There was no talk for a long time, but then the boy spoke, his voice high and quavery.

"Uncle Stavros? You know that pig at the auction . . . ?"

BOOK IV

As it turns out, the Fates know when to stick the boot in.

By the time we got out of the wagon, Night had spread her cloak of darkness across the land, or whatever it is she does with that cloak of hers.

Of course, I hadn't expected to still be in the wagon, but things hadn't gone as smoothly as I'd hoped.

A couple of preferable options might have been as follows:

(a) The mopey kid keeps his big mouth shut and, at the right moment, I slip silently out of the back of the wagon and saunter off to enjoy my well-deserved freedom in the woods.

Well, you'll be surprised to hear this, but slipping silently out of moving vehicles *isn't* one of my strong points, so option (a) wasn't the most realistic course of action. This left:

(b) Upon discovering my presence, the boy's uncle listens to my tale with a kindly ear and wishes me well . . . as I saunter off to enjoy my freedom in the woods.

Also not bad as options go. So it was particularly galling that what transpired was the rather less desirable option (c):

(c) After dealing surprisingly well with the shock of finding a stowaway who is not only a pig but also a *talking* pig, the man promptly closes and locks the backdoor of the wagon, thereby depriving yours truly of any opportunity to saunter off to the woods or, indeed, anywhere else.

I didn't exactly conceal my feelings about this turn of events, but the man remained unmoved.

"Excuse me! This would be a good spot to let me out."

"Heh, heh. Not far to go now, pig," the man said amiably.

"Here! I demand to be let out here."

"Heh, heh. Just a bit farther."

And so on. All the while, the treacherous boy stayed silent, though he cast plenty of popeyed glances back at me.

After a while I made the best of a bad lot and let the rocking of the wagon lull me to sleep. When I woke up, it was dark, and we had stopped.

Stavros slid the bolt free and folded down the back of the wagon.

"Down you get, pig," he said. He made sure I got a good look at the bow and quiver of arrows slung over his shoulder. "And don't get any daft ideas about running off now. I'm not a bad shot really."

They steered me inside a low building, into a room illuminated by a single candle. To my delicate nostrils the whole place stank of weeks' worth of fried grease.

"Stavros, is that you?" a woman's voice called from another room. It had the lilting, musical quality of a raven with a head wound.

"You'll not guess what we got at the agora, dear!" the large man replied eagerly. Meanwhile he slipped a length of rope around my neck (this was fast becoming a recurring theme of the day, and I was getting pig-sick of it). He tied the other end to the table.

The boy pressed himself against the wall like a shadow. He appeared to be settling back into his preferred habitat, in the manner of a newt returning to its pond after an extended desert holiday.

A small woman appeared at the door, her bony arms folded tight so that her elbows jutted out sharply.

"It's a pig," she declared coldly.

"It's a *special* pig," said Stavros, beaming.

The woman rolled her eyes in a way that suggested she'd had a lot of eye-rolling practice over the years.

"Have you forgotten the magic-bean fiasco already?" she demanded. "A whole month's earnings for a handful of baked beans!"

Stavros's smile froze halfway toward his mutton-chop sideburns. "But Gorgina, this is different. It's a *talking* pig, and I didn't pay a single obol for it!" He turned toward me. "Go on, say something."

I didn't give even the faintest oink.

"Brilliant!" snorted Gorgina. "Well, at least it's fat enough for the knife. We'll slaughter it in the morning and make pork pies in the afternoon."

Now, pies are just about my favorite things in the world. But to someone in my condition, they lose their charm when preceded by the word *pork*. I didn't want to end up sitting under a pastry crust, sharing plate space with a pickled onion!

"Wait!" I shouted. "I *can* speak . . . a bit."

If Gorgina was surprised, she hid it well. She scrutinized me with sharp-eyed suspicion.

"What god or goddess cursed you so?" she demanded.

"Ah, well, that's a good question. She wasn't a full-blown Olympian, but I suppose you'd have to say she was a deity of some kind, a minor one," I answered. "It was an enchantress, you see. Only I wouldn't say she gave me the power of speech, 'cause I already had that. See, I used to be human, but when we arrived at Circe's island—"

Gorgina's voice was as sharp as a brand-new steak knife. "Enough!" she cried. She pursed her lips. "Could work, could work," she muttered. There was a familiar look in her eyes. I could almost see the drachma signs in them: *ka-CHING, ka-CHING!*

"Over here, Stavros," she ordered. Like a trained bear, her husband shambled after her into the corner, where Gorgina began whispering urgently. The only words I caught were *money* and *lots*. There might have been an *of* in there, too.

Meanwhile the moon-eyed boy was staring right at me. He had apparently overcome his uncertainty and had made up his mind about yours truly. The candle's reflection shone in his dark eyes like an undying flame of hatred.

Gorgina had finished explaining her plan to Stavros. She turned now to the boy. "Prepare the cellar," she ordered.

The pale lad peeled himself from the wall. "Yes, Aunt G.," he whispered, and scurried out.

Gorgina's steely gaze locked onto me. "Here's the deal, pig . . ."

"My name's Gryllus, actually."

"Whatever. Now listen carefully . . ." She circled a hand in the air to indicate the building. "This is Big Stavros's Happy Kebab House."

My face did not light up in delighted recognition.

"Well, it wasn't always this grand," said Gorgina. "I've . . . *we've* worked very hard to create the highly successful establishment you see before you."

I gave the dump a quick once-over. It looked and smelled as inviting as a centaur's armpit, but admittedly I have never worked in the catering business.

Gorgina allowed herself a thin smile of satisfaction. "But we can't allow ourselves to get lazy and just coast along, not if we're going to expand to a whole chain of restaurants," she said. "And that's where YOU come in. . . ."

I'll spare you the details of how they got me out of the room and through the hatch to their grotty old cellar. They had to call their gangly nephew back, and it took all three of them to do it.

Before I knew it, I was landing on a pile of straw and the wooden hatch clattered shut overhead. It was dank, dark, and dirty down there.

"Hey! Wait a sec! I'm starving, I am!"

I hadn't had a bite to eat for hours, had I? That sort of starvation diet isn't good for a growing pig. The only answer to my plea was the clump of footsteps overhead.

Something with altogether too many legs scurried across the cellar floor.

"And there are bugs down here!" I yelled.

No answer.

I looked around. The cellar wasn't completely below ground level. At the top of one of the walls was one window, the bottom of which was level with the ground outside.

After a few minutes, the hatch overhead opened up again, and the boy was framed in the square of light. He was holding a bucket.

"Hey, now *this* is a series of unfortunate events, isn't it?"

I said conversationally. "Bet you didn't think today would end up like this, did you, eh?"

The boy's eyes were burning embers. (Well, of course they weren't *actual* burning embers, which wouldn't have been much use in the old optical department.)

He spoke at last, an accusation. "Why are you here?"

"Well now, strictly speaking, you'd have to talk to your aunt and uncle about that, m'boy. You see——"

"You're going to ruin everything!" he burst out. Then he emptied the bucket, and kitchen scraps rained onto me. The hatch door slammed shut with a sound I was already beginning to find distinctly irritating.

This sort of situation is almost enough to put a pig off its food, but my attitude is, *You have to keep your strength up.*

When I was done eating, I forced myself to assess the situation coolly and calmly. That's what a hero would do, and I'd spent quite some time with one of the biggest heroes going.

Okay, I thought (heroically) . . . so I was a prisoner in a third-rate kebab house. There was no way I could reach the window——and, even if I could, there was no way I'd ever squeeze my bulk through it. In fact, there was no obvious means of escape, but I didn't panic. I speedily formulated a plan and put it into immediate action.

Several minutes later, I gave up running around the tiny room squealing for help.

Obviously I'd need to come up with another plan. . . .

BOOK V

A mighty hero sings of the great deeds of yore.

I spent the next couple of days festering down in that stinking dump of a boghole of a fleapit of a crummy little cellar. Let's just say that it was no luxury apartment with an unparalleled view of the Acropolis. To make matters worse, I had to listen to the dreadful plinking of a lyre from upstairs, accompanied by a reedy, out-of-tune voice. The overall effect was that of a wailing cat with a persistent toothache.

It all added up to this—I *had* to get out of there. Yet, for some unfathomable reason, I couldn't come up with a single idea as to how to make my escape.

"What would Odysseus do in a fix like this?" I demanded of myself. I could picture my old captain's heroic, square-jawed mug well enough. But I couldn't for the life of me figure out what clever ruse the old smarty-pants would come up with in this particular situation.

In the end I gave up and tried to get some sleep. I began to take more and more naps, and I had little idea how long any of them lasted. Apart from the square of daylight or nighttime through the one little window, I began to measure the hours only by the rumbling of my belly.

Three times a day I heard the clump of footsteps from above. That was my sign to press myself against the far wall of the cellar to avoid having my meal land on my head. (Hey, I'm a fussy eater.)

For the first couple of days, the boy would glare at me as if a pig had mauled his favorite teddy when he was a toddler. Usually he slammed the hatch shut immediately, but on the third day I saw my chance to strike up a conversation. He was holding a lyre in his hand. So *he* was responsible for the endless caterwauling.

"Go on, then," I called quickly. "Give us a tune." The boy hesitated, giving me time to get in, "Do you know 'We All Live in a Yellow Trireme'? I can hum it for you."

He blinked, like a nocturnal creature that has woken up to find itself in the middle of a noontime soccer match. "I'm a poet," he said sullenly. "I don't do requests."

I smiled up with renewed confidence. "Ah, poetry . . . only the Muses' greatest gift to mankind. If I do say so myself, I've always been somewhat gifted in that regard." I cleared my throat and recited one of my finest:

"There once was a merry young Spartan.
But trouble he always was startin'.
The friends that he had
Said the smell was so bad
Because he just couldn't stop—"

"That's NOT the kind of poetry I meant!" the boy snapped. He filled his narrow chest with air. "I sing of the creation of the world and the Ocean that encircles it. I sing of the glorious pantheon of gods and goddesses. I sing of the mighty deeds of heroes and . . . stuff like that."

"Not much of a crowd pleaser, then, eh?"

Two tiny red spots appeared on the boy's cheeks. "Aunt Gorgina did agree to let me play and recite my epic poems in the restaurant, but the customers started complaining."

I grunted. "I take it you've never actually seen a god, have you, kid?"

Lank hair flopped over the boy's eyes as he shook his head no.

"Or a hero? Or a monster?"

The boy's voice dropped. "Once, someone in the village thought he'd seen a satyr . . . but it was just a goat on its hind legs reaching for a fig."

I wasn't surprised. The gods tend to show up only where the action is. Most people live their whole lives without spotting one. Me, I'd never seen one until I found myself enlisted in the Greek army during the Trojan War, and even then all I saw was just loads of flashing and rumbling in the distance. I might as well have been looking at a rainstorm. (I'd have seen more if I'd fought on the frontlines, I suppose, but I was engaged in important military work, peeling spuds in the kitchen tents.) Anyway, the far-off glimpses I'd seen of the gods were more than enough, thank you very much.

(Now, *monsters,* they were a different story. . . . Don't get me started on monsters. I'd been close enough to some monsters to count the hairs up their nostrils.)

"So let me get this straight," I said to the lad. "Your first encounter with anything supernatural is . . . me?"

Those angry red spots were threatening to take over the kid's entire head now. "Yes!" he exploded. "But I wanted it to be something special! I wanted to gaze upon the perfect loveliness of Aphrodite. I wanted to tremble in awe as Ares War-Bringer strode into battle. I wanted to glimpse fleet-footed Artemis in the hunt beneath a crescent moon. I . . . I didn't want to meet a big fat talking pig whose idea of fine arts is rude limericks!"

I nodded understandingly and dropped my voice to a confidential murmur. "Listen, kid, you're right—I'm nothing but a talking pig. So what am I doing here? What do your aunt and uncle want with me?"

"What I want right now, pig, is for you to eat your scraps and stop jabbering on!" barked a new voice. Its owner's head and shoulders joined the boy's in the hatch above.

"We were just having a chitchat," I explained.

"There'll be plenty of chance for that later," Gorgina said. As usual, her every utterance sounded like a command. "Tonight is your big night."

"Why? What's happening ton—"

But Gorgina was no longer listening. She addressed the boy. "Why don't you practice something a little more . . . upbeat for tonight? We're expecting a big crowd."

And with that she slammed the hatch shut. Her last comment hung in the air like an unwelcome smell. I sat there, thinking it over, like . . . like a statue of a pig thinking stuff over. The hours crawled slowly by like, er . . .

. . .

. . .

like crawly things, ones that don't go very fast. (I know, I know—my ability to compose vivid descriptions was fast abandoning me. I was *decomposing* in that cellar.)

The hatch didn't open again until early evening, when there seemed to be lots of noise from upstairs. Both Gorgina and Stavros were peering down at me.

"Wake up, pig," snarled Gorgina. "Your big moment has arrived."

Before I could ask for further details, Stavros lowered a ladder into the cellar.

"Up you come, me old porker," he said briskly.

It took a while—there's a good reason why you don't often see hogs whipping up and down ladders—but I made it. Once I was up, I waited for the rope to slip around my neck. It didn't come.

"Don't try anything daft, pig," Stavros said. "All the doors are locked, you know. And even if you did get away . . . I'm a pretty good shot with a bow, remember?"

Stavros led me to another room. It seemed much larger, though most of it was hidden by a heavy curtain. A steady babble of conversation told me that there were a lot of people on the other side.

There was another noise, too. A lyre was plinking away while a thin voice cracked on about Eos, the goddess of the dawn, with her rosy fingers and that sort of business. Nobody was listening and nobody noticed when the singer finished.

And then . . .

"Ladies and gentlemen," said a voice as melodious as a gargling crow—Gorgina. "Your attention, please."

36

I poked my snout through a gap in the curtain and looked out over the dining area of the restaurant (although that seems too grand a term—*slophole* might be more apt). About half the tables were occupied, by just the sort of crowd you might expect in a place like this—that is, a rabble of simple-minded bumpkins.

Over to one side of the room, the lank-haired boy was sitting with his lyre. He looked mortified and stared at his knobbly knees. Everyone else was looking at Gorgina, who was standing on a small wooden stage at the front of the room.

She announced, "It is our great pleasure here at Big Stavros's to introduce . . . for your astonishment and amusement . . . the civilized world's one and only . . . the incredible . . . the astounding . . . the truly freakish . . . TALKING PIG!"

She beckoned to me to emerge from the wings. It took a moment for the obol to drop. I was supposed to go out there!

So that was the plan! I was to be the live entertainment while the local hicks dined. I was Gorgina's latest money-making scheme to catapult her gross and greasy restaurant into the big time.

Stavros delivered an enormous whack to my haunches. "Quick as you like, pig," he boomed heartily.

Carried aloft on these winged words of inspiration, I trotted out onto the little wooden stage. Gorgina's eyes glittered greedily as she shuffled off. "Welcome to show biz, pig."

Alone onstage, I gazed at the silent audience. Their eyes would have bored holes in me if eyeballs went in for that sort of thing. The silence stretched so long it came close to snapping.

"Well?" bellowed a man with his arms folded in a gesture of not-being-very-impressed-ness. "Say something, then."

My first thought was to maintain a dignified silence. That'd show them! How would they like to explain the world's one and only talking pig that didn't utter a word? But then I considered the possible consequences. The food here wasn't exactly five star, but my captors had power over whether I ate or not. And then there was the thought of that quiver of arrows Stavros had mentioned . . .

I cleared my throat. "Er . . . Evening, all."

The crowd gasped as if they'd just had ice cubes thrown down the back of their tunics. Mouths dropped open in amazement—and, let me tell you, that is not a pretty sight at a back-of-beyond establishment like this, full of people whose mothers had never told them to swallow food before opening their mouths in total astonishment.

A man near the back began screaming hysterically. Luckily, his wife was there to calm him down by slapping him about the head and neck. There was a frantic babble as people muttered hasty prayers to their favorite gods.

I glanced offstage to where Gorgina was sporting a fixed little smile, no doubt sparked by the thought of loads of cold, hard cash.

The rednecks in the crowd were leaning forward now to

catch my next astonishing utterance. I savored the feeling of power before settling on a typically witty line.

"What are you all looking at? Have you never seen a pig before?"

And so began my career in the glittering world of entertainment.

BOOK VI

It turns out that reading is *useful, after all.*

So that's how life went for the next several days—most of my time down in the cellar, and then every evening (with a matinee on Saturdays) I was brought up to perform for the assembled masses while they shoveled food into their mouths.

Once I was onstage, I didn't have to do much. Just the fact that I, representative of another species, could talk was more than enough to satisfy the rabble. They weren't inter-ested in the hows or whys of my condition.

But what else could I talk about—the weather? The food? The price of olives these days? Just to have something to say, I found myself talking about the bad old days of the Trojan War. I mentioned Achilles and Hector and that bunch only briefly because I hadn't seen that much of the actual fighting. No, I concentrated on the *real* business of war, the behind-the-scenes stuff. We workers got on with the job of keeping a siege army fed, while the la-di-da heroes spent their time trying to brain each other. (They had it cushy, if you ask me. Try giving Achilles a potato peeler and see how he gets on with a mound of spuds, that's what I always said. We'd soon see how invincible he was if he had to make mashed spuds for three hundred hungry soldiers.)

I explained how, at long last, the Wooden Horse had brought the whole lengthy war to an end. The audience looked pretty impressed when I told them that this brilliant plan had been mine. (Well, strictly speaking, my idea had been to build a Wooden Cow. It was almost identical to Odysseus's Wooden Horse idea, only mine would have had a snack bar and lounge housed in the udder.)

Once I'd run out of war stories, I started telling them about the long journey home to Odysseus's kingdom of rocky Ithaca. I told how Odysseus had promised us that it would be an easy trip: "Cheer up, lads. It'll be a pleasure cruise!"—those were his exact words, as I recall. Yeah, right! Not much chance of an easy trip after Odysseus incurred the wrath of Poseidon, God of the Seas. (Here's a bit of advice for all wannabe heroes. If you're planning a long voyage, do *not* anger Poseidon.) Right from the start we had nothing but bad luck—tempestuous seas, raging winds, allies of Troy attacking us when we put ashore, the whole shebang. You name it, it went wrong. I even got a nasty splinter in my thumb first day out, though I bravely did not put in for sick time.

It's hard to tell what the restaurant crowd made of all this. Judging from the slackness of their jaws, I might as well have been reciting a shopping list. But then again, it did seem that every night more and more people came to see me. Word of the talking pig must be spreading.

I more or less went through the events of the crew's journey in order; so I suppose, if I'd stopped to think about it, I would have realized what the next bit was going to be. The problem was, up there on that stage with all those yokels listening to me, it was much easier to run off at the mouth than it was to stop and think.

Which is how I ended up starting to tell them about the one island I wanted to forget more than any other.

"Go on, then!" yelled an impatient voice when I paused. "What was on it, then?"

"It . . . it was the home of a tribe of giant, man-eating monsters."

"AND?"

And what? How could you begin to explain the feeling when you see a one-eyed giant stomping toward you? It's not the sort of thing you expect of a Tuesday morning, is it?

"Well . . . one Cyclops trapped us in his cave."

Just then a fluting voice spoke up. "Weren't you afraid?" It was the boy with the lyre, leaning forward to catch every word. Something about the lad's rapt expression enabled me to pull it together for a moment.

"Afraid?" I scoffed. "Let me tell you something, sonny boy. I laugh at Fear! I do, right to its face. I call Terror a big baby and then I tell all its friends that it wears diapers. I . . . er . . ."

But I couldn't keep this up for long. The terrible memory of our time with the Cyclops barged into my mind and held me in its sweaty grip.

All of us huddled together in the clammy darkness of that cave, we were, with torches throwing madly dancing shadows up the walls and that one-eyed monster stamping around and going on and on about how hungry it was, positively starving for a bit of red meat, that was what it had said. The bloke next to me whispered that the captain had a plan, but I knew in my heart that Odysseus couldn't get us out of this mess, not this time. There was no chance, no hope of escape, no hope. . . .

I was suddenly aware of the uncomfortable silence in the restaurant. "Er . . . sorry, where was I? Oh, yes . . ." I tried to shake the memory away. "Yes, well, anyway, Odysseus came up with a plan in the end—I helped him, mind you—and we escaped, and that was that. It, er, all turned out right in the end."

The audience didn't seem troubled by this abrupt ending. Only the boy with the lyre looked cheated. His brow furrowed, and it stayed furrowed for the rest of the evening.

Once the restaurant had closed and I was back in the basement, I found out why. After he'd delivered my supper, the boy made no move to close the hatch.

"I . . . I've got more questions for you," he began. "About Odysseus's journey . . . I want to know more."

"Go on," I said between mouthfuls.

"Okay . . . how did you get turned into a pig?" he asked.

"I was getting to that part," I said. "This was a while after we'd left the island with the you-know-what."

"The Cyclops?"

"Yes!" I snapped, eager not to dwell on the topic. "Anyway, our ship was blown off course, and we ended up on this unknown island. Odysseus sent a few of us to scout the place out. So we're wandering through the woods, and guess what we come across? Only a great big palace, that's what. And that's not all. There were all these exotic animals wandering around—lions and wolves and bears and such—but the funny thing was, none of them attacked us. Not that we were complaining, mind you. But we're just thinking, *This is a bit unusual,* as you would.

"Okay, so then the lady of the house shows up, says her name is Circe. You can tell right away she's no peasant. Has to be at least a demigod. She invites us in and gives us all a drink of wine and a bite to eat. All very hospitable. Then she gives us a big grin and waves this stick thing, and next thing I know, I can hear grunting all around me—and some of it is coming from me! She'd turned us into pigs, see! Real, live pigs!

"You could tell the lads weren't overjoyed by this, but there wasn't much they could do about it except, you know, go *oink, oink.* Well, there was nothing for it, was there? We all got herded off to the sty!"

"So are the others still there?" asked the boy. "In Circe's pigsty?"

I shook my head. "No, no, Odysseus sorted it all out in the end. Before the captain came to see what was going on, the god Hermes zoomed down and gave him this plant that protected him from Circe's magic. So it was nothing for him to march up, knowing full well he couldn't be transformed. He gave Circe a bit of the old smooth talk, and she agreed to change the crewmen back into humans."

The boy frowned. "Then . . . why are you still a pig?"

Ah, well that was the sixty-four-million-drachma question, wasn't it?

"I'd managed to squeeze my way out of the sty earlier on, hadn't I? Through this gap in the fence."

"So you were heading back to the ship to warn Odysseus?" the boy asked hopefully.

"Um, not exactly. I'd run out of food, you see. I was looking for a bite to eat."

"So . . . you weren't there when Circe transformed everyone back again? She missed you?"

"Yes . . . and no. I was there, but I was hiding behind a tree."

The kid was silent, but his expression screamed *I don't get it.*

I struggled to find the words. "I . . . I just didn't want to turn back into a person. Okay? It's better being a pig!" I couldn't stand the silent accusation of his stare anymore. I turned to the food at my pig's feet. "Do you mind," I grunted. "I'd like some privacy when I'm eating."

The boy began to protest, but my snout was down in the grub. I didn't even glance upward when the hatch shut with a careful click.

The slop was no better than usual—not exactly ambrosia of the gods, if you get my drift. I'd begun to notice that my girth was shrinking from its former splendor, but that wasn't the only thing shrinking. So, too, were my hopes of escape. Would I ever get out of this place?

I was thinking about how nothing was ever going to change my miserable situation . . . and then something happened.

"Pssst!"

The noise came from the narrow window.

I looked up just in time to see a pale hand framed against the moonlight. It flicked a scrap of papyrus into my room, then disappeared. I heard the muffled sound of footsteps scurrying away outside.

Aye, aye. Very interesting.

With my snout I nudged the papyrus to the patch of floor illuminated by the moonlight. It was full of that squiggly writing stuff.

Okay, confession time—when I was little, my dear old ma always wanted me to learn to read. Every week she dipped into her savings jar and gave me the money to take lessons. I knew that these coins represented years of blood, sweat, and tears. Naturally every week I played hooky and bought as many pies as I could. Well, how was I to know it'd turn out she was right?

I looked now at the note with a grunt of irritation. I had no idea what the words were, but squiggle for squiggle they looked like this:

Sit tight, stupid pig. And keep away from the tall man!

I snorted with excitement. I might not understand every word—okay, *any* word—but this note had to mean good news. Escape! Freedom! A one-way ticket out of kebab central! My heart leaped like . . . er . . . like Heracles leaping up. (You know, he could leap really high because his legs were so muscly?)

A sudden thought smacked me a good one. What if my captors saw the note? They wouldn't be too pleased, would they? I was the best thing that had ever happened to their cruddy restaurant. They'd do anything they could to ruin the plans of my mysterious helper.

There was nothing else to do. I began to eat the papyrus.

It could have used a little pepper, but it was quite tasty.

BOOK VII

Stars are not only in the heavenly firmament, actually.

Breakfast was late the next day, and I was starving by the time the hatch opened up.

The boy peeked down warily.

"Mornin', sunshine!" I called up.

"Er . . . hello," he mumbled suspiciously.

I was dying to get cracking on breakfast, but I forced myself to wait.

"So . . . how're things upstairs?" I asked, all cool and casual.

"Okay." His eyes narrowed. "Why?"

"Can't a pig make polite conversation?"

The boy glanced nervously over his shoulder. "There *is* something going on, actually," he hissed. "There's a fancy-looking visitor from down south. Says he's come to see you special. Aunt Gorgina's been talking to him all morning."

"Oh, yes? What's he like?"

"Very sophisticated," answered the boy. "Must be from the big city. Skinny, he is, and tall—*very* tall. He wants to see your act tonight. Says he might want to use you."

"Your aunt would never sell me!" I exclaimed, adding with a hint of pride, "I bring in too much money."

The boy shrugged. "I think she'd sell you if the price was right," he said, then he closed the hatch.

That gave me plenty to think about, no mistake. I could safely assume that the deliverer of the mysterious note last night and the sophisticated out-of-towner were probably one and the same. There were still lots of unanswered questions, but one thing was for sure: anything that got me out of this basement and away from this stinking place couldn't be a bad thing.

The rest of the day went by so slowly, I couldn't help wondering if Apollo hadn't parked the Chariot of the Sun and slunk off for a bag of chips. It seemed as if evening would never arrive. Stavros delivered the next meal, and there was as much point in asking him questions as there was in interrogating the bucket in the corner.

Finally, evening did arrive. At long last I found myself waiting to go onstage again.

Stavros was particularly nervous. "Just be yourself, pig," he mumbled. "Can't ask any more, can we, me old porker?" His nerves were the kind caused by the possibility of large sums of money.

Out in front of the diners, the boy was finishing his recital—a long poem about how Cronos, the father of Zeus, vomited up all the gods that he had previously eaten. (To my mind, that's just sick.) The sound of his lyre helped to mask several snores from the dining area.

At least his poem gave me the opportunity to give tonight's crowd a thorough once-over from behind the curtain. It was the same old bunch of scruffy bumpkins, all guzzling their drinks and shoving greasy food into their great fat cakeholes . . . apart from one.

An elegant, thin man perched at a side table near the stage. He was clearly not used to being in this sort of establishment (which is to say, a total dump). His toga looked as if it had been made-to-measure in the swankiest tailors' row in Athens. His hair was Adonis-perfect, his eyelids heavy with disdain of everything here. (And who could blame him?)

Oh, one other thing—he was very, very tall. He practically had to fold himself up to fit into one of the restaurant's chairs, but he managed to do so with elegance. In my book, that's class.

Among the regulars, this guy stood out like Ares, God of War, at a sit-in for peace. He stood out like beautiful Helen of Troy in a lineup of ugly-mug Cyclopes. He stood out like . . . well, let's just say he stood out.

He *had* to be the person who'd written me the note!

When the man's plate was brought out, he squinted as if attempting to identify it as a foodstuff. He sensibly decided that it wasn't and pushed the plate away with slender fingers.

I wasn't entirely surprised that someone like this had arrived. An act as astonishing as mine shouldn't be stuck in a grubby little restaurant out in the middle of nowhere, should it? Naturally this guy wanted to whisk me away to the finest theaters and restaurants in all of Greece. It stood to reason.

I knew immediately that this was my best chance. Of course, Gorgina and Stavros would be asking for big money, but this chap didn't look short of an obol or two, and he was clearly someone I could reason with in a civilized manner. We could work out some kind of a split of the profits. Failing that, then at some point on the long journey to Athens, there'd surely be an opportunity for me to scamper off into the woods and resume my life of leisure.

Besides, anything had to be better than staying in the cellar of Big Stavros's.

A rusty nail of doubt punctured the balloon of my excitement. What if the man didn't think that my humble little act was good enough for metropolitan theaters? Something that wows the yokels out here might meet nothing but yawns in the big city.

There was only one thing for it. I had to get out of here, and so I would have to dazzle him with my performance. I would have to do more than just ramble on about Odysseus and all those endless old stories about gods and monsters.

I could do better than that. Tonight I would be a star! I would bring the house down.

When Gorgina was finished with the usual introductions, I burst out through the curtain on all fours and hopped nimbly onto the little stage. I turned my snout to survey the whole room, taking care to make eye contact with the tall man. I gave him a big wink. (He didn't react, but of course a professional in the business wouldn't, would he?)

You're a star, I reminded myself. *Now shine!*

"Good evening, ladies and gentlemen," I said. "It's wonderful to be here."

The usual chorus of gasps bubbled around the room, and a dull thud told me that we had another fainter in the house.

"Gryllus is the name," I continued, "and entertainment is the game."

I pressed on over the mutters and prayers and so on.

"So . . . is there anyone here from Thrace?"

A couple of travelers near the back raised their hands tentatively.

"Great, great," I continued. "I went to Thrace for the weekend once. . . . It was closed."

The silence that followed gave me a chance to consider what to say next.

"Hey, who's your favorite god?" I asked a woman near the front.

"Er . . . Demeter."

"Great, great, nice choice. I mean . . . her followers

sacrifice pigs to her—but, hey, no one's perfect. Am I right, or am I right?"

A cough from the back of the house echoed around the room. Pigs don't sweat, so I wondered why I felt a sheen on my brow. Remembering the commotion back at the market-town temple, I made a mental note to steer clear of religion for the rest of the act.

"Hey, you'll never guess what I saw the other day," I continued. "It was a dog with no nose. What's that, you ask . . . how did it smell? I'll tell you. It smelled terrible! Actually, it was Cerberus, the three-headed dog, so it smelled three times as bad."

"Not as terrible as you!" yelled a burly man with a mound of food on his plate. "I can smell you from here. You stink, you big fat stinkin' pig!"

The crowd guffawed at this classic line from the *Bumper Book of Backwoods Wit*.

My bristles bristled. I couldn't allow a heckler to throw me off my stride, not tonight. I had to be a seasoned pro. Luckily my lightning wits came to the rescue.

"Back off, fatso," I quipped.

As you can see, I was on fire that night. Humor poured from my mouth like a babbling brook full of . . . humorous stuff. The only problem was that here, in the outer reaches of the back of beyond (make a left turn at Nowhere), big-city wit often goes unappreciated. All these outdoorsy types, with brains no bigger than an olive pit, are not known for their sophisticated sense of humor.

In fact, several people were now glaring angrily at me. Talk about a tough crowd. It was time for something different. I tossed a glance at the boy, who was still sitting sulkily at his lyre.

"If you will, maestro . . . hit it! And make it peppy!"

The lad still looked as if he had a couple of lemons tucked inside his cheeks, but, amazingly, he began to pluck the strings. Once the music got up to speed, I hopped onto my hind legs and began to dance. The sound of my hooves made a *tap-tap-tapping* on the wooden floor that was uncommonly pleasant if executed with enough rhythmic ability (of which the gods have blessed me with an abundance, thanks be to Apollo, Lord of the Dance). I accompanied the whole thing with a jaunty refrain that I made up on the spot.

Okay, let's be honest—when was the last time you saw a singing, tap-dancing pig? Not the sort of thing you see every day, is it? Well, you'd never guess that from this audience. You'd think they were sick to the back teeth of watching singing, tap-dancing pigs day in, day out. *Oh gods, not another singing, dancing pig!* they all seemed to be muttering. *I wish I'd stayed in and taken a bath.* (Actually I wished they'd stayed in and taken a bath, too, for obvious reasons.)

By the time the music ended, I was feeling a bit frantic.

"Okay, okay . . . you'll like this," I panted, still out of breath from my virtuoso dancing display. "There . . . once was . . . a merry young Spartan—"

I didn't get a chance to finish, because a piercing voice tore through the smoky air.

"You can come out now!"

BOOK VIII

Battle rages at the kebab-and-grill.

The comment came from the darkness of an alcove at the back where a lone figure sat.

"'Scuse me?" I asked.

The voice was a young woman's, and it was depressingly familiar. She rose from the shadows, but her face was still shrouded by the hood, as it had been when we'd first met. "I'm talking to the person BEHIND the curtain. . . . Come out and show us how you are throwing your voice to the mouth of this dumb beast!"

I attempted a calm smile. "I can assure you, miss, that—"

"Assure all you like." Her voice was louder now. "But that doesn't mean I'm going to be fooled. We're not *all* as stupid as Boeotians, you know." She said this last sentence with particular emphasis.

There was a pause of a few seconds while her insult sank in. Then an outraged voice piped up. "Oi! I'm from Boeotia! Who are you calling stupid?" It was the man who had heckled me earlier. He was on his feet and looking angry.

"Oh, be quiet!" said the hooded woman. In a single motion she swept up something from the table and hurled it at the man, who reacted by stepping into the path of the oncoming missile (thus nicely illustrating how Boeotians

53

had earned their bad reputation). The meatball struck him in the left ear before exploding into a shower of mini-meatballs.

"OW!" he protested. He grabbed the nearest thing at hand—a bread roll—and threw it back. But Sibyl—for, of course, 'twas she—was too quick. She hopped nimbly to one side and ducked. The bread roll landed on the table beside her. More precisely, it landed in a bowl of lentil soup, splashing it all over the man who had unwisely been about to spoon the soup in the general direction of his mouth.

That's more or less the moment when things began to go downhill. I watched in horror as food, fists, and folding chairs started to fly. The whole restaurant tumbled into chaos as the crowd took it upon themselves to brain one another. The air was filled with curses and yells and various noises along the lines of *CRASH!,* "OW!," "WHOOPS!," *BYOINGGG!,* and *CRUNCH!*

I glanced nervously at the elegantly tall man, who was sheltering behind an overturned table. Gorgina was calling for order and whacking people on the head with a tray. Stavros was busy trying to protect what was left of the shattered crockery.

I was following my usual tactics—strategic hiding behind a large vase—when there was the loudest crash yet. A scrum of diners had fallen into the room's outer door. I poked my head out to see that the door now hung half off its hinges. This was my chance! I hopped off the stage, narrowly avoided a flailing foot, and scurried under a table. I made my way across the room from table to table as bottles and plates exploded all around me.

And then, finally, I was at the last table. Just a short dash and I would be free. I took a deep breath.

Suddenly I heard a voice to my side. It was the boy. He still clutched his lyre, though the frame was broken and one string stuck out at a crazy angle.

"Wait!" he cried. "I want to hear the rest of your stories . . . for my poems."

I didn't have time for this. "What's your name, kid?"

"Homer."

"Listen, Homer, lad. Don't take this to heart, but you really ought to drop the poetry." I ducked a flying pita bread. "Learn a proper trade. Like plumbing."

"But—"

"Mark my words, you'll thank me." There wasn't time to explain how much better the career opportunities were outside of epic poetry. I just charged for the door. "Bye, kid," I snorted over my shoulder.

Out of the din behind me, I could hear one voice rising above the rest. It was Gorgina, shrieking, "He's getting away!"

You bet I was getting away! I shoulder-charged my way between two diners who were smacking each other with breadstick and cucumber, respectively. Up ahead, Stavros moved to block me. For once, he wasn't looking quite so jovial. He was fast for such a bulky guy, and something pointy and arrowlike lay in his hand. There was no way I'd make it to the open door in time . . . but then suddenly Stavros flew into the air and fell backward. He had slipped on the large dollop of minty yogurt dressing that had just landed on the floor in front of him.

I glanced back. Through the crush, I could make out Homer. One hand was dripping with the yogurt dressing he had just scooped up and hurled. The other was raised in mournful farewell.

I nodded once and then raced through the doorway. It took my eyes a while to adjust to the darkness outside, but then I spotted the tall man. He was dashing toward a carriage, twenty or thirty yards down the dirt road, shouting something or other.

"I'm coming!" I yelled, but my voice was drowned out by the din coming from the restaurant behind me. I started toward the carriage myself, but then a voice hissed from out of the darkness to one side of the road.

"This way!"

It was Sibyl, hood still up over her head. I might have known she'd escape after starting the whole ruckus.

"Come on, stupid pig!" she hissed urgently. "There isn't much time."

I looked ahead at the tall Athenian, who was now kneeling by a figure lying on the ground next to the carriage and trying to shake it awake.

This was a tough choice. Should I go with an obvious gentleman—someone clearly my equal in matters of good taste and intellect? Someone to whom I could no doubt explain my predicament? Then again, should I run off with a hooded weirdo with a mission from the god Apollo and a tendency to throw meatballs in public?

I put my head down and set off for the waiting carriage.

At least, I tried to. Sibyl had other ideas—she leaped forward and tackled me. I had only an instant to notice that she was holding something in one hand, and then she was saying, "This is for your own good." (Those six little words make up one of the most chilling sentences ever uttered—it ranks up there with "This is going to hurt me more than it hurts you" and the dreaded "What happens when I press this?")

And then everything went black, which it often does, I've noticed, when you've been clobbered on the head.

"Aren't you full yet?"

I grunted, "No," and went on eating. The way I saw it, the least she could do was give me a proper feed.

Our fire was a tiny bubble of light and warmth in the darkness all around. You could hardly see the pale moon through the tangle of branches overhead. We were deep in the woods, which meant that we were surrounded by all those deep-in-the-woods-in-the-middle-of-the-night noises.

"I could have been on my way to perform in one of the swankiest theaters and restaurants in all of Hellas," I grumbled, "but *you* had to go and muck it up."

"I told you to keep away from the tall man. Good thing for you I knocked out his servants. He's bad news. Didn't you even see my note?"

"Yes," I replied huffily. "Sort of."

"I couldn't let you go with him because I need you. I told you that, too." She made an effort to inject a little sympathy into her voice. "How's your head now?"

"Maybe a tiny bit better . . . no thanks to you." I shifted uncomfortably. "My back hurts, too."

Sibyl nodded. "Probably from when I rolled you down the hill."

That explained why I had woken briefly and found myself looking at sky, ground, sky, ground, sky, ground, et cetera.

"You mean you rolled me all the way here?"

"No, I rolled you all the way to the wheelbarrow. Then I pushed the wheelbarrow all the way here."

We fell into an uneasy silence, broken only by the sounds of chomping.

"You *must* be full by now," Sibyl said a few minutes later. She had pulled the hood of her robe back now. Her pale face was framed by short, straight hair, and it was currently sporting a look of disgust.

"It's not just a question of being hungry," I explained with my mouth full. "I get a great deal of comfort from food, and after what I've been through, I need all the comfort I can get." I eyed the ear of corn she'd left half-eaten. "Are you done with that?"

The girl rolled her eyes.

Much scoffing later, I let out a satisfied burp and got to my feet.

"Well, it's been nice catching up with you," I said. "If we

meet again, I'd suggest not doing the rolling thing, but I'm happy to let bygones be bygones. . . ."

"Er . . . where do you think you're going?" Sibyl demanded.

"I thought I'd toddle off and find somewhere to sleep. After that, I'll see how things go. Probably just stick around the woods."

The girl laughed, but it was one of those short, bitter laughs that often come right before people say things you really don't want to hear.

"What, did you think I rescued you—*twice*—out of the kindness of my heart? Think again, pig." Sibyl was rummaging around in her backpack.

"What are you doing?"

"Right now? I'm moving up to Plan B." Her voice was all business.

"Oh yes? What was Plan A?"

She didn't look up. "Plan A was 'Find the big, fat, talking pig and use reason to show that it must help save all the heavens and the earth below.'"

I didn't like the sound of Plan A for obvious reasons.

"And Plan B is . . . ?"

"'Find the big fat pig and create so much terror in its cowardly, piggish heart that it has no choice but to help save all the heavens and the earth below.'"

I sucked in air. "Hmm. This terror thing . . . I have to say, it doesn't work for me. You see, I've never reacted well in stressful situations—I just . . ."

Sibyl wasn't listening. She pulled a small clay jar out of her bag. Its neck was stoppered with a cork, and there was a handle with a piece of string running through it.

"Do you know who the Erinyes are?" she asked.

I thought it over. "Aren't they a girl band on the Mykonos nightclub circuit—Erika Eta and the Three Erinyes? They sang 'Zeus Only Knows What I'd Do Without You,' right?"

"Sadly not." Sibyl's eyes flashed. "Sadly for you, that is."

The jar in her hand seemed to glow orange, as if there were an unearthly fire inside it. There was a faint sound like a cross between a distant scream and the buzz of a hive of disgruntled bees.

"The Erinyes are spirits of vengeance. Their sole purpose is to right wrongs. Let's say a hero is killed dishonorably in battle. . . . The Erinyes are the ones who will take vengeance on the dog who slew him."

I nodded glumly. "Oh, *those* Erinyes. I get you."

"No, I don't think you do get me," said Sibyl. "You see, there's one inside this jar. Summoning an Erinys was the last thing we did while the temple was still operational." She held the jar closer to me, and for some reason the light inside it glowed even brighter and that hideous wail grew louder. There was definitely something in there, and it didn't seem to have taken a shine to me.

I tried to shrug with piggy nonchalance. "I haven't done anything wrong," I said.

"Ah, but it's not just a matter of doing something wrong, is it?" Sibyl gave me a tight little smile. "I'll tell you a true story about the Erinyes. You see, once upon a time Hera, Queen of the Heavens, granted a horse the power to speak with human tongue. Anyway, the Erinyes felt rather strongly that this sort of thing was an offense against the laws of nature, didn't they? So they did what they do best. They set about righting the wrong."

I didn't like the sound of this. "They gave that horse a serious talking-to, I expect . . . ?"

"Not exactly." Sibyl shook her head. "Let's just say poor old Dobbin didn't win many races after that. Or do much of anything . . . if you get my meaning."

"Loud and clear," I said miserably. I edged away from the jar and glanced at the darkness of the woods to my side.

Sibyl followed my gaze. "I wouldn't even think of making a run for it," she said pleasantly. "Because the Erinys knows all about you. And once she's out of the jar, it would take her . . . oh, about four seconds to catch you. Five seconds tops, and that's if you're really fast on your hooves." I got the impression she was enjoying this.

I sighed. Saying the next few words was like getting money out of my old crewmate Stingy Petros.

"So what do you want me to do?" I grimaced. "Something about saving the world, wasn't it?"

Sibyl's smile bloomed into a grin, but not a very jolly one— more your grimly-determined-in-the-face-of-impossible- odds kind of grin. "Like I told you, Apollo stopped talking to us at the temple. And the problem wasn't just at Delphi. The whole pantheon of gods just stopped showing up at temples all over the country. We were all going crazy with worry. And then, one night I had the dream. I was standing in Olympus itself, but the home of the gods was deserted. The great marble temples lay in ruins. Even Zeus's throne was empty and upturned. One god alone ran through the great courtyard. It was Apollo and he was . . . he was scared."

She drew a breath, as if about to jump in at the deep end. "This is what Apollo told me in my dream. He said, 'Find the pig that talks and go to Mount Ouranos. There you must find a simple goatherd on whose shoulders rests the fate of the Cosmos.' And then he ran off, and I woke up."

I considered her dream for a moment. "Maybe you just ate a bad bit of cheese? I had some olives once that made me dream I was at the Acropolis with no clothes on."

"The dream was true," said Sibyl flatly. "The one about Apollo, I mean. We can only hope and pray yours wasn't true."

Lit by the eerie glow of the Erinys's jar, her face looked altogether too spooky. She spoke at last. "There was one other bit of Apollo's message," she said.

"Oh, yes?"

Sibyl's eyes met mine. "It was . . . 'Death will be waiting for you.'"

It took a moment for these words to sink in. I listened to the mad whine of the Erinys in the clay jar.

"Well, that's just fan-bloomin'-tastic!" I said at last.

BOOK IX

The road is long (and a certain pig's feet are acting up).

Sibyl made us set off at a ridiculously early hour.

"I need eight hours of beauty sleep," I muttered as I stumbled through the unfamiliar darkness of early morning.

"Eight *years* of beauty sleep wouldn't be enough," commented the girl frostily. "Anyway, it's the early bird that gets the worm."

"Yeah, but it's the second mouse that gets the cheese."

We didn't talk for a while after that.

I'd describe the terrain and the trees for you, but—and this might come as something of a surprise—that sort of business isn't really one of my strong points. If you've seen one tree, you've seen 'em all. Name one that isn't made of wood with a few leaves stuck on top. As for the land, it was sort of bumpy and sometimes it went up and sometimes it went down. Enough of a mental picture?

It seemed as if we'd already been walking for ages when Dawn finally waggled those rosy fingers of hers up in the east. Sometime after that, the sun deigned to make an appearance, and then it wasn't looking too healthy; it distinctly wobbled as it climbed the skies.

Sibyl eyed it nervously. "Apollo's Chariot of the Sun isn't moving very smoothly today," she said. "And look, it's blood red."

I studied the glowing orb. "More beetroot-ish, I'd say."

Her voice hardened. "Trust me: I work for Apollo—I know these things. That sun is the color of blood after it's spilled to the earth."

So anyway . . . the sun climbed the vault of the heavens like an immense root vegetable.

Soon these pig's feet of mine were aching like nobody's business. The ground was getting rockier, and we were at the beginning of a long slope upward that showed little sign of having too many down stretches.

"Can we stop for a rest now?" I asked.

Sibyl's only answer was to keep on walking.

"What about now?" I pleaded a while later.

This time I got a brisk shake of the head.

"Now?" I tried a bit later. "I'm close to total exhaustion here!"

My campaign to wear Sibyl down must have been working, because this time she actually answered, whirling around to say, "Quit your whining, will you? We've got to keep moving!"

It was time to make my stand. I parked my bum by the side of the path. "I'm not going anywhere," I declared. "Not until I've had a rest and a bite to eat."

Sibyl's hands were already on the Erinys as she walked back down the path toward me. "Have you forgotten something, Gryllus?" she said. Her fingers danced threateningly over the jar's cork stopper. The contents of the jar buzzed alarmingly, but I didn't budge.

"I've been thinking about that," I answered as calmly as

I could. "See, if I'm so essential to this god-given task of yours, you can't go letting that Erinys kill me straight off, now can you, eh? Get out of that one!"

For a second Sibyl's face looked like one of those tragedy masks. Finally she said, "We can have a *quick* rest." (Yes! Pigs 1, Weird Prophetesses 0.)

She flopped down onto a rock, and for the first time it occurred to me that she was probably a bit on the tired side herself. How long had she been searching for me? Weeks, maybe?

We snacked on some dried fruit from Sibyl's backpack.

"I usually prefer something a bit more substantial, to tell you the truth," I said. "Got to keep my strength up."

"Don't push your luck, pig . . . and keep your mouth closed while you're eating, will you?"

I thought I should get to know my traveling companion better. (I wasn't being friendly for its own sake, you understand. The more I knew about her, the more chance I'd have to make my escape when the opportunity arose.) "So tell me . . . how did a nice girl like you end up working at Apollo's Oracle at Delphi?"

Sibyl's eyes met mine but didn't give them much of a friendly hello.

"I joined the temple when I was a little girl. I've always had this . . . *gift,* I suppose you'd call it. My dreams would show me glimpses into the future."

"Yeah? Like what?"

"Well . . . I dreamed that one day people will be able to talk to each other over long distances."

I snorted. "Excuse me, Mystic Meg. We have that already. It's called SHOUTING."

"And they'd have horses made of metal to pull them."

"That's better than horses made of horse, is it?" I rolled my eyes.

Sibyl was smiling, but her eyes were sad. "It doesn't matter anyway. You see, my dreams . . . they're just glimpses into possible futures. It isn't certain that any of these things will come to be." She sniffed and wiped her nose on her sleeve. "And recently all my dreams have been . . . very different."

"Oh yes? What have you seen lately? 'Cause if you could glimpse the result of next week's Athens-Sparta soccer match, we could make a pretty obol or two."

"That's just it," said Sibyl. "Lately all my dreams of the future have shown . . . nothing."

"What, nothing at all?" I commented. "Maybe you've just lost the knack."

"You don't understand," she said, her face suddenly set again. "I'm still seeing the future, I know it. It's just that the future I see contains complete and utter nothingness." She looked nervously at the skies. "We've got to get moving."

"Hold on! Walking right after you've eaten isn't good for the digestion. We should—"

But Sibyl was up and moving, and I had no choice but to follow.

I won't give you a step-by-step account of the whole wretched walk. All you need to know is, it was long, it was hard, and it was endured in the company of someone without even a shred of sympathy for a creature in suffering.

"My legs hurt," I said for the ninetieth time. "My back hurts. My tail hurts. My bu——"

"Stop!" Sibyl spat. She blocked my way with an outstretched arm.

We were at the edge of a forest.

"What is it?" I asked. "Nothing dangerous?"

Sibyl was pointing to a slender silver-white tree that stood by the path and towered over the trees around it.

"See the silver birch?" Her voice trembled.

"Ah, well, you'll be amazed to hear this, but trees aren't exactly my strong suit," I began.

"It's a dryad," Sibyl said softly.

"What? That's absur——"

The word died in my snout.

It was true.

If you squinted, you could make out a face halfway up the trunk. The eyes were closed, the mouth just a little bit open, as if speaking, though there was no sound but the dry rustle of leaves. And even as we watched, the face seemed to sink deeper and deeper into the tree, until there was really nothing but the hint of a face—a triangle of indentations where eyes and mouth had been, a slender bump of bark for the nose.

But it didn't make sense. Dryads were wood nymphs. They should be prancing around the forest scattering petals and singing or something, shouldn't they?

"What's going on?" I asked.

"When they are in great danger, dryads have the power to turn into the trees they protect," said Sibyl sadly.

"Well, that's handy," I commented, but Sibyl's eyes shone with tears. "Isn't it?" I asked.

"Not really," she said. She was arranging a bunch of wildflowers in an intricate pattern in front of the birch. "It's just a last resort. You see, they can't turn back again."

Sibyl didn't look up as she worked. I had plenty on my mind, too. If the dryad's reaction was anything to go by, perhaps Sibyl wasn't such a fruitcake after all. This terrible thought gripped me by my short and curly tail and wouldn't let go.

We took a last look at the ghostly-white tree, which was now entirely treelike and nothing more, then we plunged into the forest. For the next couple of hours I complained to Sibyl about how much my poor old pig's feet were aching only when it was absolutely essential.

BOOK X

A mysterious young goatherd lets it all hang out.

On the other side of the woods, the ground climbed steeply. Mountaintops rose before us like a bunch of overgrown bumps. A river snaked through a valley like a silver ribbon, blah, blah, blah, blah-de-blah. It was one of those landscapes that artistic types are always rambling on about, saying it's "majestic" or "breathtaking" or whatever—only of course it's not all that majestic when you have to plod right through it.

"That's where we're going," said Sibyl, pointing to a tiny dot on a hill just above the wooded valley.

"What, that tiny speck?"

It was late afternoon by the time we neared the tiny speck, which turned out to be a shoddily constructed stone hut. It was much less impressive close up than it had been as a speck in the distance.

The mountainside here was dotted with goats. They were so intent on munching every last scrap of grass that they paid us hardly any attention. (The goat has always struck me as a disagreeable animal, with its bulging eyeballs and its ridiculous little beard—all in all, it has nothing on its barnyard companion, the noble hog.)

Sibyl peeked inside the hut. It provided some shelter from the wind, which was as bitter as an unripe lemon with an attitude problem. The hut was empty of both furniture and goatherds. There was a pile of filthy rags in one corner, a scattering of bird bones on the dirt floor, and a persistent odor—three domestic touches that, taken together, failed to create much by way of an ideal homes exhibition.

"Well, that's that, then," I announced. "May as well pack this little quest in."

But Sibyl was already looking around outside. There was a shallow rocky pit a bit farther up the hill, and that's where the boy was sitting. He was about eight years old, and he was covered in muck. His hair was matted and

69

filthy. By the looks of it, the last time it had been washed and combed was . . . oh . . . never.

The lad wore a cheerfully dopey expression but nothing else . . . including any item of clothing whatsoever. He didn't seem troubled by his total nudity (which is more than you could say for me).

"That must be him," said Sibyl.

"Did Apollo mention that he'd need a bath?" I asked. "You haven't got any fragrant oils in that bag of yours, have you? Anything to mask the stink?"

When he heard our voices, the boy looked around and hopped up. Brilliant-white teeth flashed on his grimy mug.

"Er, hello," said Sibyl. She raised a hand in formal greeting. The boy responded by jumping up and down and shouting, "Bek, bek!"

"I think he's happy to see us," said Sibyl.

"Yeah," I commented, "but when he jumps around, he wafts the smell this way."

Sibyl gave me a funny look and muttered something under her breath about pots and kettles, but I couldn't catch the rest.

"What's your name?" Sibyl called to the gyrating boy.

He took this as the cue to intensify his mad, naked jig. "Bek! Bek! Bekos!" he hooted. "Bekos! Bek!"

As far as I was concerned, we should just have given up there and then. It was curtains for the Cosmos if we were pinning our hopes on this kid.

I let out a sigh and turned to Sibyl, who looked suddenly unsure of what to do next.

"Well, what did Apollo *tell* you to do?" I asked. "After all, he's running this show, isn't he?"

"Apollo wasn't able to go into details," she said. "I was hoping the goatherd might tell us, but . . ."

The lad's arms were flapping like a chicken struck by lightning. I snorted at the idea that he could impart any information whatsoever.

Sibyl bit her lip thoughtfully. Finally she rolled up her sleeves, fixed the best smile she could on her chops, and got to work.

The lad didn't have much of a clue, but he was happy enough to let Sibyl lead him to the little stone hut.

I lurked around outside until he had been cleaned up a bit. By the time I popped my head around the door, his brown hair was still long and straggly, but at least it no longer looked like a weekend getaway for an assortment of minibeasts. I was also relieved to see that he was no longer swinging free in the breeze—which is to say, he was now dressed. In fact, he was sporting a tunic several sizes too big for him. Sibyl had pinned it up as well as she could, but it still flapped like a trireme's sail on a gusty day.

"Got him all spruced up then, eh?" I said.

The boy's eyes glowed with wonder as they lit on me. The thing is, I don't think they were showing wonder at seeing a talking pig. It was simple amazement at seeing a plain old pig. I couldn't help thinking that this lad's entire worldview was altogether too . . . *local.*

"Any chance of an early dinner?" I asked Sibyl. "You have to admit, we worked up a healthy appetite getting here."

"First things first," said Sibyl, a bit on the snappy side (just for a change). "I want to see how much the boy knows."

"That shouldn't take long then."

Sibyl glared.

"Right, then," I sniffed. "I'll leave you and Bumscruff the Goat-Boy here to it. I'll be outside having a snack."

I marched away and decided to sample what this hillside had to offer by way of food. The goats were all merrily chomping on the scrubby, long grass, but of course the goat is a notoriously unfussy eater. I nibbled a blade of the grass and spat it out immediately.

Then I hit upon a clump of darkish-green weeds that were really quite tasty: crisp, refreshing, and with a certain lemony zing. Say no more! I scoffed the whole clump in one bite and looked for more.

There was only one other patch of the weed, but when I sidled over to it, a strapping young billy goat marched up. His bulgy yellow eyes were trained on me.

"Morning, Bill," I said, and I bent my head to grab some more grub. Immediately, the billy goat lowered his head and pawed the ground. I didn't like the look of those horns. He was ready to charge.

I took a step back. The goat raised his head from the attack position, but his unblinking eyes were still trained on me.

"Go on, buzz off," I said. "Shoo! Go and . . . do whatever you goats like to do. Go and climb a mountain or something."

The goat didn't appear interested in my advice. I stretched forward to eat again, and once more the goat readied himself to charge. As before, he raised his head only when I pulled back.

This happened several times. Outrageous! I wasn't going to be pushed around by some numbskull mountain goat. It was time to assert the natural superiority of the pig, which meant flexing my mental muscles.

I threw an indifferent look at the weed and tutted loudly as I wandered away.

"I spat on it anyway," I said over my shoulder. "AND I've got a cold."

I took care not to glance back at the goat until I was at a safe distance. Clearly lacking the necessary brainpower, my enemy had already begun to drift back to the rest of the herd.

"Oh dear, oh dear, you disappoint me," I muttered as I made a wide loop around a ridge of rocks. "It seems that you picked the wrong pig to mess with today, my friend."

When I'd cleared the rocks, I was some way behind the goat, which was no longer near the patch of food. The wind carried his somewhat confused "Meeeeh!" down the hillside to me.

I tiptoed down to the patch of weeds, skillfully weaving my bulky frame through all the rocks. Then I began chowing down. My victory made the plant taste sweeter than ever!

I was vaguely aware that the goats around me were all

going *maaaah,* and these seemed rather more urgent than the usual *maaahs.* Frantic even, but then the goat is not known for its smarts.

I only looked up when I heard the thunder of hooves. Maybe I'd celebrated victory a tad too soon? Because then I glanced down the mountainside and what I saw froze the blood in my veins.

BOOK XI

The chimeras give chase, which is no laughing matter.

"We're still not eating yet," snapped Sibyl when I barged into the hut.

"M-m-m—"

"Spit it out," she said. "You're hungry and you'd like some melon? No? Moussaka? Mrs. Mycene's Marvelous Muffins? What *is* it?"

"M-MONSTERS!" I screamed. "Monsters coming up the hill!"

Sibyl threw me an if-this-is-your-idea-of-a-joke scowl, but she went to the door. One glance down the hill and she changed her tune fast.

"Erm, yes, well . . ." She blinked rapidly. "I think we'd better . . . er . . ."

You can't blame her for being flustered. It's a funny thing about monsters. You can see a picture of them on a vase or a wall frieze in a temple or something, and think they look a bit dumb. I mean, really . . . head of a lion? Body of a goat? Tail of a serpent? "Come off it, pal!" you scoff knowingly.

But then you find yourself actually staring at a real chimera—lion's head, goat's body, snake's tail, the works—and the scoffs tend to sputter and die in your throat.

The chimera bounding up the hill didn't look silly at all. More terrifying and horrendous, I'd say. The two others charging behind their leader were no less terrifying and horrendous. Their terrible jaws drooled, their red eyes blazed, and all in all, they gave the impression of being very cross indeed. I wasn't going to wait and find out what about.

"RUN!" screamed Sibyl.

Yes, well, I was already running, but young Bumscruff the goatherd didn't seem too troubled by this turn of events. He gazed down at the rapidly approaching monsters with the same glassy-eyed smile he had turned on just about everything.

There was no time for lectures on the food chain and our place in it. Sibyl grabbed the back of the boy's baggy tunic and began to drag him along, charging after me. We raced to the top of the hill and then started down the other side.

"Don't look back!" yelled Sibyl.

I looked back.

I couldn't help myself, though I immediately wished I had more self-control. What did I have to go looking back for? The chimeras were closing the distance between us as they loped through the trees and boulders that dotted the slope. All this exercise seemed to be putting a nice edge on their appetite.

"Try and get to the river!" Sibyl called to me. "There's a bridge there."

True, there was a river at the foot of the hill, but we had no chance of reaching it before they reached us.

"No good!" I panted. "Too far! Need to . . . climb tree!"

I began to scramble up a pine tree. Or at least, I *tried* to. The body of the pig is perfectly designed for many activities, but shooting up trees at high speed is not one of them. My front feet clawed frantically at the lower branches, but my back legs remained resolutely on the ground.

Sibyl and the boy reached the same tree. Help at last!

The first thing Sibyl did was shove me down so that all four feet were on the ground.

"Oi!"

"Stand still!" she snapped, and she helped Bumscruff step onto my back to reach the lower branches.

"Hey, that hurts! My back's not what it once was . . ."

Luckily, Bumscruff scurried up into the branches before my spine gave out. I could hear the throaty snarl of the monsters getting louder and louder.

"I'm not letting *you* climb on my back," I informed Sibyl. "You're a lot heavier!"

But Sibyl wasn't trying to step on to my back. She was trying to push me up the tree trunk. She gasped with the effort. I found a foothold with one of my back feet and kicked as hard as I could. Sibyl was shoving on my rump with all her might, but it was no use. I had as much chance of getting up that tree as snake-haired Medusa has of getting a job advertising dandruff shampoo.

But then a smiling Bumscruff reached down and grabbed one of my forelegs. With him pulling, Sibyl pushing, and me kicking like mad, I managed it. I was up in the tree.

Only Sibyl wasn't.

Still on the ground, she was clearly out of breath, perhaps from the enormous effort of transporting a full-grown pig vertically. But there wasn't time for her to catch her breath. The chimeras were almost here. Sensing that the end was near, they had put on a blistering sprint. Any second now . . . Sibyl and I may not have got off to a wonderful start to our relationship, but I really didn't want to see her get eaten by chimeras (and not entirely because I'd only just finished my own lunch so recently).

But the gods—or whichever one is patron of tree climbing—were smiling on her. She whizzed up that tree, just in time to avoid the first chimera's ravening jaws. SNAP!

The beasts were not well pleased to have missed their snack. Having established that they could not climb the tree themselves, they spent a while roaring and snarling up at us. When they got bored with that, they went in for a bit of prowling and pacing below the tree. Their reptilian tails swished through the air angrily. Finally they just plunked themselves down in the shade a few yards away and kept a watchful eye on us.

I did what any hero would do under the circumstances and made a calm, thorough evaluation of our situation.

"We're stuck," I wailed.

"Duh!" said Sibyl, eloquently suggesting she had reached the same conclusion. "Well?" she demanded, staring at me. "Haven't you got any ideas?"

Boy, she had some bloomin' nerve!

"Me? ME? Are you forgetting something? You're the one who dragged me along on this little pleasure trip! Why don't YOU pop down there and do something?"

Sibyl's eyes flicked to the dreadful beasts below us. I saw a flash of anxiety in them, but she tucked it away quickly.

"I would, but I've got to keep the boy safe. Nothing else is as important as that. That's what Apollo told me."

"Ye-es, but in this sort of situation, it pays to be flexible. I'm sure Apollo would see the sense in that."

Only Bumscruff seemed unfazed. He was currently breaking leaves off the tree and sniffing them one by one. He popped one into his mouth and chewed experimentally.

I looked at the ferocious beasts below. "I wish they were the other way around," I said glumly.

Sibyl tutted. "What, you mean goats' heads and lions' bodies? I expect then you'd jump down and heroically feed them all carrots, would you?"

"Ha, ha!" I replied. Then I added sulkily, "We haven't *got* any carrots."

"We *did* have, but *you* ate them," Sibyl muttered.

"Well, if you're going to be like that." I turned and edged along the branch, farther away from the lippy trainee-priestess.

"Er, Gryllus?" she said. "I think you'd better not—"

78

"W
A
A
A
A
H!"

This was the sound I made after the branch snapped under my weight.

CRUMP!

This was the sound I made as I landed on the ground like an enormous pink sack of spuds.

Only my catlike agility prevented me from crunching a few ribs (that and the extra padding I was carrying, which is mostly muscle, you understand). I lifted my head and saw the pack of chimeras leap up, snarling and drooling in a way that could only be described as . . . hungry.

And then I was on my feet and running. Flat-out terror gave me that much-needed boost of speed.

As I fled, Sibyl shouted encouragement from the safety of the tree. "You're doing brilliantly, Gryllus! Keep your knees up and control your breathing!"

Even Bumscruff joined in with some choice advice: "Bekos! Bek!"

I hadn't given much thought to the direction I was heading in. It was more a matter of charging off any old way in a desperate attempt to save my bacon. But then I realized that I was barrelling downhill toward the river . . . and the bridge!

Don't go picturing any grand stone bridge spanning the

79

water. This was one of those ratty little footbridge jobs made of old rope and planks of wood. These were set wide apart, presumably to stop the goats from making their escape off the hillside.

The bridge looked as if it could hardly bear my weight, but I didn't have much choice in the matter. I picked my way across the gaps, my hooves clacking on the rickety planks.

I hadn't even made it to the other side when a chorus of feral snarls struck up behind me. The biggest of the three chimeras pushed in front of the other two and raced onto the bridge.

It didn't get far before it lost its footing. One front leg fell between a gap in the planks, and it slammed down, face-first. The two chimeras behind snarled furiously at the holdup. Meanwhile, the bridge creaked ominously under the weight of three good-sized ravening monsters.

I hopped off the other end of the bridge and plunged headlong into the tall grass in front of me. Unable to see more than a foot* ahead, I charged through that grass in the manner you might expect of a deeply intelligent pig being chased by three drooling carnivores. Blades of grass whipped against me, causing untold damage to my hide, which is particularly delicate as pigskin goes.

*This Ancient Greek measurement was based on the length of a human foot. Standards varied from place to place. The Olympic foot was taken from Heracles' foot (18 inches long), whereas the Samian foot was 13½ inches. The Melian foot was just 3¾ inches, taken from the foot of Tiny Toes Timios.

"Don't slow down!" came Sibyl's voice in the distance. "They've nearly crossed the bridge! They'll be in the grass any second now!"

Sure enough, the snarls I could hear behind me sounded somehow *faster*. The beasts were clear of the bridge. They would not be able to see me in this tall grass, but they could simply follow their noses. (Pigs have many distinguished qualities, but a lack of smell is not one of them.)

I suddenly burst out into the clearing—right in front of the bridge I'd already crossed. I had cunningly run in a wide loop. Well, okay, I hadn't planned to do this, but I was brilliant enough to turn it to my advantage.

I high-stepped back across the rickety bridge. The beginnings of a NIFTY IDEA were tickling at my brain—if I could just force myself to ignore the roaring behind me, which meant that at least one of the chimeras had also made it back to the bridge.

Once I'd recrossed the bridge, I stopped and began gnawing at one of its support ropes. It was thicker than it had first looked.

"What are you doing?" yelled Sibyl. "They're coming!"

"Bek! Bek!"

It was true! The first chimera was already on the bridge. Somewhere in its monstrous brain it had learned the lesson not to go too fast here. It picked its way carefully from plank to plank.

My jaw was working frantically, but the stinking rotten rope wasn't close to breaking yet. (Typical, eh? If you found yourself hanging off the side of a cliff holding on to a rope, you could bet your bottom drachma it'd unravel and break in a flash. But for once in your life you find yourself *wanting* to break a rope and suddenly Heracles himself couldn't pull it apart. This must have something to do with living in an unfriendly universe. Either that, or there's someone at the rope factory with a very nasty sense of humor.)

The bridge let out a painful groan. All three chimeras were on it now. Their growls were idling as if they sensed there was little sport left in this particular hunt. Somewhere in the middle of the ocean of fear in my heart, a tiny voice was saying, "Maybe it wasn't such a nifty idea after all. . . ."

"Run!" screamed Sibyl, but my legs had chosen this of all times to become immobile through all-consuming terror.

Only at the last minute did I hear the rapid thunder of hooves approaching behind me. Another chimera? I didn't have time to look around. I hadn't even taken the rope out of my mouth when I was struck a mighty blow in the rear end. I tumbled forward into the mud.

I looked up to see a familiar sight. It was my old enemy, the billy goat from the hill. He had waited patiently to have his revenge, and nothing—not even a pack of monstrous carnivores and all-around abominations of nature—was going to stop him. He gave a little victorious *meeeh!* and strutted away, satisfied that his honor had been regained.

It was only then that I noticed the enraged roars coming from the river. Not just enraged . . . enraged and *wet*. When the billy goat had struck me, the force of the blow

82

had been enough to sever the rope clamped between my jaws. The bridge had collapsed, and the chimeras had tumbled into the water.

They hissed and spat their rage. Having lions' heads, the chimeras were part cat and, like all cats, they were not at all happy about getting their hair wet. All three attempted a sort of panicked doggy paddle for the bank, but the current was too strong for them.

I just watched contentedly as the river swept them away.

BOOK XII

The meaning of existence is not on offer to certain species.

The next day found us—surprise, surprise—plodding along on the road again. The only difference was that now we had Bumscruff in tow.

At least we'd waited and camped for the night before setting off. By the time we'd made sure the chimeras were well and truly gone, Sibyl had decided that there was no point in leaving so late in the day. Instead the plan was to get a bite to eat and a good night's rest.

Back in the hut, Sibyl had set out most of the remaining food from her backpack. It wasn't much: some bread (hard as a rock), a bit of cheese (on the wrong side of aromatic), and a few figs (overripe).

Still, no use complaining—that's my philosophy when it comes to food.

The thing is, it wasn't easy to concentrate on your meal. It was the goat-boy—I couldn't take my eyes off him as he lifted a fig to eye level and studied it carefully. It was like watching a housecat trying to figure out its next chess move.

Sibyl lifted some food to her mouth. "Like this," she explained. She made little smacking sounds as she pretended to eat.

Bumscruff the Goat-Boy nodded vigorously and crammed a loaf of bread into his mouth. The half that didn't fit jutted out at a right angle.

"For gods' sake, don't ever give him soup," I observed.

The exposed part of the loaf fell as Billy Bekos chomped down. He began to chew, taking care to leave his mouth open.

Now, I was always taught that it is impolite to draw attention to others' lack of manners, but then again . . .

"By Heracles' hairy nostrils, you are the most clueless twit I have ever set eyes on. I know the job requirements for goat-boy aren't high, but I can't help thinking they've taken a turn for the worse these days. How did you ever manage to herd the goats? Weren't they constantly outsmarting you with their superior goat intellects? I mean—"

When he realized I was talking to him, the boy shouted an enthusiastic "Bek!"

"Leave him be," Sibyl told me. "You're no slouch in the

bad manners department yourself, Gryllus." Her eyes flashed angrily. "Tell me something, anyway . . . Just why did you want to stay like this, a big pig?"

"For your information, pigs are nobler creatures by far than most people, thank you very much," I answered huffily, not looking her in the eye.

Sibyl shook her head. "Do you know what words are inscribed above the entrance to Apollo's temple at Delphi? 'Know thyself.' I always thought it was good advice, but in your case, Gryllus, I'd make an exception."

The rest of the evening passed in much the same way, with an all-around lack of banding together in the face of the horrible dangers that lay ahead. I didn't get much sleep either, what with Bumscruff shouting, "Bek, bek!" in his sleep and the goats outside making a din. But what really ruined my beauty sleep was something Sibyl had said right before lights out.

"The question is . . ." she had pondered aloud, "was it just chance that a pack of chimeras stumbled upon us? Or did someone send them, knowing we'd be here?"

Terrific! Just what I needed to set me up for a night full of nightmares.

So, as you can imagine, the following morning I had no enthusiasm for yet more walking; my get-up-and-go had gotten up and gone. Bumscruff, on the other hand, appeared to have limitless energy. He strode along with an annoying bounce in his step for hour after hour. The same puppyish grin was plastered on the lad's face at all times. Sibyl had been concerned that he had no sandals to protect his feet, but he hardly seemed to notice the jagged rocks beneath his bare soles. Not bright enough to feel pain, I reckoned.

"Can't you go any faster?" Sibyl called to me when, once again, I was lagging.

I thought the question over, remembering that the fate of the entire universe apparently lay with us.

"No."

Sibyl and I played out this exchange several times during the morning. After yet another replay, Bumscruff turned and marched back toward me. He grinned as amiably as ever as he bent down and lifted me up effortlessly. He put me across his shoulders and then he walked forward and past an astonished Sibyl, with the same enthusiastic vim he had shown the whole day.

"Bek!" he said jovially. It wasn't the most comfortable ride, but I'm not one to complain, as you've probably gathered.

I'll say one thing for that lad. He might not have been the brightest constellation in the nighttime sky, but he was strong and he had bags of stamina. I'm not all that petite as pigs go, but he didn't appear to know the meaning of *tiredness,* or indeed the meaning of any other words, preferring instead to stick with "Bek!" as a sort of one-size-fits-all utterance.

All things considered, the lad was more rewarding to talk to than Sibyl, who had a nasty habit of wrinkling her nose in distaste whenever she looked my way. However, if it was hard information I was after, I did need to consult the prophetess rather than the monosyllabic lad.

86

"Where are we going, anyway?" I asked her.

"There should be a village a few stadia ahead," she said. "If I'm right, there's a temple of Apollo there. We'll be told what to do next."

"That's good," I replied. "I wouldn't want you to have to think for yourself or anything."

Sibyl gave me a look as sharp as a Hydra's eyetooth and walked on.

The distance turned out to be more than just a few stadia. It was well into the afternoon by the time we passed a sign that Sibyl read aloud to us:

THE VILLAGE OF
MICRODUMPOS
WELCOMES CAREFUL DONKEY DRIVERS

In fact, it looked the sort of place where someone riding through on a donkey would be the talk of the town for weeks. There wasn't much more to the place than a scattering of houses and a high street with one taverna and one shop. Both were closed. In fact, the whole place seemed to be shut.

"The temple should be a little way out of town," said Sibyl.

"You go right ahead," I said. "I'll stay here."

"Naturally," replied Sibyl. "You probably need to re-gather your strength after being carried all day."

While she and Bumscruff set off to find the temple, I took the opportunity to stretch my legs. Of course, I thought about really stretching them—stretching them right out of there. Unfortunately, after we'd picked up Bumscruff, Sibyl had taken the precaution of tying that little clay jar around my neck, explaining carefully that if I tried to flee, the stopper would pop off and the Erinys would burst out.

Great—so not only couldn't I flee, but I was stuck with a necklace that really didn't suit my coloring.

It was on one of the side streets of Microdumpos that I came across the only villager still in residence: an old woman sitting outside her house. Hunched over in jet-black clothes, she resembled an enormous crow.

"Afternoon," I said. I considered explaining how black actually absorbs heat and so isn't a very sensible fashion choice in a hot climate, but just the idea of this conversation tired me out.

"Who are you, then?" she asked, displaying the open friendliness I had come to know and love from rural types.

Better get it out of the way fast, I thought.

"I'm a pig."

The old woman's face split into an unexpected grin. "My first husband was a pig, too," she remarked with a cackle. "Couldn't get him to put his undies in the laundry basket for love nor money, the dirty old swine."

As I got closer, I noticed milky-blue cataracts on both eyes. The old woman could not see me.

"Where's everyone else?" I asked.

"Gone," she answered.

"I can see that. . . . Gone where?"

She gave a shrug. "Off to hide in the hills, I suppose, or down in the big city in the valley. There was talk of monsters roaming this area, see."

I was indignant. "What, and they just left you behind?"

The old woman gave a dismissive shrug. "Nah," she said. "They wanted me to come, but I said it'd take more than a few crummy old monsters to have me running off like some frightened little wood nymph."

I looked at her ancient and wizened face. There were so many wrinkles, it resembled a detailed relief map of the mountainous north.

"I don't think there's much chance of anyone mistaking you for a wood nymph," I ventured diplomatically.

"Lived my whole life in this village, I have," the woman declared proudly. "You'd never catch me running off to the bright lights of Macrodumpos."

"How far away is Macrodumpos?" I asked.

"Twenty stadia." She shook her head in wonder at such an immense distance. "Listen, stranger. I'm a hundred and nine years old and I'll tell you something. . . . I didn't reach this age worrying about monsters, OR about what I eat, or any of that nonsense. Want to know how I did it?"

"Er, okay," I said.

She tapped the side of her nose with a bony finger. "I know the *answer*."

"The answer to what?"

Her toothless mouth opened in a toothless laugh, and I was reminded of the Cyclops's dank cave.

The old woman's cackle mutated into a series of explosive coughs. Finally she was able to say, "There's only one question worth asking, laddie. . . . Why are we born to suffer and die? Your basic mystery of existence."

My heart was pounding so hard I wasn't sure the old rib cage could stand it. "Strictly speaking, that's two questions," I said carefully.

Another shrug.

"And?"

"And what, sonny?"

"And what IS the answer?" I did my best to cloak the urgency in my voice.

"I'll whisper it to you. Come 'ere." Her clawlike hand reached out and rested on one of my ears. It ran down the length of my snout.

"Get your hog out of the way, lad, and lean in," said the woman.

"Er, no, that's MY face you're touching. It's a long story," I said quickly.

The woman's hand disappeared back into the folds of her black robe as quickly as a rabbit that's popped out of its hole only to find that the visitor ringing the bell is in fact a starving ferret with a napkin tied around its neck.

"You're a pig!" she exclaimed.

"I *told* you I'm a pig."

"Yes, but I didn't think you was a PIG pig, did I?" She got huffily to her feet. "Hundred and nine years old, I am! If you think I've waited all this time to pass on the secret of existence to some bloomin' talking pig, you've got another think coming. When I was a girl, pigs knew their place. . . . Snufflin' around in the sty, that's where they belonged and they knew it. Pigs was proud to be turned into pork chops back then. They didn't go around striking up conversations with decent, gods-abiding human folks."

"But—"

It was no good. The old woman was shuffling to her door at what appeared to be her top speed.

"I'll bid *you* good day," she declared with finality. She scurried inside, and the door slammed with even more finality. A glowering silence emanated from the house in yet another dollop of finality.

I was still sitting there when Sibyl turned up.

"We've found the temple," she informed me. "It was locked, but Bumscr—but the boy's opening it right now."

I didn't have the energy to summon an answer.

"What are YOU doing?" asked Sibyl.

I sighed. "There's a woman in here says she knows the answer to the mystery of life."

Sibyl folded her arms in a no-nonsense manner. "Oh yes? And what is it?"

"She wouldn't tell."

By now Sibyl's patience had worn as thin as a flamingo's leggings. "How can I put this, Gryllus?" she began with a humorless smile. "If we don't shake a leg, there might not *be* any existence left to explain."

Bumscruff had joined her on the dirt path now. He contemplated the subtle ins and outs of our philosophical debate before making his contribution: "Bek!"

BOOK XIII

The god of music doesn't feel much like giving us a tune.

The temple was nothing grand—as you'd expect out in the sticks. The front doors were flanked by two columns, one of them displaying a distinct lean. The doors themselves were boarded shut, but Bumscruff had little trouble ripping them open. (The lad was even looking taller and stronger now. He had clearly benefited from all that healthy mountain air.)

We stepped inside. It was still and heavy in there, as only the air inside a temple can be. In the darkness you could just about make out the wall friezes—Apollo playing the lyre, Apollo dancing, Apollo steering the Chariot of the Sun, Apollo feasting, Apollo playing beach volleyball. If you liked Apollo, this was the place to be.

Sibyl quickly arranged an offering of food on a stone step at the far end of the temple. Then she piled a stack of twigs into a pyramid shape nearby. She took a stone from her pocket and began striking it against the stone floor to spark a flame. I wisely hung back. (*It never hurts to be near the exit*—that's my philosophy.)

"Having a campfire, are we?" I asked. I was about to launch into one of my favorite singsong ditties, but Sibyl shushed me.

The fire had caught, and now she pulled a small purse

from her pocket. She took a handful of something—dried herbs?—and sprinkled it onto the fire.

The effect was immediate and impressive. The flame whooshed upward. It blazed brighter and brighter, throwing the rest of the temple into a carnival of dancing shadows.

I watched in astonishment as the column of fire climbed until it was close to the ceiling. And then slowly the shimmering flame began to take form. There was someone *in* there.

The figure was twice the height of a mortal man. Encircled by a laurel wreath, his hair was a radiant cascade of golden curls; his face was shockingly handsome. In one perfectly muscled and tanned arm he held a lyre, in the other a golden bow. He didn't seem quite real—I sensed that if I'd reached out to touch him, my hoof would have settled on nothing more substantial than dancing flame (before quickly becoming smoked bacon).

I knew that we were in the divine presence of the god of medicine and archery, of music and prophecy, the immortal driver of the Chariot of the Sun and the Olympian tender of flocks and herds around the world.

"This better be good," grumbled Apollo.

Sibyl stepped forward. "O great Apollo," she called in her "work" voice. "As you foretold, so it was. We have done your bidding and found the boy on Mount Ouranos."

The god blinked his golden eyes. "Oh right. Yes . . . you have served me well."

His heavy-lidded gaze turned my way. "So this is

the pig?" The god's aquiline nose wrinkled in Olympian disgust.

I wasn't sure what etiquette demanded when addressing a god, so I decided to combine religious formality with a certain casual charm. "Wotcha."

But Apollo had already turned his attention to Bumscruff. He leaned down to get a closer look at the goatherd.

"And this is the boy," declared Apollo, pursing his god-like lips and furrowing his godlike brow. "Tell me, boy. What do you make of the great god Apollo?"

Bumscruff treated the great god Apollo to one of his inexplicable, blank grins.

"Er, he can't speak Greek," said Sibyl quickly. No doubt she was going to explain that the poor lad was several gods short of the full pantheon. But before she could say any more, she was interrupted . . . by Bumscruff!

"Grape god A-polly!" sang the goatherd. "Polly lolly oodallolly!"

The boy's voice was as croaky as a frog with tonsillitis, but he babbled on like a merry toddler.

I felt this was a good moment to state the completely obvious. "He can talk! . . . Well, sort of."

"Great!" snarled Sibyl, glancing nervously at the god's expression of distaste. "But can he shut up?" She hurriedly indicated the bits of food on the stone step. "Accept these humble offerings, great Apollo," she said.

The god gave the cheese, honey, and oil a long, sniffy look.

"Is that all there is?" he said. "No meat?"

"I'm sorry. That's all we had left."

The god's immortal forehead creased in Olympian annoyance. "What, no bread? Not even some pita or a cracker?"

Sibyl shook her head. A heavy silence elbowed its way into the temple and sat there as if it owned the place. Finally Bumscruff broke it.

"POLLY WANT A CRACKER!" yelled the goatherd. "POLLY WANT A CRACKER!"

"I do *not* want a cracker!" snapped the god. "And stop calling me Polly!"

"POLLY WANT—"

A muffled, metallic clank rang out, silencing even the newly talkative Bumscruff.

"What was that?" hissed Apollo, looking around urgently. Those immortal golden-blue eyes, more used to admiring themselves in the mirror, were suddenly wide with . . . well, the only word for it was *fear*.

I could hardly believe this—the gods were experts at inspiring fear in us mortals, but everyone knew they were strangers to the feeling themselves. Well, apparently not. . . . Fear is a subject I know a lot about, and fear is what I saw in the deity's eyes at that moment.

But of what exactly? I looked around. There was no one else in the temple.

"Quick! Tell us what to do next!" Sibyl urged the god.

Apollo was rubbing his noble brow with golden fingers. "Er . . . yes. What to do next? The . . . the future is cloudy, but . . ."

The metallic clank sounded again, louder this time. It

seemed to be coming from within the very flames that Apollo occupied. He looked over both shoulders in alarm.

"Please!" shouted Sibyl.

The god was flustered now. "Yes, erm . . . take him back to Delphi, to the Omphalos,* that's what you have to do."

Apollo threw another fearful look behind him. "But be careful! The Cosmos is out of balance, everything's messed up—there are monsters on the loose! They'll be looking for the boy, and I can't help you. No gods can help you—you're on your own! You must take the path through the mountains to Delphi! Um, what else, what else . . . ?" His eyes darted around wildly. "Er . . . beware of mushrooms! I see a mushroom that will bring disaster . . . er . . ."

My ears perked up. "Mushrooms? I'm quite partial to fried mushrooms."

"Forget about mushrooms!" hissed Sibyl, then to Apollo, "What must we do at Delphi?"

But the god wasn't listening. He had swung the quiver from his shoulder and was scrabbling for an arrow with trembling fingers.

"What's he doing?" I asked out of the side of my mouth.

Whatever it was, he wasn't making a very good job of it. Arrows spilled forward. The god bent to pick them up, and

---

*Located in Apollo's temple at Delphi, the Omphalos was a large stone block, known as the Navel of the World, which marked the center of the Cosmos. To identify the spot, Zeus released two eagles from the far corners of the world. Where they met was deemed to be the center of the world.

that's when I saw it—another figure in the flames behind him.

It was small, but that's because it was some way in the distance. With another metallic-sounding footstep, the figure came closer and I got a better look. It was covered from head to toe in tattered black rags. No face was visible beneath its torn cowl, and I for one was grateful for this.

Apollo had seen it now. The god's hands trembled so much he was unable to thread his bow.

"Quick!" he shouted in desperation. "Put the flames out!"

As Sibyl rushed forward, so too the dark figure in the flames moved implacably toward the god. Apollo was immobile with distinctly ungodlike terror. As Sibyl stamped on the burning twigs, the dark figure raised one ragged arm and began to reach up to its cowl.

I didn't want to see what lay under there, thank you very much, but I couldn't drag my eyes away from it either. Slowly the cowl began to move back and . . .

"Quickleeeeeeeeeeeeeeeeeeeeeeeeeeeeeeeeeeeeeee!" called Apollo, but the end of his cry was nothing more than an echo in the smoke, as the fire died under Sibyl's speedy footwork. Darkness reclaimed the temple. Both the figures in the flames were gone.

Bumscruff was looking sadly at the dying embers.

"Bye-bye!" he called tearfully, as if bidding a favorite aunt a pleasant trip to the seaside.

Sibyl was waving one smoking sandal in the air to cool it off. "And what do you think you're doing?" she asked me.

I looked up from the untouched offerings on the stone step and burped discreetly.

"Waste not, want not."

The temple had begun to give me the willies, so it was a relief to be outside. We had moved to the sanctuary, which is a fancy way of saying the temple's backyard.

Bumscruff occupied himself jumping for lemons from the trees that surrounded us, while Sibyl and I discussed what we had just seen. Neither of us quite trusted our own memories.

"So . . ." I said carefully. "That isn't how Apollo usually acts?"

Sibyl shook her head. Her face was as pale as feta cheese.

"Never."

"And who was the other one, then? The one whose laundry had fallen into the shredder?"

Sibyl bit her lip in that pensive and worried way in which some people tend to bite their lips. At last she spoke.

"I think it was Thanatos."

What? The name alone made acid flare in my belly as if I'd been eating red-hot chili-pepper sandwiches.

Thanatos!

But that didn't make sense. Okay, Thanatos was an immortal also, but you wouldn't call him a god. More of a cosmic force really. I mean, no one gave offerings to Thanatos as they did to the proper pantheon of Olympians. There was no eager audience for tales of his amazing exploits. Thanatos simply dispatched people to the afterlife and the Underworld, where Pluto reigned. Pluto might be the lord of the dead, but Thanatos was the very embodiment of death.

"Well, I told you Apollo's prophecy," Sibyl said. "You know, the end of the world, death and destruction all around, that sort of thing."

An icy chill tap-danced the length of my spine and back again. Why hadn't we moved a little farther from the temple before having this chat?

"But he can't have been talking about the gods, too. The gods are immortal!" I exclaimed. "They can't die, so why should Apollo be so afraid of Thanatos?"

"That's a good question," said Sibyl. Unfortunately, she didn't seem to have much by way of a good answer.

"YUCK!" shouted Bumscruff, looking down at the half-bitten lemon in his fist. He popped the rest of the lemon into his mouth and went on chewing.

"Close your mouth when you chew," said Sibyl absent-mindedly.

BOOK XIV

The travelers take the high road (even though one of them has been known to get nosebleeds at high altitudes).

"Isn't there a route that's a bit . . . flatter?"

"No."

Geography has never been a big interest of mine, so I had no choice but to believe Sibyl when she said that the mountain path was the only route connecting this corner of northern Greece with the mainland to the south. We plodded on.

Sibyl's social skills didn't pick up, but at least Bumscruff offered fresh opportunity for conversation now, after the sudden expansion of his one-word vocabulary.

I was glad to have something not quite so apocalyptic to think about. What's more, though I have never received formal training, I am a natural-born teacher, and I selflessly passed the hours giving the lad Greek lessons.

"See those bright things? They're called *noses*. Say *noses*."

"Noses!" barked Bumscruff.

Sibyl butted in. "They are NOT called *noses*. They're *flowers*! And those flying things are *butterflies*, not *underpants*. Stop telling him the wrong words for things, Gryllus!"

We didn't encounter anyone to break up the monotony of the journey. Once or twice we'd spot an isolated hut in the distance. I was all for making a brief detour so we could stock up on essential items such as pies and . . . well, pies would have been a good start.

Sibyl wouldn't have any of it. "We're not doing anything that isn't part of the task Apollo set us," she said firmly, not to mention bossily. "No leaving the path until we reach Delphi."

We'd walk until close to sunset—each one looking more ragged and wobbly than the last—and then look for a place to make camp. It was on our third evening that I made an astonishing discovery. Sibyl was busy assembling the various fruits and vegetables we'd foraged into something approximating a meal, and Bumscruff was enthusiastically gathering more wood for the fire. I was occupied gazing dreamily into the flames of the campfire.

"Is it me, or is Bumscruff getting bigger?" I commented thoughtfully.

I couldn't help thinking that in the brief time we'd known him, that lad had aged a couple of years, not to mention grown taller by a foot or so. Suddenly the lad's tunic was looking perilously short.

Sibyl didn't look up. "Must be all the exercise he's getting, what with having to lug an enormous, fat pig everywhere."

"It's not my fault I've got bunions!" I sputtered.

Sibyl made a little noise that I would have to label a snort of derision. "I don't think you can get bunions on pigs' hooves, can you?"

"I don't intend to find out!" I fired back.

At that moment Bumscruff strode into the campsite and

set down the impossibly large stack of wood he had been cradling in his skinny arms. He grinned hugely and pointed at a scrubby bunch of flowers at the edge of the campsite.

"Me like noses!" he boomed.

"Good," I said, glad to fall back into my role as wise old mentor. "So why don't you pick one?"

The next day started out in much the same way as usual. I walked as far as I could—twenty minutes or so—then Bumscruff hoisted me onto his narrow but tireless shoulders. I was struck again by how much farther away the ground was since he'd first provided this service.

We continued this way for some time. The only problem with this travel arrangement was that it gave me a little too much chance to think, and none of my thoughts were very comforting.

The world around us didn't seem especially aware that anything was wrong with the fabric of existence—insects wandered from flower to flower, plants grew, et cetera, et cetera. If I hadn't been present in the temple of Apollo, I might have been able to convince myself that Sibyl had gotten it wrong. I certainly *wanted* to believe this. Unfortunately, I knew better.

"So . . . how long do you think we've got?" I asked. "Until the end of the universe as we know it, I mean?"

Sibyl's eyes flashed. "Let me put it this way. At least I won't have to repaint my bathroom."

"You're joking, right?" I said.

"Yes, I'm joking. . . . It's actually my living room I won't have to paint. I did the bathroom last spring."

Nobody likes a prophetess with a smart mouth.

I was about to try again, but then suddenly Bumscruff was shouting and pointing to a thin plume of smoke in the valley to our east. (At least I *think* it was east—somewhat surprisingly, navigation is not one of my strong points, as Odysseus discovered after I had once steered the ship in entirely the wrong direction for several hours, leading us to the stretch of water known as the Shipwreck Reefs. It was the sort of silly little mistake anyone could make, so I really can't say why he got so snippy about it.) The smoke rose from a clearing in the blanket of trees.

"House!" yelled Bumscruff. "House!"

"Terrific," growled Sibyl, "but we have to keep going. There's a lot of ground to cover before—"

She paused, mainly because there wasn't much point carrying on. Not when Bumscruff the Goat-Boy had left the path and was striding toward the pine forest that led to the smoke. Given my status as his passenger, there wasn't much I could do but enjoy the scenery.

"Stop!" yelled Sibyl. "We can't leave the path! Apollo said not to!"

But Bumscruff kept on walking. Sibyl legged it after us. "Gryllus!" she wailed. "YOU stop him!"

"Okay," I called from the lad's shoulders. "Any ideas how?"

When we reached the edge of the woods, Bumscruff paused and waited for Sibyl to catch up.

"You *can't* go this way," she said, panting.

For once Bumscruff wasn't smiling. "Muss go," he said seriously. "Muss go ta house."

The prophetess was chewing her lower lip again. "Why?"

"He's probably hungry!" I exploded. "Maybe he doesn't want to eat your Olive and Vine Leaf Surprise again for supper!" (This was what Sibyl had prepared three nights in a row—the only surprise being that it tasted worse than it sounded.)

"Go ta house," Bumscruff repeated. His words were underscored by a rumble of far-off thunder, though the skies directly above us were cloudless still.

Okay, time for me to brush up my legendary rhetorical skills. "What harm will it be?" I said to Sibyl in my most velvety tones. "We'll take a quick detour, grab a bite to eat, and then we'll be back on the mountain road before you can say 'Aristotle's your uncle.' You have to admit, it'd be nice to have some different grub for a change."

Sibyl wasn't convinced, but she looked once more at the determination on the goatherd's face. This was something she hadn't expected, that the lad would not follow her every order to the letter. But he clearly wasn't going anywhere other than the source of that smoke. At last Sibyl gave a quick, anxious nod, and we entered the woods.

Away from the vantage point of the high road, it wasn't so easy to see where we were going. I kept on bumping into branches until I reluctantly had to ask Bumscruff to set me down.

One thought kept me going as we made our way through

those woods: where there was smoke, there had to be fire—
and where there was fire, there was a chance of a decent
fried breakfast. I knew Sibyl was fretting that we'd get ourselves lost, but Bumscruff seemed to have a good idea
which direction to take. Then, after a while, I was able to
let the trusty old snout take over, and we just followed the
scent.

Before we could see anything, we heard a whirring
sound and a low hum. When we reached the edge of the
clearing, we peered through the pines and found ourselves
looking at an old man—much like any other skinny, old,
white-haired guy really, though what he was wearing was
rather more exotic than the usual garb.

"He's got trousers on!" I hissed, failing to stifle the
incredulous smirk in my voice. (I'd heard tell that men in
far-off Persia sported trousers on their legs, but I'd always
assumed this was just an outlandish tale.)

Well, okay, I wouldn't expect Bumscruff to see the
humor, but Sibyl didn't offer up even the flicker of a ghost
of a hint of a smile. "One day all men will wear trousers
instead of tunics," she declared loftily. "Plenty of women
will, too, actually." She hesitated. "Well, as long as there's
anyone around *to* wear trousers, that is. . . ."

But it wasn't just the trouser wearing that was so weird.
What the old man was *doing* was a bit on the odd side,
too. He was sitting at one end of some sort of mysterious
contraption. He had both feet on a kind of handle with
pedals, and he was turning it around at a steady speed. This
handle rotated something that looked like a metal bar with

lots of copper wire wrapped around it. The other end of this wire was wrapped around another, even larger, metal bar, which dangled over a small wooden table at the opposite end of the gizmo. The whole contraption was held up by rickety-looking bits of wood and string.

As we got closer, we saw that there was something hanging from the larger metal bar.

It was a fork.

"Listen," Sibyl said in an urgent, low voice. "I'll do all the talking, okay?"

Bumscruff nodded solemnly, though who knew whether he understood. He clearly lacked the newfound words to express his thoughts (if any). Or perhaps he was feeling guilty about forcing Sibyl to depart from Apollo's plan. Either way, he fell back on his trusty old standby.

"Bek."

Sibyl turned to me. "Okay, Gryllus?"

"What are you trying to say?" I demanded.

"Just that a talking pig can be a bit of a shock to less open-minded folk . . . so keep your big trap shut."

And then the disapproving frown on her face metamorphosed into a great big beamer of a grin as she strode out into the clearing. Bumscruff trotted after her.

"Good afternoon!" called Sibyl in an unfamiliar tone that took me a moment to identify.

It was open and friendly.

BOOK XV

The "Father of Science" displays his incredible performing fork.

When the old man stopped turning the pedals, the buzzing abruptly ended. The fork at the far end of the contraption fell onto the table with a dull clang.

The gaze with which he greeted Sibyl and Bumscruff was one of those unblinking ones that are a bit on the worrying side. It was matched by the fixed grin farther down his face.

"How can I help you?" he asked.

Introducing herself, Sibyl said that Bumscruff was her younger brother. She didn't bother mentioning me, although I too had wandered into the clearing. The old man was called Thales, he said.

"If it isn't too much trouble," Sibyl continued, "we'd love a bite to eat. It's been a while since we had any food."

"Food!" Bumscruff echoed. He was holding up the fork at the wooden table. A casual observer might have assumed that he was appraising the utensil in anticipation of eating something with it. I knew better—Bumscruff was evaluating the fork itself as a potential foodstuff. Sure enough, he lifted it to his mouth and tested it with his teeth.

"Yes, food . . . Quite so! Yes, I know just the thing!" declared Thales, doing his polite best not to stare at the goatherd. "I shall be back before you can say . . . erm, back in two shakes of a . . . I shall return momentarily!" And he scurried off toward a small hut at the other end of the clearing.

"Hope he isn't making a mushroom omelette," I muttered, remembering Apollo's warning about mushrooms.

Meanwhile, Bumscruff continued to inspect the old man's mysterious contraption. The goat-boy ran his hands across the iron, copper, and wood gizmo with his customary blend of enthusiasm and incomprehension. He turned the pedals with one hand, much faster than the old man had done. Once more, the entire contraption began to hum. The fork whizzed upward again to the metal bar.

"Don't touch that!" Thales was hurrying across the clearing with a tray of food in his hands. "It's a very delicate instrument," he added more calmly, once Bumscruff had let go and the fork had fallen again.

"What is it, anyway?" asked Sibyl.

"I'm sure you've heard of something called a magnet?" Thales began with a proud little smile.

"Yeah, sailors use them to navigate," Sibyl said with a nod.

"Well, this is a most special kind of magnet," continued Thales. "When I push the pedals, I rotate magnet A inside this copper wire, and this creates a form of energy that flows along the wire. When it flows through the big coil, it turns the large iron bar into a second magnet, enabling it to pick up the fork, or indeed any metal object."

I was about to say, "Why don't you just go and pick up the fork?" It would've been a lot easier than fiddling around with all these magnets and pedals and such like.

As it turned out, all I managed was "Wh——" before Sibyl's knee caught me a good one in the ribs.

Meanwhile, Thales was getting the grub ready.

The good news was that it wasn't mushrooms; the bad news was that it didn't appear to be any known foodstuff. He emptied a load of dust and dried-up twigs into a serving bowl.

"This is a little something I have been working on. Haven't had a chance to try it myself, but I think you're going to like it," Thales declared, beaming. Oblivious to the look on our faces, he poured boiling water from a jug onto the dried-up dust. "I call it Desiccated and Rehydrated Noodle in the Pot."

With the addition of the water, the food lost its dustlike appearance, but it failed to take on much of a foodlike quality. What's more, the aroma of Desiccated and Rehydrated Noodle in the Pot did not get the old gastric juices flowing. It smelled as appetizing as a Spartan's socks after a ten-mile forced march.

"You are about to taste the foodstuff of the future," Thales announced. I could only pity the diners of the future (until I remembered that there probably wouldn't *be* a future).

Unaware that only Bumscruff was shoveling the food into his mouth (noisily and with fingers), Thales set about getting the bread, which he placed on the table with a theatrical flourish.

The reason for his proud grin was clear: the bread was already neatly sliced into a dozen perfectly equal rounds!

"Incredible!" I gasped. "Pre-sliced bread! That's the best thing since . . . I don't know what!"

"Thank you," began Thales. "It was really just a matter of perfecting the slicing machine so that—" He paused, and his eyebrows shot up in surprise.

"Wh-What did you say?" he asked me.

"Not sure it tastes all that great, though," I declared through a mouthful.

"Extraordinary!" Thales gasped, turning to Sibyl. "Young lady, were you aware that your pig had the power of locution?"

"It's hard to forget," growled Sibyl.

"This is simply astonishing!" said the old man, his gaze flicking like a Ping-Pong ball back and forth between the prophetess and me. "It's imperative that I cut open this specimen and see how its vocal apparatus differs from that of most pigs."

"Oi! I like my vocal apparatus where it is, thank you very much." I took a hurried step backward. "On the inside of my neck."

Thales hesitated. "But . . . you'll be broadening the horizons of human knowledge. Adding your footfalls to the glorious march of progress to a better tomorrow."

"Tomorrow won't be much better for me, though, will it, if you cut me open?"

"But . . . but the insides of your skull must be a treasure trove of information!"

"You keep your mitts off my treasure trove," I exclaimed. "I like my brain where it is, too."

"Gryllus is planning on using it one day," added Sibyl.

I ignored her and set the old fellow straight. "You can't look at my brain because I'm a human," I said.

"No, no, no," Thales responded with an indulgent smile. "You see, man is a rational biped, and you, clearly, are no biped."

"He isn't very rational either," Sibyl chipped in.

Before I could unleash one of my more scathing put-downs, Bumscruff started jumping up and down and yelling, "Birdie! Lookit the birdie!"

If Thales really wanted to unravel a mystery, he ought to be having a look at *Bumscruff's* brainbox. The poor, thick lad was pointing to an unremarkable small bird flapping over-head. Who knew why he was so excited about this one rather than any of the others twittering around the place?

As it happens—and this might be a bit of a shocker to you—ornithology is not one of my strong points. I'm really only interested in two kinds of birds—ones you can teach to say rude limericks and ones you can roast after stuffing sage and onion up their bums. So I didn't pay much attention to Bumscruff's little bird . . . not until it let out a raucous *CAW!* and swooped down from the pine it had perched in. It was aiming straight at my head.

"Watch out, Gryllus!" yelled Sibyl.

Luckily, repeated brushes with danger over the years have honed my reactions, leaving them sharper than the stylus of a schoolroom bookworm.

Unluckily, that bird was fast too, and one of its wings did graze the back of my neck.

"YEOW! That thing's wings are like metal!" I gasped. "It's shaved off some of my bristles!" Judging from the breeze I could suddenly feel, I was now sporting a strip of skin as smooth as a baby's bottom.

The bird had banked and come to rest on a nearby branch. It watched us with an eye as beady as a bead necklace.

"Birdie give da owee!" Bumscruff hooted excitedly.

"Oh gods," gasped Sibyl, a look of horror on her face. "I know what that is. It's one of the Stymphalian birds."

"One of the what?"

"Don't you know *any* history?" she snapped.

"History repeats itself," I replied knowledgeably. "I can catch it the second time around, can't I?"

"The Stymphalian birds live up in the northern marshes," explained Sibyl quickly. "They'll attack anything. Heracles had to fight a flock of them as one of his Labors. They're not normal birds—they've got razor-sharp iron beaks and wingtips."

"Ah, well . . ." Thales cleared his throat in a professorial manner. "I'm afraid that can't be, miss. You see, a bird's ability to fly is dependent on the lightness of its body. A bird with iron-tipped feathers could never become airborne. It's all a matter of what I like to call *physics*. . . ."

Thales would have continued his lecture on the impossibility of the Stymphalian birds, but he was distracted by the rapid approach of the Stymphalian bird, which had not been informed that it couldn't fly. Indeed, as the sun glinted off its beak and wingtips, it did give every impression of being both airborne and metallic, not to mention very, very dangerous.

It was also hurtling toward Thales' head.

"Erm, yes—" sputtered Thales. Then he chose to give up talking in favor of warbling like a panicked turkey and ducking his head so that it wasn't punctured by the deadly spear of the bird's beak. He only just made it. "WAAAAH!" yelled Thales, and he began legging it toward the wooden hut.

"HOO-HAH!" Bumscruff chipped in happily.

I would have joined in this chorus, but I was focusing all my attention on running around and around in frenzied circles.

Not Sibyl. "Here, birdie," she shouted coolly as she hopped onto the seat of Thales' contraption. She let out an encouraging whistle as if trying to coax a kitten out from behind a couch.

The bird was completing a wide arc over the trees at the edge of the clearing. It switched course so that it was flying straight at Sibyl. The prophetess carried on whistling, apparently unconcerned that the murderous bird was about to do something a bit more radical than sit on her shoulder and eat a cracker.

As it folded its wings back into a terminal dive, the bird became a dark streak of doom against the sky. There was no time for Sibyl to make a run for it now. This wasn't going to be a pretty sight.

But then suddenly Sibyl began pedaling Thales' gizmo. The metal bars started spinning, and the whole contraption began to hum. The fork clanged up into the larger metal bar . . . and so did the Stymphalian bird.

It wobbled in the air and then veered left, straight into the "special" magnet, where it was stuck fast . . . and clearly not happy.

Sibyl, still pedaling, shouted, "How about that, then?"

"Not bad," I answered. "It must be your magnetic personality. Get it? Your MAGNETIC personality?"

No one else seemed to appreciate this, leading me to reflect on a sorry truth about this imperfect world of ours: *The path of the gifted pig is a long and lonely one.*

BOOK XVI

A visionary maps the road to the future while making a round of toast.

It was late in the day — too late for us to hit the road again, thankfully — but Thales made no further mention of dinner. The old boy was too busy staring at the Stymphalian bird and scribbling notes on a large piece of papyrus. He used a writing stylus the like of which I had never seen. (He called it a Ball-Pointed Writing Stylus. His fingers were stained black where his "revolution in the development of the written word" had leaked.)

Meanwhile, the Stymphalian bird was not a happy camper. One of its legs was tied to a short cable, the other end of which was attached to a metal peg sunk into the ground.

The setup had been Sibyl's idea, but only Bumscruff had been physically able to do it. That lad might have looked as weedy as a sloth's backyard, but he was as strong as a bodybuilding ox on a high-protein diet and as quick as . . . Well, he was very quick.

"What's all this, then?" I asked Thales.

He gave up a tiny part of his attention to me. "Making *scientific* observations."

Fair enough. I had a shot at this myself, and I watched as the bird flew around and around in ever-faster circles. After a while, it stopped and tottered around dizzily before falling over. I immediately formulated a theory to account for this behavior: "This bird's stupid."

I knew I was on solid ground as Thales chose not to contest my view. Instead he went on writing. In the middle of the papyrus was a diagram of a bird with lots of that squiggly writing stuff all around it.

On the ground by his feet lay another papyrus. I flipped it over with my snout and said, "What's on this one, then?"

"Preliminary notes on the other . . . erm . . . specimen," murmured Thales.

There was a sketch on this papyrus too, but of a beast that occupied a rung on the Ladder of Being much higher than any mere bird. It was, in fact, a pig. The picture wasn't very realistic-looking, though, mainly because Thales had drawn various bits that you can't usually see, as they're tucked away on the inside—all tubes and tendons and gross stuff like that.

I was the other specimen!

"And what does *this* writing say?" I asked, pointing to one scrawled sentence.

"It says 'How can an ordinary man of limited intelligence be transformed into a talking pig?'"

I rose above that "limited intelligence" crack, because that's the sort of pig I am. Big-hearted.

"And what about this bit you've underlined five times?"

"I don't know," answered Thales.

"You don't know?" I snorted. "But you wrote it!"

"No, you misunderstand," said Thales. "You see, the starting point of what I call Science must be a clear-eyed admission of what we do NOT know."

"Well, I can't speak for the sparrow of doom here, but I can tell you how I got turned into a pig. You see, there was this goddess-type on an island, and—"

"Enough!" cried Thales, and even the Stymphalian bird quit cawing for a moment. "That is precisely the sort of explanation that will not do. It is not sufficient to say, 'Oh well, the gods did it!' or 'By Zeus, it was magic!' What are these but ways of saying we have no idea how something really happened? The correct question should be '*How* did the gods do it?' And Science is what will supply the answer."

"The answer to what?" said a weary voice from behind us. Sibyl had caught just the end of Thales' minispeech.

"Well . . ." declared the old boy, "the answer to every-thing."

The prophetess slumped into a chair and sighed. "Oh yeah? I wish it could tell me where Apollo has gotten to." Clearly, her attempt to contact the god again had failed.

Thales was blinking rapidly as he processed this new information. "So . . . you have been trying to contact an Olympian?" he said in a hushed voice.

"She works for one," I chipped in cheerfully. "Apollo." I gave Sibyl a big wink.

Thales' brow was creased with the effort of keeping his disapproval in check. "And what is it that you do for this . . . deity?"

Judging from the way she glared in my direction, Sibyl didn't want to be having this conversation. "I work at the Delphic oracle."

"She's a junior prophetess," I added helpfully, just in case he thought she only worked the cash register at the snack bar or polished the marblework or something.

Thales could contain himself no longer. "This is exactly what I'm talking about!" he exclaimed. "Predicting the future should be no divine mystery. The whole thing is just a matter of extrapolating from the present evidence. When I see thunderclouds, can I not predict that there will be a storm? Your 'god' Apollo is simply privy to more such evidence on which to base his predictions. But that's not to say that we mortals can't gain access to the same evidence. . . . Knowledge is power!"

I cleared my throat tactfully. "Quite right, too! And speaking of knowledge . . . do you know what's for supper?"

Sibyl whirled to face me. "Oh for gods' sake, Gryllus, stop thinking about your belly for *once,* will you!"

But the old boy was nodding his head vigorously. "No, no, your . . . erm, friend here is quite right," he said. He hopped up in a sprightly fashion. "Now is an ideal moment both to have a little nourishment and also to witness a proper demonstration of the potential of this enterprise called Science." He began to stride off toward the back of the hut. He got halfway before he realized that no one was following him. "Erm, walk this way, please."

"I don't think I can walk that way," I whispered to Sibyl out of the corner of my mouth. "I think *he* only walks that way because his trousers are too tight."

Bumscruff was sitting around the back of the hut. He looked deep in thought, though I wouldn't like to speculate what thoughts were actually ricocheting around his skull. (They say the eyes are the windows to the house of the soul. I couldn't help thinking that in Bumscruff's case the windows looked in on a disused storage room.)

The four of us made our way to a second building set away from Thales' dwelling quarters. This one was smaller—more a shed than a hut. Thales paused outside the door, which was secured with several serious-looking chains. The look on his face suggested someone who has been asked to explain advanced Pythagorean mathematics to an unschooled guinea pig.

"Are you familiar with the *atom*?" he began.

I nodded intelligently. "'Course I am! I figured you must have a load of atoms stacked up in there. Collect 'em, do you?"

Thales was looking nonplussed.

"We don't know what atoms are," Sibyl cut in. "DO we, Gryllus?"

118

"Not as such . . . no."

Thales had freed one of the chains. "Okay, okay . . . Think of it this way," he began with daunting enthusiasm. "Imagine a flea."

(Easily done—every bed I'd ever slept in came with a handy supply of fleas.)

"Well, now imagine that the flea itself has a sort of flea upon its back." A little smile was peering out from behind his beard again. "And that flea—the flea's flea, if you will—has another flea. And so on. Imagine something as tiny as a flea on a flea on a flea on a flea on a flea on a flea on a flea."

"That's a lot of fleas," I said thoughtfully.

"Precisely!" Thales grinned as if all were now clear. "I contend that the entire world is made up of particles as small as this."

"What, the world is made of fleas?"

"No, no, the world is made up of tiny particles so small that you could never see them," said Thales with unnerving eagerness. "Billions of them."

I grunted in disbelief.

"Erm, anyway, some thinkers argue that the atom is indivisible, as its very name implies," Thales went on. "I, however, do not believe this to be the case." His voice grew louder. "The atom can be split, I tell you! The device I am working on in this very shed is designed to do just that—to split open the indivisible atom itself!"

With all the chains now removed, he threw open the door. We peered in. The room was dominated by a large, squarish object with several holes on top. The whole thing was connected by metal tubes to a much smaller device with two slots on the top. One end of the room was blocked off by a low stone wall.

Thales bustled off to the other end of the room and knelt by a pit dug into the floor.

"I've got a question," said Sibyl, stepping inside. "Why? What's the point of splitting an atom, then?"

"To release the energy stored within," said Thales, as if it were obvious. "So that humankind might finally stand on its own two feet, of course. So that we might stop relying on the gods to do everything." He patted the bulky object proudly. "When we can truly harness the power of the atom, we can do anything. Why, we . . . we could be more powerful even than the gods themselves."

Still at the doorway, I looked nervously up to the skies. People have received lightning bolts to the head for saying much less than this.

But no lightning bolt arrived to punish Thales now. Somehow that silence from the skies was even scarier than thunderbolts whizzing all over the place. What were the gods playing at? Did they no longer care? Was any Tom, Dick, or Harrios now free to mouth off about the Olympians?

Using tongs, Thales lifted a small, thin tube out of the pit. It glittered with silvery yellow light.

"This substance is highly toxic," said Thales, stepping carefully toward the larger device. "However, I am taking all necessary safety precautions." (I think he was referring to the spotted hankie he'd put over his mouth.)

I took a step back. So far Thales hadn't done much to put an edge on my appetite.

"What is it?" asked Sibyl.

Thales was inserting the rod into a hole at the top of the machine.

"Perhaps the rarest substance in the Cosmos," he explained. "All the more amazing that I found traces of it lying around in my backyard. It's mostly found deep in the Underworld, as you would expect Pluto's Iron to be."

"Pluto's Iron?" echoed Sibyl. "You mean that's . . . PLUTO-nium?"

Thales nodded enthusiastically. He had now gone behind the low wall to a small table from which he took two slices of his pre-sliced white bread.

"Er . . . what's the bread for?"

Thales gave a series of blinks. "Eventually my Atomos Device will provide unlimited power—to heat our cities, drive our vehicles, anything. . . . But for the prototype, I have chosen to harness its energy to meet a need shared by all humanity—the desire to enjoy a slice of bread rendered crisp and warm."

He popped both slices of bread into the slots in the small device.

Sibyl's mouth hung open. "It's a toaster?" she said. "You're using Pluto's Iron and splitting the atom and what-not, all just so you can make some TOAST?"

As far as I was concerned, this was the first interesting thing anyone had said in ages.

"Great!" I said. "A piece of toast would really hit the spot."

Thales began to crank a handle on the side of the big square machine.

"I, um, I recommend that you stand behind the protective wall," he said. "Just in case, you understand . . ."

I was behind that wall before he could finish the sentence. Sibyl followed, dragging Bumscruff with her.

When the machine began to hum, Thales hitched up his trousers and charged behind the wall, too.

"It's really a matter of controlling the energy so that——"

A thunderclap and a flash of light cut him off. The shed was filled with black smoke. Sibyl let out a businesslike scream of surprise, and I believe a squeal or two even made their way out of me. (Okay, two squeals exactly—one at each end.) Bumscruff jumped up and down with excitement and yelled, "Ker-pow!"

We slowly emerged from behind the barrier. The spot where the toaster and bread had been was now occupied by a small pile of powdery black dust.

"Erm, I do hope you like your toast well done," said Thales.

It wasn't so much well done as vaporized.

While Thales wasted time with the machine's settings, promising he could sort it all out in a jiffy, I gave the remains of the bread an experimental sniff. After all, food's food, and the stomach of a pig is itself a beast to be fed on a regular basis.

"Got any marmalade?" I asked.

BOOK XVII

The "Mushroom of Doom" is neither fried nor grilled.

I don't count myself among those poetic types who rattle on and on about the glories of the dawn and all that. If the sunrise is so wonderful, why don't the powers that be put it on at a more reasonable time of day when normal folk have had enough sleep?

The next morning was an exception, however. I woke up so early that it was still dark out. I did so because, for one thing, I was starving. After the toast fiasco, we'd ended up eating the only thing Thales had left in the pantry, more Desiccated and Rehydrated Noodle in the Pot.

Discomfort was the second reason I found myself up at this absurd hour. Thales' living quarters were what you'd call Spartan—which is to say a dump with not much in it. (By the way, you have to be careful about making this sort of observation to actual Spartans, who can be a bit touchy and are often armed with sharp swords.) There were no beds in the room Bumscruff and I had slept in so we'd had to sleep on the bare floor.

I didn't expect anyone else to be up, leaving me free to explore the kitchen in case our host had overlooked any scraps of food. But, as I trudged into the main room, Thales was there, in the same place from where he'd said good night. Scrolls were spread on the table in front of him.

They were illuminated by a lamp that appeared to light up without the aid of a fire.

I sighed deeply. "Still trying to figure out what went wrong with the toaster, are you?" I asked.

There was a pause of a few seconds while Thales' brain underwent re-entry into the world of everyday conversation. "The road of Science cannot be expected to proceed without a few . . . um, potholes."

He set down his Ball-Pointed Writing Stylus and gave me a long, bleary-eyed look. "Would you care to know why I'm doing all this?" He waved an ink-stained hand to indicate everything around us.

I vetoed the answer that first sprang to mind—"No!"— on the grounds that it might stop our host from rustling up some breakfast at any point in the foreseeable future.

"Okay," I sighed.

"Each of my inventions is no more than a skirmish in the same long war. In all my work, I am engaged in a fight against Chaos," Thales said gravely. "You see, before the world was born, there was nothing but Chaos—shapeless matter and void in an endless swirl—a sort of primordial soup."

That got my attention, as I have always been fond of soup.

"The creation of the universe was a process of imposing order on that Chaos," Thales went on. "Shapeless matter took form and became the world we know. The history of the Cosmos is one of steady ascent from disorder and Chaos."

He paused to give his brain a chance to squeeze out a few more Big Thoughts.

"But the journey is far from over, and we humans are the ones who must complete it. The gods had their chance with the so-called Golden Age, when the race of humans lived in a world of darkness and superstition. Now only Science can—"

I never did find out exactly what only Science could do for humanity because suddenly

B O O O O M !

the world shuddered with the loudest noise I'd ever heard or felt in my life. It was like listening to thunder from the inside of a thundercloud. It was like being a gong. Even in my fear, a tiny thought dashed itself onto the shores of my consciousness: the gods have done this. They may have taken their own sweet time, but they got around to it in the end. Thales had put their backs up, rambling on in the way he had, and now they'd decided to teach him a lesson.

"What was THAT?" gasped Sibyl from the doorway, and then more urgently, "Where's the boy?"

As soon as she said it, I knew the answers were connected. I hadn't even bothered checking on the lad when I had left the room.

Thales ran to the window. What he saw made even

him forget his principles for a moment. "By the gods . . ." he gulped.

Sibyl rushed to the door and pulled it open. By the time I got to the window, Sibyl was already racing toward Bumscruff, who was swaying gently in the gray light of the dawn. His face was blackened by ashes, and his hair stood on end. Smoke rose from it in lazy strands. For once, Bumscruff wasn't smiling. He held one hand to his head and let out a glum little groan.

"Ow!" moaned the goatherd.

It was easy to see why he might have a touch of a headache. Behind him, where the shed had once stood, there was nothing but a large pit surrounded by a black scorch mark on the ground. And rising into the air was the strangest-looking cloud I'd ever set eyes on. It was like a column of smoke that bloomed at the top into a billowing cloud.

"Hey, look at that!" I marveled. "Looks just like a mushroom, doesn't it?"

Sibyl had her arm around the lad's shoulders now. As she looked back, she drew in her breath sharply. "Oh gods, Apollo's prophecy!" she gasped. "Beware the mushroom! He called it the bringer of death or something. . . . We've got to go!"

I shook my head. "I don't think that's what he meant—"

But then I saw it, a huge, raggedy, black shape rising above the trees far behind the cloud, shimmering like a heat haze. We had seen that dark figure before. It was Thanatos, and it was coming this way.

As the dark shape came closer, it was just about possible to make out the rapid flittering of dozens and dozens of knife-sharp pairs of wings. And then suddenly it burst apart into dozens of smaller shapes, and the truth slapped us about the head.

It *wasn't* Thanatos. It was more of those Stymphalian birds. Lots more.

"Erm, perhaps you'd better come inside," Thales called with the calmness of utter disbelief. Sibyl half-carried the still-dazed goatherd toward the doorway. By the time everyone was inside and Thales had slammed the door and closed the shutters, I was safely under the table. Not that I was cowering under there—in a hairy situation like this, your common-or-garden-variety hero requires a quiet, dark, and, above all, *safe* place to muster his heroic stuff and cook up a suitably valiant course of action.

"Keep it down, will you?" I snapped when the first *THUNK!* sounded. "I'm trying to come up with a plan."

"Er, Gryllus?" said Sibyl. "That wasn't us. That was one of the birds."

There followed another *THUNK,* then another, and another. Soon we could hear nothing but the constant drumming of the birds' beaks as they hurled themselves at the hut. *THUNK! THUNK! THUNK!*

"Head hurt," groaned Bumscruff, clapping his hands over his ears. "Go 'way!"

"What are we going to do?" yelled Sibyl over the racket.

Thales was hunched over the table, scribbling furiously.

THUNK! THUNK! THUNK! And then suddenly there

was a noise that wasn't exactly a *THUNK!* It was more a sort of *CRACK!* followed by a kind of irate *CAW, CAW!*

I peeked out. One of the birds had smashed right through the wall. Its beak jutted in like a dagger. The dagger began to twist, then the beak was pulled out, leaving a split in the wall.

CRACK! Another razor-sharp beak poked its way in on the other side of the house. *CRACK! CRACK! CRACK!* It was beginning to sound like a woodchoppers' convention, and I was already missing the good old days when all we had to listen to was those *THUNKS*. Dozens of beaks were now thrusting into the hut.

Thales leaped to his feet and waved his papyrus about in an agitated way. "According to my calculations," he shouted, "the domicile is sturdy enough to withstand the attack! I designed and built it myself, you know."

There was just time for me to contemplate the true terribleness of this information, and then the *CRACKS* were joined by another sound—a sort of long-drawn-out *CREAAAAAAK!,* a sound of infinite sadness and pain. It was coming from the walls of the hut.

The next instant, one entire wall simply fell forward. It did so without fuss, as if it had just decided that, all things considered, it would be better off having a bit of a nap now. That might well have been true for the wall, but it was hard to see that we were better off. After all, the Stymphalian birds were now free to hurtle into the hut and peck us to several hundred bits.

"There's a possibility I may have miscalculated," mumbled Thales just as a second wall decided to join in and topple over. We had to get out of there before the two remaining walls gave up and allowed the roof to fall and splat us.

Outside, the birds were regrouping into an attack formation. Their squawking had taken on a triumphant tone.

Well, I wasn't going to stick around to see who they picked first for slicing and dicing. I ran toward a line of trees. In a situation like this, it's every pig for himself.

Behind me I could hear the metallic whirring of the assassin-birds' wings. The cawing got louder. There was no way I'd be able to make it to the safety of the foliage in time.

But then a plan leaped into my mind like the newborn goddess Athena leaping out of Zeus's head. (Only, of course, she leaped OUT and this brilliant idea of mine leaped INTO my head, so the comparison isn't perfect. Also, one of them was a goddess and the other was a plan. Okay, so the idea didn't leap like Athena at all. I just had the idea, sort of suddenly.)

As I came to a halt, the birds zoomed past me. Their flight path went right where my head would have been if I hadn't stopped.

I had reached the magnet gizmo that Thales had shown us the day before. There was nothing else to do. If Sibyl could do this, it would surely prove no problem for me! I hopped up onto the seat and began to turn the contraption's pedals, just as the priestess had done. Or at least,

I *tried* to. The anatomy of the pig, though wonderful in many ways, is not designed to perch on a narrow seat while turning pedals with its back feet. I promptly fell off.

"Get back on!" Sibyl shouted from the hut.

I did so, more gingerly this time, and got my hooves to the pedals. I was turning them as hard as I could, but it wasn't fast enough to work Thales' magnet gizmo.

"Faster!" screamed Sibyl.

I felt as if my heart had traveled up to my cranium, where it was about to explode.

"You . . . come and . . . do it!" I panted, but Sibyl was (conveniently) too far away and looking after Bumscruff.

Meanwhile, the birds were banking back toward me. The sight of them helped me to dig deep into unknown inner reserves. The pedals whooshed around beneath my hooves and . . . nothing! The magnet thingy still wasn't working! And now the birds were aiming right at me.

Suddenly there was another cry from the hut behind me. "No!"

I turned to see Thales racing forward. He held his arms up and waved his hands in the air. If this was an attempt to distract the birds, it worked. At the last second, they changed course and headed toward the accelerating scientist.

But Thales was no easy target. No doubt those trousers allowed him greater leg-mobility, and he managed to dodge the birds' attack.

"A wire must have come undone!" he called to me. "Don't move!"

He zigzagged the rest of the way to the contraption and began to inspect it, starting at my end.

"Er . . . Thales? The birds are turning around again," I explained.

Half crouching, Thales continued to check the machine.

"They're coming this way!" I wailed. But Thales began reconnecting two bits of copper wire.

"They're—" Oh, forget it—there was no point in offering further commentary. I closed my eyes. So this was the end. What a way to go: sliced into a mound of shaved ham by a flock of stinkin' birds!

The birds shot by me with the sound of zipping arrows. They weren't aiming at me—they were aiming at Thales!

I opened my eyes just in time to see the elderly scientist leap to one side. Again, the birds just missed him.

"Try it now!" Thales shouted.

I had a shot at turning the pedals, I really did, but by this stage I was well and truly pooped. It wasn't my fault that the machine hadn't worked when I did have enough energy!

Thales scrambled to his feet. I recognized the look on his face, no longer one of fear. I'd seen that look before, usually on the faces of heroes as they readied themselves for glorious combat outside the Trojan walls. It was the look of someone going into battle. Thales was going to pedal the machine himself.

There was just one tiny problem. He was immobile. Something was holding him back. Thales looked down at his feet in alarm and dismay. One of the Stymphalian birds was still there. It had pierced the bottom of his flared trousers and nailed them to the ground like a tent peg.

Desperately Thales tried to pull his trousers free. He glanced up to see where the rest of the flock was. The look in his eyes told me they were close.

But then there came a terrible ripping noise as the fabric of Thales' trousers tore. The bird remained beak-first in the ground, but the scientist was able to rush forward, his pale white shin now on display through the rip.

He shoved me sideways off the seat with a bony hand, then hopped up and began to pedal like crazy.

Foolishly, I peeked upward. The birds looked like a comet plummeting to earth. Well, not quite to earth, because there was something in between, which was me.

But then Thales' magnet began to hum. The scientist pedaled faster still, and the hum grew louder.

The killer birds were almost upon me. I closed my eyes because I have never liked the sight of blood, especially my own. But no blow fell.

I opened one eye just as the birds whooshed straight toward the magnetic bar as if pulled by invisible threads. They struck with a mighty *CLANG!* All of them were stuck there. . . .

At least, they were stuck there for as long as Thales could keep pedaling. He wasn't showing any sign of slowing down. I was amazed at the old scientist's gutsiness.

"You're doing a grand job," I yelled encouragingly. "Keep it up just a bit longer while we get out of here, okay?"

"He'll do no such thing!" snapped Sibyl. She was leading the goat-boy out as fast as the dazed lad could go. "We'll get a net or something."

"Not possible . . ." gasped Thales. "Couldn't . . . hold them. Afraid pig's right. . . . I suggest . . . you get . . . out of here!"

Sibyl made no move to go. Thales was still whizzing those pedals around, though he did seem to be slowing a bit. Understandable, really—I mean, we're not talking about an Olympic athlete here.

"Come on, my son!" I shouted. "Go for the burn!"

"Go!" cried Thales. "I will . . . fight the . . . forces of . . . Chaos!"

It was clear he couldn't last too much longer. His face had turned a plumlike shade of purple that might look jolly on a flower or a party dress but was a bit alarming on a human face.

Sibyl nodded in grave acknowledgment that Thales' plan was our only chance. The day before, Bumscruff alone had been able to take hold of a single Stymphalian bird. With the lad out of action now, how could we possibly hope to subdue an entire flock of them? And, after all, there was always the Cosmos to save.

So we made like one of Thales' atoms.

And split.

BOOK XVIII

There is yet more running for a footsore hero.

Consider, if you will, the anatomy of the pig. In essence, what you've got is a large, splendidly round body perched atop short, thin legs that taper down to four petite hooves. Artistically, it's an unqualified triumph. But, when it comes to usefulness . . . well, let's just say we're built more for short bursts of speed than for long distances. (You know that guy who ran from Marathon all the way to Athens? Not a pig.)

You'll understand, then, why I was struggling somewhat as we ran and ran through the woods.

"Can't . . . go on!" I managed to gasp through enormous rasping breaths.

"Shut up and keep running!" barked Sibyl, perfectly showcasing her lack of sympathy toward those not of her immediate species. She was guiding Bumscruff with one arm around his narrow, pimply shoulders and the other hand in the middle of his chest. The lad stumbled along with a dazed expression indicating that even by his own dismal standards, he had less of a clue than usual what was going on.

"Owee, gotta nowee," he mumbled occasionally. "Wanna sleep."

As for me, I couldn't maintain this pace much longer.

My body was on the verge of mutiny, with heart, lungs, and muscles plotting to explode rather than put up with any more of this running business.

"I . . . really . . . can't—" I began, but Sibyl had already lined up her counter-argument.

"MOVE IT!" she yelled.

The only thing that stopped me firing back a choice helping of sarcasm was my inability to speak or breathe at the time. Also, I couldn't think of anything.

After what felt like eons, Sibyl finally decreed that we could slow to a brisk walk. Judging from the way his feet dragged and his head lolled, I wasn't sure that Bumscruff was up to even that.

The ground had started to rise again, and I realized that we were making our way back to the mountain path.

"You bet we are," Sibyl confirmed. "I should never have let us leave it."

Every minute or two she kept glancing back over her shoulder. Finally, she said, "Thales has stopped."

I looked around—"How can you tell?"—just in time to see a cluster of tiny birds rise as one above the trees in the distance below us. "Oh."

The Stymphalian birds executed a perfect loop-the-loop and then dived back down.

Sibyl and I exchanged grim looks. We carried on in silence. My thoughts were now weighing me down like cast-iron sneakers. Had the forces of Chaos finally claimed Thales? It was hard to see how anyone could come up with a plan to get out of a scrape like that. Then again, perhaps . . . "EEEEEK!" I squealed as a pinprick of terror punctured the bubble of my thoughts. "They've found us!"

I nipped behind Sibyl and the ailing goatherd for a little protective cover.

Sibyl lifted her eyes to the bird I had spotted. It cooed menacingly from its branch. "That's a pigeon," she said wearily.

I edged out. "Of course it is," I said. "But perhaps you failed to notice the nasty glint in its eye?"

"Sleep!" moaned Bumscruff, swaying around alarmingly.

After a moment's thought, Sibyl nodded briskly. "I think we're far enough away," she said. "And he can't carry on, not in this condition."

It was spitting rain, so Sibyl set about gathering branches and sticks to construct a lean-to shelter. Meanwhile, I volunteered for the vital job of keeping an eye on Bumscruff. He wasn't actually doing much beyond sitting with his arms wrapped around his knees, rocking back and forth. The important thing is that I was *ready* if he did decide to do anything. (Sometimes the tough jobs involve purely mental exertion.)

When the lean-to was finished, Bumscruff collapsed on the ground inside it. He was asleep as soon as his head hit the rock that Sibyl had supplied in place of a pillow.

He was just in time to avoid the proper rain that now started to fall. There was enough space for Sibyl and me to sit at the other end of the lean-to. The prophetess didn't seem all that comfortable with the arrangement, judging from the odd way her nostrils quivered and she kept waving a hand in front of her nose. We sat and watched the rain.

"Oh, that's just typical, that is!" I complained. "I mean, isn't it enough that we've been chased all over the place by monsters? That Thanatos is on our tails? That the Cosmos is supposed to end? You'd think we could at least have a bit of decent weather."

There's nothing wrong with weather as a topic of conversation—in some countries it's all people ever discuss. (In the legendary northern islands of Hyperborea, for example, it is said to rain 85 percent of the time, but the pasty, grim-faced locals still derive countless hours of pleasure discussing the possibility of rain.) But Sibyl had other matters on her mind.

"No normal mortal could have survived an explosion like that," she said, jerking a thumb toward the sleeping lad. "Who do you think he is, Gryllus?"

The goatherd seemed to be in the middle of some unpleasant dream, and behind closed lids his eyeballs were as restless as a five-year-old at an eight-hour performance of a Sophoclean tragedy on ice.

"I think he might be a hero of some kind," Sibyl continued. "You know, the child of a god and a mortal?"

It was hard to believe. True, most of the great heroes of the past came from mixed mortal/divine families— Theseus, Heracles, Perseus, Clifford (okay, I'm not sure about Clifford—you don't hear many epic poems about him these days and, now that I think about it, defeating a short-haired rabbit in one-on-one combat isn't all that heroic). Bumscruff might well be strong, but he was also a spindly scruffbag of a kid who seemed out of place in such square-jawed, musclebound, knock-back-some-ale-then-slay-the-foul-monster company.

"Aren't heroes generally a bit more . . . heroic?" I ventured. "Broadly speaking?"

"I suppose so." Sibyl was again indulging in the bad habit of biting her lower lip. (I would have said something, but I was myself indulging in one or two bad habits, which common decency prevents me from describing. Suffice it to say that I was only living up to my family's ancient motto, "Better Out Than In.")

"There's definitely something . . . *different* about him," Sibyl sighed. "I just wish I knew what's supposed to happen when we get him to Delphi. *If* we can get him there . . ."

Outside, the rain was coming down harder now. "The birds'll never follow us in this," Sibyl said. She tried to stifle a yawn with the back of her hand. "While we're waiting for Bum—for the lad, we may as well get some sleep ourselves."

And with that she leaned her head back and fell immediately into the land of Hypnos—which is to say, she nodded off.

To tell you the truth, I could have done with forty winks myself after the day's early start and overexertion, but I forced myself to stay awake.

Here's why. Since I had become acquainted with Sibyl and Bumscruff, what had happened to me? I had *nearly* been torn apart by a pack of chimeras. I had *nearly* been blown up by a poorly designed plutonium-driven toaster. I had *almost* been pecked to smithereens by a flock of psychokiller birds. Oh yes, and I had apparently come to the personal attention of Thanatos, God of Death!

It didn't take a genius to work out that these people were hazardous traveling companions. So *logically,* wouldn't it therefore be a smart move to part company with them?

Of course, there was still the Erinys to worry about. I subjected this problem to the glare of my incisive mind.

Fact 1: I hadn't heard a peep from the clay jar since Sibyl first abducted me, had I?

Fact 2: Sibyl had shown herself on numerous occasions to be untrustworthy and basically unsympathetic to the plight of the pig.

Conclusion: Maybe the whole thing about the Erinys had been nothing more than a trick. I wouldn't put this past Sibyl (see Fact 2).

Well, it was worth testing out. I got slowly to my feet. Sibyl muttered something in her sleep, but she didn't wake up. I stepped out of the shelter. We were surrounded by trees, but the rain drove against me like loads and loads of drops of water falling from the sky. The wind had picked up too, and—just to complete the drama—I could hear thunder.

Guilt flared in my belly as I looked back at the sleeping pair. *No,* I told myself, *that's not guilt—it's indigestion, brought on by all the dangers I've had to meet. Face it, I don't have the digestive system necessary for this kind of lifestyle. Any more perilous situations and my innards will be a total mess.*

Besides, whatever awaited Sibyl and Bumscruff at Delphi, surely they didn't need *my* help to face it. If the Cosmos really was going to end—and let's be honest, it was looking decidedly poorly—what use would I be?

I took a few more steps. Not a peep from the clay jar around my neck.

A few more steps. Not a sausage.

A few m—

Suddenly a dazzling red light burst out from the jar. It didn't actually break, but it let out a shriek that gave the howling wind a run for its money.

"I'm going back!" I yelled, hastily retreating to the shelter. But even when I reached it, the light didn't fade. In the gloom of the storm it flashed out like a beacon.

"Wh-What's going on?" asked Sibyl. She managed to infuse her next question with a more suspicious tone. "What are you up to, Gryllus?"

"I was stretching my legs!" I answered, doing my best not to babble. "You know, popping behind a tree, answering Nature's Call and all that. I've got no idea why the—"

But Sibyl was staring up and over my shoulders. The narrow look of suspicion in them widened to one of alarm. I turned to see a tattered shape hurtle through the trees. It didn't fly so much as barely steer itself as gusts of wind tossed it along. The wet, shabby bundle of feathers landed in the mud behind me with an undignified *SPLAT!*

An owl sat up and tried to shake out its bedraggled wings. Then it fixed us with baleful eyes.

"Well?" it demanded.

BOOK XIX

The Bright-Eyed Lady reveals what she had for lunch.

Being a bit of a traditionalist at heart, I'd been expecting the customary *TWIT-TWOO*.

"Well, what?" I fired back. "Who *are* you?" (I admit, part of me was a little put out to encounter another talking animal. I mean, you trundle along in life thinking you're unique . . .)

The bird's saucerlike eyes were fixed in their sockets so that she—the voice gave that away—had to turn her neck to redirect her gaze. The spotlights of those big, bright peepers aimed right at me. In the gloom of the storm, they were almost all pupil, with just a rim of gray shot through with fiery yellow.

"Oh gods, a talking pig!" said the owl without apparent delight.

Her tone was regal and aloof, as if she had a bad smell under her beak. (Well, *technically,* she did, but I wasn't about to back away for the sake of a hoity-toity barn owl.)

"I beg your pardon, madam," I sputtered. "Have you looked in a mirror lately? At least I'm a mammal!"

"Pipe down, Gryllus," hissed Sibyl. "This is Athena."

The bird ruffled its soggy feathers and turned those searchlight eyes on Sibyl. "The full title, if you please."

The prophetess took a deep breath. "Bright-eyed Athena,

Goddess of Wisdom, Queen of Owls, Daughter of Zeus, Lady of the Citadel, Bringer of the Olive Crop, Patron of Craftsmen, Wearer of the Aegis, um . . ."

"Yes?" demanded the owl. One of her talons tapped irritably in the mud.

"Erm . . . oh yes, Helmet-Head!"

"Correct," said Athena. "Why does everyone always forget the helmet bit?" The owl took a hop closer. "Well?" she repeated. "Are you going to get out of the shelter or not?"

That was the Olympian way, I suppose—immortals got whatever they wanted. It never crossed their divine minds to question this. It was merely a reflection of the natural order that the goddess should enjoy shelter while we poor mortal stiffs got good and soaked.

Sibyl shook Bumscruff awake. "Wakey, wakey," she murmured.

The boy looked as if he'd grown even more, and his face seemed leaner and older, as if his sleep had burned away yet more of his childhood.

His eyes fluttered open. He let out a great groaning yawn . . . and then saw the owl. His face lit up with instant delight, and he lunged for the bird. Athena hopped backward in alarm, but not before the goatherd had thrown his wiry arms around her neck.

"Birdie!" hooted Bumscruff in unadulterated joy. His nap had clearly done him the world of good.

"Get this oaf off me!" Athena managed to squeak from the depths of the lad's hug.

I gave it a go. "Get off her, oaf!"

I couldn't tell whether Bumscruff heard and understood or whether his hug just came to a natural end. Either way, he let go and sat back with an inscrutable smile on his face.

The owl took up position in the shelter.

"Avert your eyes!" she commanded.

"That means look away," Sibyl explained.

So we all looked down at the wet ground. Was the goddess transforming back into her normal divine form? It certainly didn't sound that way. It sounded more like she was emitting a series of low burps.

"You may lift your eyes once more," said Athena in a dignified fashion.

I was disappointed to see that she was still an owl. However, a little gray-brown pellet of something lay at her feet.

"What's that?" I asked.

Sibyl dug an elbow into my side. "It's an . . . um . . . it's an owl pellet," she explained hastily.

I didn't get it. "I don't get it," I said.

"Well, when an owl eats something, it sort of . . . and then it . . . you know . . ."

"No, I don't know."

"Oh, by my father's throne, I can't stand this!" Athena burst out. "Owls eat their prey whole. We regurgitate the compacted skin and bones in pellets."

I took in this information carefully. "You mean you, Goddess of Wisdom, Daughter of Olives, Queen Citadel Head, Whatsit of Thingamajig . . . you eat little woodland creatures?" I asked.

"When I am in this form, yes," she huffed.

"And then you *throw up* the bits you don't want? Isn't that sort of gross?"

I wasn't trying to be impertinent to an A-list deity who under other circumstances might be inclined to smite me from on high, or transform me into a potted plant or something. But that was just it: I didn't really feel as if I *was* talking to the goddess Athena. I mean, she didn't *look* like a deity. No, I was just talking to a rather tatty-looking owl. Okay, it happened to be a talking owl, but you could hardly expect me to be too impressed by that.

Meanwhile, Bumscruff was beaming away at the owl. "I like birdies!" he announced grandly. "Twit-twoo!"

"Wait a minute," said Athena, glaring at the goatherd with sudden intensity. "Let me see your head, boy."

Bumscruff nodded enthusiastically and without a scrap of understanding. "Oh yes!"

Sibyl helped, gently easing the boy's head forward and lifting his hair as the goddess directed. "I never noticed it before. . . . He *has* got a scar here," she declared, looking down at Bumscruff's skull. A thin red zigzag was visible under his straggly mop of hair.

"Where did you get that scar, boy?" demanded the queen of owls.

"He had a nasty accident with a toaster," I offered, but Sibyl shook her head and murmured, "No, this scar's old."

Insofar as the face of an owl can wear much of an expression, Athena's shouted puzzlement. "Who is this boy?" she demanded.

"We don't exactly know," said Sibyl. "Apollo told me to take him to the Omphalos at Delphi. He said it was the only way to save the Cosmos. The only problem is . . . we haven't been able to contact him for further instructions."

"You're not the only one." The owl goddess did her best to sniff disapprovingly, though this wasn't easy through the pinprick nostrils of her little beak. "No one has seen my brother in days. We can only hope that he has fared better than the other gods."

"What happened to them?" asked Sibyl.

The anxiety that clutched at me in anticipation of the goddess's answer was even less comfortable than the rivulets of rainwater that were running down the folds of fat at the back of my neck.

"Thanatos took them," said the lady of the citadel simply. "Dionysus was taken in the middle of a party on Olympus. Demeter was hiding in a cornfield. Poseidon had assumed the form of a giant lobster, but he was still found. Hera, Aphrodite, Pluto . . . all of them taken by Thanatos. Artemis tried running, and so did Hermes. All they found of him was a pair of winged sandals." The owl sighed. "Fighting proved no more successful—Ares, God of War, tried that. He transformed himself into a giant boar and attacked when Thanatos came for him. He didn't last two seconds. . . . All I know is, I'm taking no chances. . . . I'm staying in this form."

"But what's the problem? Gods can't die," I exclaimed. "*Can* they?"

My question was met with an unnerving silence.

"What about Zeus?" asked Sibyl.

"He was the first to disappear," said the goddess of wisdom.

Meanwhile, Bumscruff was trying to reach an apple that hung from a branch just out of reach. On each attempt he would look over at Athena and give a merry thumbs-up. Then he'd leap up and try to grab the fruit with one whippet-thin arm. On the fourth or fifth try, he managed to get his fingers to it but then slipped on the wet leaves and fell on his backside. Seconds later, the apple dropped, striking him on top of the head with a hollow *CLOP!* before rolling into the mud.

Athena sighed. "Did you consider the possibility that my brother might be mistaken about this boy?" she said. "I mean, Apollo isn't the god of wisdom, you know."

Sibyl didn't reply, but it was clear that this comment had shaken her—the possibility that Apollo might *not* be right. That he had only seen a part of the future, perhaps an insignificant part? Rain rolled down Sibyl's face as she considered this awful possibility.

Bumscruff was wiping the mud off the apple on his wet tunic. He strode over and offered the worm-riddled fruit to Athena.

"For you," he said with a smile like sunshine. "Eat!"

"I don't eat apples," Athena declared imperiously.

"Me neither!" I joined in, happy to find common ground with this deity. "Apples give me gas like nobody's business.

Is that why you don't eat them either, 'cause they make you f—"

It felt as if those gray saucer-eyes were staring into the depths of my soul and didn't much like what they found there.

"Er, never mind," I mumbled.

The rain had eased off now, and Athena hopped out of the shelter.

"Where are you going?" asked Sibyl.

"I must return to Athens," said the owl. "Olympus is no longer safe, but the citadel in the city that took my name . . . that must be." She cast a final glance at Bumscruff, who had shoved the entire apple into his mouth and was munching it contentedly, worms and all. "Maybe there'll be a hero in Athens who can help," she said pointedly.

The owl spread her wings ready for takeoff.

"Wait!" I cried. "You're the goddess of wisdom! Before you go, have you got any words of wisdom for us?"

Owl-faced Athena blinked thoughtfully. "Always have a good breakfast, don't eat yellow snow, and change your underwear every day," she said at last.

"But I don't wear any—"

The owl goddess had no time for petty objections. She ran forward, flapping her wings like crazy. It didn't look much like the sort of thing that has poetic types going on about "gliding gracefully through the woods like a silent ghost" and whatnot, but it did the trick. The goddess began to fly away.

"No!" cried Bumscruff, spraying apple in his distress. Lightning flashed overhead, the thunder hot on its heels, and the rain returned, harder than ever.

"Farewell, Bright-Eyed Athena, Goddess of Wisdom, Queen of Owls, Daughter of Zeus, Lady of the Citadel, Bringer of the Olive Crop, Patron of Craftsmen, Wearer of the Aegis," called Sibyl in her best ceremonial voice.

"Helmet-Head!" came a distant, haughty reply through the trees. "Don't forget Helmet-Head!"

As we continued our trek later that afternoon, we were all lost in our own thoughts. Sibyl was muttering to herself about the need for full details in mystical predictions or else what was the point. Bumscruff? Well, he had seemed oddly upset at Athena's departure, and his bad mood lasted longer than I imagined any thought *could* in the inhospitable terrain of the lad's head. But his mood slowly improved, and by the time the rain had fully stopped, he was no doubt back to contemplating deep philosophical questions such as, "Which is better, red or green?"

Me, I was thinking about the gods. This was something of a first for yours truly. For as long as I could remember, they had been distant figures of awe and dread. Right through the long siege at Troy, we'd lived in fear of the Olympians. After all, they ran the whole show, didn't they? It had never really occurred to me to question whether they made a good job of it.

I mean, I'd heard priests go around saying how Olympians were fond of playing chess with the Cosmos.

Their whole point was that we mere mortals couldn't understand the grand game because we were no more than unwitting pawns in it. It's true (if somewhat surprising) that theology is not what you might call one of my strong suits. Nor, for that matter, is games theory. . . . But, from what I'd seen of the gods lately, a game of *checkers* was beyond their abilities. Perhaps tiddlywinks was more up their alley — games that didn't guzzle too much of the old intellectual juice. Twister, perhaps?

The way had become steeper and steeper, and the trees began to peter out. It wouldn't be long before we were back at the mountain path. Sibyl reluctantly allowed us one quick final rest in the woods. While I was recouping my energy, the prophetess went ahead to scout out the best route. She had gone only a short distance when she let out a little gasp.

Curiosity beat laziness (narrowly), and I rose to my four feet. "What is it?" I asked.

"Nothing."

"What's that in your hands, then?"

Sibyl clenched her fist shut. "NOTHING," she repeated.

"Looks like an owl pellet," I said suspiciously.

"Nope," came the answer. "Well, that's enough chitchat. We'd better shake a leg."

I tried to see past her legs, which weren't yet shaking. "And what's that mark on the ground?"

"Nothing! It's just where some lightning struck."

I grunted. I'd heard of lightning striking the ground

before . . . but I'd never heard of it leaving an owl-shaped scorch mark.

Both Sibyl and I looked back at Bumscruff, who was currently struggling to master the arcane art of whistling.

"Time to go," said Sibyl heavily, and all I could do was nod.

BOOK XX

The ancient gaze of the stony Sphinx is enough to give everyone the willies.

Once we were out of the valley and back on the mountain path, we made better time. There wasn't much by way of scenery, just soaring mountains and plunging valleys and the like.

A different kind of bird circled overhead now, too big to be either Stymphalian bird or owl. Bumscruff took to waving at it contentedly.

"It's probably waiting for us to die of exhaustion," I explained, "so it can pick our bones clean."

The huge bird remained high overhead, like an airborne reminder of stuff you don't especially want to be reminded of. It was still there when we moved out from under the shadow of a smaller mountain and saw the peak of Mount Parnassus towering in the distance ahead. That's where we were headed—Delphi lay on the slopes of Parnassus.

The mountain was majestic and awe-inspiring and all that stuff, but most of all it was big. The problem was, however much we walked, it never seemed to get any closer.

"Is that a trick mountain or something?" I inquired miserably.

"We *are* getting closer," Sibyl assured me. "Once we reach the top of that hill"—she pointed up ahead—"I think we'll be able to see Delphi."

The good news was that she was right. Delphi was visible in the distance, lying on the lower slopes of Mount Parnassus like an inkblot on a skirt.

The bad news was that something else was visible, and it was a lot closer. About half a mile ahead, something was blocking the path.

As we neared it, the shape became recognizable: a huge rocky figure rising out of the ground, as long and tall as an ocean-faring ship. It had the body of a lion but the giant face of a human. The whole thing seemed carved out of the very rock.

"Lookit the big kitty!" yelled Bumscruff enthusiastically after setting me down.

"I don't know," I tutted. "Who'd go and build something like that, way out here? What a waste of taxpayers' money!"

But Sibyl was staring at the immense figure grimly. "Er . . . Gryllus, I don't think a sculptor made this. . . ." Her voice wobbled. "I think that's the Sphinx. You know, the *real* Sphinx."

"Not possible!" I scoffed. "The Sphinx guarded the gates to Thebes, donkeys' years ago! How could it be here? You're just being para—"

The Sphinx's great stone eyes opened. Slate-gray pupils leveled their steady gaze at us. If the cold look in those eyes was anything to go by, it wasn't about to win any Cuddliest Monster competitions. The rest of the stone creature's body didn't even twitch.

"—noid."

Terror grabbed me by the roll of fat at the back of my neck and gave me a good shake. My bristles stood on end like a crack squad of Spartan soldiers on parade.

"Then again, you may have a point," I said hurriedly, "in which case, we really ought to be getting out of here." I turned to go back the way we had come, but Sibyl blocked my path.

"We *can't* go back," she said firmly. "We can get past the Sphinx—I know we can. All we have to do is answer a riddle."

She rested a hand on my back. Was she attempting a friendly gesture or making sure I didn't bolt?

"Gryllus, you're good at riddles and stuff, aren't you?"

I could see where this was leading, and I didn't like the scenery. I might not be one of those bloomin' bookworm braniacs up at the Academy in Athens, but I have graduated with honors from the University of Life, which is where I learned the golden rule: *Never—and I Mean Never—Volunteer. For ANYTHING.*

"Not a chance!" I said.

Sibyl folded her arms crossly. "But Gryllus, you told us you were brilliant at riddles! You said you had a million of them!"

True, I had heard a great many riddles during the long years of the Trojan War. I knew all the classics: "How many Spartans does it take to screw in a torch-holder?" "Why did the Hydra cross the road?" "What time is it when Pluto, Lord of the Underworld, sits on your fence?" I probably did know a million of them.

"But what if today's question is number one million and one?" I whined. "Like I said, NO CHANCE."

There was a terrible sound like rock grinding and crumbling. In fact, it *was* rock grinding and crumbling, as the Sphinx turned its tree-trunk-size neck to get a better look at us.

"I am the Questioner," said the Sphinx, its voice stone on stone. "Who shall be the Answerer?"

And without another word, Sibyl took a step forward.

At that moment, despite the many differences we'd had along the journey, despite all the squabbles and bickering, I couldn't help truly admiring the bravery of that simple act.

"He is," said the prophetess, pointing at me.

Rock groaned painfully as the Sphinx nodded.

"I am not!" I sputtered. "YOU be the Answerer."

"It's just one little riddle," Sibyl hissed.

"Oh, that's easy for you to say, but what happens when I CAN'T answer it?"

"Riddly diddly!" offered Bumscruff happily.

"You WILL answer it," said Sibyl. "But . . . erm . . .

well, just supposing someone *didn't* answer correctly . . . not that I'm saying you won't be able to . . ."

"Yes?"

Sibyl seemed to be having difficulty meeting my eye all of a sudden.

"Well, according to the legend, if you can't answer the Sphinx's riddle, then . . . the earth opens up and swallows you."

"What!" I exclaimed. "I'm not sticking around for this cartload of Cretan crud! I'm outta here!"

Barging my way past the prophetess, I took a couple of steps back up the mountain path. The earth rumbled ominously beneath me, then it ripped open into a jagged scar of a crack. Two of my feet were on one side of that crack, and two on the other. Contrary to what you might expect, I have never been able to do a split and did not relish the prospect of that crack widening.

"Um, I don't think the Sphinx will let you go," explained Sibyl. "Not now you've been accepted as the Answerer."

I whirled around and looked up at the stone monstrosity. "Hello, up there! I'm afraid there's been a bit of a mix-up, your Sphinxness," I shouted. "You see, I'm not even supposed to be—"

"Silence, Answerer!" commanded that stony voice.

"But I'm not—"

"Silence!"

"No, I was just trying to explain—"

"SILENCE!"

"There's no need to get snippy."

"SILENCE!"

"I think you'd better shut up," Sibyl hissed to me.

"SILENCE!" roared the Sphinx, now switching its dreaded gaze to Sibyl. Its voice echoed around the mountains, a diminishing chain of,

"Silence,

silence,

silence,

silence,

silence,"

and then all was quiet.

"Si-lence!" called Bumscruff joyfully. "Kitty big-head wanna silence!"

"SILENCE!" roared the Sphinx.

By now, the Sphinx didn't seem quite as calm as it had been at the beginning. Centuries-old rock rose and fell while the beast took a calming breath.

"Here is your riddle, Answerer. . . ." It glared as if daring me to pipe up. "What creature walks on four legs in the morning, two in the afternoon, and three in the evening?"

What? This wasn't the sort of riddle we used to tell back in the service tents during the Trojan War. Riddles back then were more along the lines of:

"Knock, knock."

"Who's there?"

"Euripides."

"Euripides who?"

"Euripides tunics and you'll have to pay for them."

Or:

What's an Athenian urn?
About eight drachmas a week, if he's lucky.

Or my personal favorite:

Why is Zeus only 12 inches from top to bottom?
Because he's the RULER of the gods.

You know, proper riddles, none of this bloomin' "four legs in the morning" malarkey.

I frantically searched my encyclopedic brain, but the bright ideas all seemed to be hiding in the corners.

"Can I consult a friend?" I asked in desperation. "I'd best get going then, 'cause my friend lives four days' march away. . . ."

"Time is up," said the Sphinx. "What is your answer?"

"Just give me a sec, will you? It's . . . um . . ."

"Ye-es?"

I heard myself answering. My voice sounded small and faraway and a bit on the dumb side. "Is it . . . a squirrel?"

I was faintly aware of Sibyl's groan from behind me. The Sphinx's face betrayed no reaction.

"No, wait!" I cried. "Not a squirrel . . . a chicken! I mean . . . a hippopotamus!" Still no help from that stony visage. "A camel? A goldfish? A parakeet? Give me a clue at least!"

"Is that your final answer?" asked the Sphinx darkly.

"Yes, er, no, I don't know!" I wailed.

"The answer is a human," declared the Sphinx. "A baby crawls on all fours. The child and the adult walk on two legs. Then, in the twilight of life, the old must use a walking stick—three legs."

The Sphinx's stony lips shifted ever so slightly into what might have passed for a smile.

"I cannot accept your answer," said the Sphinx. "Goodbye!"

The earth let out another rumble, then it shuddered, and the crack beneath my feet widened and gaped. The sulfurous stench of rotten eggs wafted up to my snout. (Don't ask me what rotten eggs were doing in the depths of the earth—geology is not a strong suit of mine, amazingly enough.)

"Wait!" I screamed. "That's not right! I mean, what about me? I'm walking around on *four* legs, aren't I?"

The crack in the earth stopped widening as if the very ground were concentrating.

The Sphinx blinked slate eyelids as big as gongs. "You are not even human," it said at last. "You do not count."

"Well, okay, but I wasn't always a pig. And when I was a baby, I didn't crawl. My old ma told me I used to shuffle around on my bottom, but I never once crawled on all fours."

The earth let out a faint, uncertain groan. The crack beneath my four feet was not widening. If anything, it had closed up slightly.

"I'm just saying that your answer isn't fair," I pressed on. "Lots of people don't fit that description. What about my old pal, Johnny Hopalong? He only had one leg. And not all old folks use walking sticks either. My uncle Xerxes trained two goats to walk by his side instead. . . ."

"No one ever complained before," said the Sphinx, a hint of petulance creeping into that granite voice.

"They were probably just being polite," I said, choosing not to add that complete terror might have accounted for such impeccable behavior. (For the same reason, most people will demonstrate perfect table manners under threat of decapitation, even when eating spaghetti.)

The creature seemed unsure what to do. "I could ask another question," it began.

And then it hit me — an idea so red-hot and brilliant it could have melted the wax off Icarus's wings at fifty paces.

"Wait!" I said. "I should be allowed to ask YOU a question. That's only fair, and if you can't answer it, then you let us past."

The Sphinx smiled with renewed confidence. "Very well," it said serenely.

I took a deep breath and moved to a patch of sandy ground. With one front hoof I carefully traced three words in the ground. When reading is *not* one of the strings to your bow, it isn't easy to replicate even a few words, but the squiggles seemed to match my memory of what I'd seen.

I DON'T KNOW

I took a step backward.

"My question is—what does this say?" I asked.

The Sphinx's enigmatic smile became even more enigmatic. "You are a simple-minded fool, hog. I know every human tongue ever devised and many more not yet dreamed of. I can read hieroglyphics, cuneiform, and even doctors' handwriting."

It squinted down at the letters on the ground. There was one of those silent, wobbly moments when the entire Cosmos holds its breath. Then:

"I don't know," said the Sphinx smugly.

There was a deafening boom as the earth cracked open under the immense monster.

"No, wait!" wailed the Sphinx as it tumbled down into the crevice. "You don't underst—"

But, with no regard for grammatically complete sentences, the earth swallowed the monster and just as quickly closed up again. The only evidence that anything unusual had happened was a long hairline crack in the rock and a crescent-shaped blade that may have been one of the Sphinx's toenails.

"Kitty fell down the hole! Kitty fell down the hole!" hooted Bumscruff, as if we'd been watching a conjuring trick. "Again! Do it again!"

Sibyl was looking down at the writing on the sand with disbelief stamped all over her face. I could tell she was impressed.

"That was . . . incredible," she told me. "How on earth did *you* think of a trick like that?"

Unable to tap the side of my snout, I settled for a knowing wink. "Easy, kid," I told her. "I saw those same words in Thales' notes. I asked him what they meant and he just looked at me, didn't he, and said, 'I don't know.' I figured that if someone as brainy as Thales didn't know, then the Sphinx probably wouldn't either."

Sibyl rolled her eyes and started laughing. It had a brittle, hysterical tone to it. Perhaps in her nervous state this was the only way the poor girl could find to express admiration for my brilliant and heroic ruse.

"A simple 'Well done, Gryllus, that was magnificent!' would have done," I sniffed. But Sibyl was unable to stop laughing. Bumscruff joined in for a while, but Sibyl was still laughing when the lad's butterfly attention had moved on to other matters.

She still hadn't stopped as we started down the mountain path, toward the sacred city of Delphi.

BOOK XXI

There is, in fact, no place like home.

Most people who visit Delphi only see the tourist stuff in the town center—the various temples of the gods and, most famous of all and set high above the rest, the temple of Apollo that houses the Delphic oracle. There are plenty of B&Bs, too, and little shops that sell useless items to the tourists. (You can buy a scrap of wool that's supposed to have come from the Golden Fleece, or a tunic that says *My mom went to Delphi and all I got was this lousy tunic.*)

But, of course, that's not all there is to a town like this. Some locals always have to keep such towns running, and these people have to live somewhere. We entered Delphi through one of these residential suburbs that lay outside the city proper. It was the sort of neighborhood where locals pride themselves on keeping the front lawn tidy and making sure their donkey cart is as nice as the one next door.

The only problem was that *these* lawns were all overrun with weeds. The only donkey cart we saw was up on blocks, without wheels. Several doors gaped open, but we didn't see a soul. An unsettling quietness covered the area like a heavy fog.

Sibyl seemed to know the streets inside and out. She led us in silence for a while, but I knew a comment was building inside her.

"I used to live in this neighborhood," said Sibyl, looking around in wonder. "I can't believe I'm really back. After all this time, I can't believe I'm home again."

"Gods, do you know who you sound like?" I said. "Odysseus, that's who! He couldn't talk about anything else except getting home to dear old rocky Ithaca. I mean, have you ever seen Ithaca?"

"No. What's it like?"

I snorted. "Let's just say, if there was a contest and first prize was a week in Ithaca, second prize would be *two* weeks in Ithaca. I tell you, the island's a dump: no decent beaches, the tavernas all close early, no miniature golf or anything for the kiddies. If Odysseus ever *does* make it home, I reckon he and Penelope should just sell up and move to a nice little bungalow on the mainland. They could call it 'Dunroamin' or 'Dunfleeingods' or something."

But Sibyl wasn't listening. She had stopped in front of one of those crummy little houses.

"Speaking of dumps . . ." I muttered. I rolled my eyes at Bumscruff, who joined in by echoing, "Dumpo!"

"This is where I was born," Sibyl said quietly.

"Ah." I took a step back and reappraised the property. "Loads of rustic charm, though."

"I haven't even set eyes on it in years," Sibyl went on. She was having one of those moments when people's bottom lips start to wobble as they dredge up the memories. "I had to leave when I was only four, but I can just about remember it." She put a hand on the wall as if the feel of it might bring her lost childhood into clearer focus. "We used to sit around the hearth and listen to stories about the gods. It all seemed so wonderful and exciting back then."

As you know, I'm more sensitive than your average pig. I could tell this meant a lot to the kid.

"So, is your family still here or what?" I asked.

Sibyl shook her head. "They moved south, I heard. Couldn't stand being so close to the oracular temple and not being allowed to see me. Those were the rules when I was training, you see. Even though we were only an hour or two away, trainees weren't allowed to see their families except on feast days." She stared in through the front window as if watching some long-gone domestic scene only she was privy to. Her voice was a whisper. "I suppose it's a mistake to try and go home."

"I learned I can never go home," I said soberly.

The prophetess nodded in bittersweet agreement. "Wise words, Gryllus. . . . No one can truly go home because nothing ever stays the same, right? You can't step into the same river twice, and you can't return to the past. . . ."

"Well, yes, there's that," I said. "But mostly I can't go home because the island I grew up on sank."

"It SANK?"

"Yep—sank without a trace," I explained, "right into the deep blue Aegean. You see, there was this volcanic eruption on the island next door. Some folks said it was an accident, but I blame Poseidon."

"And why is that?"

I shrugged. "Apparently our island blocked a nice view of the sunset for him."

Sibyl shook her head and laughed softly. "Sometimes I actually appreciate your warped insights into the world, Gryllus."

This was possibly the nicest thing she'd ever said to me— maybe the nicest thing *anyone* had ever said to me, come to think of it. I may be a battle-hardened veteran warrior of the Trojan War, but the tender heart of a lyric poet beats beneath these spareribs. I gave in to the sentiment of the moment.

"You know what, guys?" I said, looking mistily at the

trainee-priestess and the mysterious, aromatic goat-boy. "We need a group hug."

Bumscruff seemed up for it, but Sibyl recoiled in inexplicable horror.

It didn't matter anyway. The moment was spoiled by the large mob that had appeared at the street corner. Most of them were wearing long dark robes with hoods.

"Let's get going!" I urged, but Sibyl didn't budge.

"We'd never make it," she said calmly.

She dug out a black garment from her backpack and gave it to Bumscruff.

"Here—put this on, quick! It's my spare." Then she pulled the hood of her own robe up over her head.

As they drew closer, I saw that several of the black-robed mob were carrying chunks of white marble. As they drew closer still, I realized these were pieces of a statue. One person carried a section of arm, another a chunk of torso. One poor guy was struggling along with a complete thigh and pelvis.

The figure at the front carried the smallest chunk, so that probably meant he was the leader. Judging from the winged sandal on the stone foot in his hand, it had once belonged at the bottom end of a leg on a statue of the god Hermes.

This man pulled back his cowl to reveal a pale face in need of a good shave and some sleep, or perhaps just a thunderbolt from on high.

"Praise be to Thanatos," he said matter-of-factly.

"Yes, erm, praise be to Thanatos," Sibyl parroted.

164

The rest of the mob mumbled the words, too.

The mob leader gave me a suspicious look. "What are you doing with this pig?" he demanded of Sibyl. He said it in the tone people usually reserve for official comments like "Have you got a ticket, then?"

The prophetess didn't miss a beat. "What? Are you telling me you haven't heard? About the feast?"

Fear paddled through the man's watery eyes. "Er . . . what feast's that?"

Sibyl gave him a pitying look. "Duh! The feast Thanatos ordered, of course! All sorts of animals are being brought into town. . . ." She caught my eye and added gratuitously, "To be ritually slaughtered."

"No one told us about any feast," said the man indignantly. The mob behind him murmured in agreement. They sounded in need of decent all-you-can-eat feast to boost morale.

That's when Sibyl played her trump card. "No problem," she said brightly. "It's *good* to be cautious, so why don't you just toddle off to town and check with Thanatos. That way you can explain how you felt it necessary to question his direct orders. I've heard he *encourages* initiative. . . ."

The man in the cowl didn't strike me as the imaginative sort, but he apparently formed a good-enough picture of what Thanatos might do to him. His eyes bulged as big as poached eggs—*scared*-looking poached eggs.

"No, no, that won't be necessary," he blustered. "You can be on your way."

The mob began to stagger off, lugging the shattered

statue with them. Sibyl bent and picked up a thin stick from the ground.

"This is just for realism's sake," she whispered as she tested the stick for springiness. Then she whacked me with it, right on the hindquarters!

"YOW!"

We set off in the same direction as the mob.

"That's quite enough realism, thank you," I hissed the umpteenth time the stick flicked my way.

"Sorry," Sibyl said quietly, though I could hear the satisfied smirk in her voice (highly attuned to this sort of thing as I am).

After a few long minutes of this, we came to the town center. Sibyl kept her eyes looking forward, but she spoke under her breath. "The temple of Apollo is on the other side of town. Just follow my lead, okay?"

The center of Delphi was bustling with activity. Lots more black-clad figures were coming from all directions to the middle of the square. Like the first group we had encountered, they were all carrying broken pieces of statues, which they hurled onto a huge pile of marble body parts. A jagged assortment of elbows, feet, and handless arms jutted from the mound. Dozens of marble eyes stared blindly from the bodiless heads.

"'Sbad," said a voice darkly. To my surprise, it was Bumscruff, who was scowling at the jumbled heap of smashed statues. Several of the followers of Thanatos sat around the pile and hammered at bits of statue, intent on reducing everything to rubble.

Sibyl bent and picked up a marble arm that lay at her feet. It was broken off just above the elbow and ended in a fist clenched around a sword hilt.

"Probably a statue of Ares," Sibyl murmured, examining the muscled forearm. She looked in despair at the followers of Thanatos as they continued to demolish all signs of the Olympian gods. She gave a curt nod, as if urging herself on. "Let's get going," she whispered. "Try and look as if we have official business."

We set out across the square at a brisk walk, forcing ourselves not to run. Sibyl was probably ready to pull that routine about the feast again, but no one challenged us.

Right up until we had almost reached the far side, it seemed that we were going to make it. But then suddenly—*SPROING!*—my bristles sprang to attention. You probably wouldn't understand—it's an animal thing. We nonhumans are just more in tune with the rhythms of the Cosmos, you know. This was one of those mystical moments when I could hear the beat of reality, only I didn't much feel like dancing. Something was wrong, I knew it; something bad was about to happen.

"We're being watched," I hissed. I could feel unearthly eyes drilling into the back of my neck like . . . loads of sharp objects that were not of this earth, only they were also eyes.

"Just keep going," murmured Sibyl. We were nearly out of the square now, heading for the narrow alleyway between two temples.

But then, from behind us: "Stop them!"

BOOK XXII

The eagle has landed.

That voice sounded exactly like a rusty eight-inch nail being dragged across a granite wall in an underground cavern. Or perhaps like the dying breath of a vast and ancient serpent. Or maybe it sounded like some guy with a really nasty sore throat, the kind you just can't get rid of, no matter how many leeches the doctor sticks on your neck. No, come to think of it, a mortal could never make a sound like that.

I looked back in panic and saw where the wailing voice *was* coming from. It emerged from the mound of broken statues. It got worse—suddenly all the eyes in all the broken faces appeared to be alive. The white marble pupils darkened into black pits, and the black pits were all staring straight at us with a shared, unblinking gaze. All the lips in all the smashed heads moved as one, and a single, terrible voice came from them, saying, "Get the boy with the pig!"

The assembled followers of Thanatos didn't wait for further instructions. They jumped to it, casting aside bits of statue and hammers and charging toward us, robes flapping in the wind.

So off we ran.

We burst out of the other end of the alleyway just in time to come face to face with a smaller group of followers of Thanatos, rushing forward to cut off our escape route.

We were trapped.

Sibyl drew a deep breath and stood with her back to the temple wall, with Bumscruff alongside her. She still had the arm of Ares, and she was gripping it with both hands.

As the first batch of Thanatos's followers arrived, Sibyl crouched into a fighting stance and began to swing the marble club threateningly.

"Right, then, who's up for a knuckle sandwich, courtesy of Ares?" she growled.

The mob slowed. Understandably, no one wanted a punch in the head from the god of war, even if it was just the bodiless arm off his statue.

Everyone was so intent on watching the arm's hypnotic sway that no one really paid attention to me as I began to tiptoe stealthily toward a nearby colonnade. Behind me, one foolhardy man had made a lunge at Bumscruff and Sibyl, only to be felled by a straight-arm jab from Ares.

I positioned myself behind a column. I couldn't tell you whether it was Doric or Greek Ionic. My chief area of architectural interest was whether the thing was wide enough to hide behind.

I peeked out. Sibyl was still swinging the arm in wild arcs, but it looked as if the mob was mustering the courage to make a group charge. Bumscruff moved out of the marble arm's range. Someone tried to grab him, but they hadn't figured on the lad's uncanny strength. The goatherd shoved the attacker away so hard that he bowled over two of his co-chasers.

You have to help! insisted an unfamiliar voice in my head.

Maybe we can get away before the main group gets here. All you have to do is charge them from behind. No one will expect that, and then maybe—just maybe—the three of you will have a chance.

It wasn't much as heroic plans go, but it was all I had.

You've got to try! I told myself. *Okay, one, two, three . . . GO!*

Nothing. My legs had formed the opinion that my brain was no longer acting in their best interests and chose to ignore its command.

GO!

But, once again, fear held my body immobile in its cold, pinching grip. I couldn't do it. I couldn't move.

And then it was too late anyway, because the rest of the followers of Thanatos ran out from the alleyway. Made bold by reinforcements, our pursuers rushed Sibyl and Bumscruff. The two fought valiantly—I heard several sickening crunches and saw a couple of black-robed figures hurtle through the air like uncoordinated crows. But there were just too many of them. There was no way Sibyl and Bumscruff could win. It would take a miracle now for them to escape.

"ARRRKKKK!" screamed a miracle from above.

It was an eagle—the biggest bird I'd ever set eyes on. It would have taken an awful lot of birdseed to keep it happy (assuming that eagles eat birdseed—dietary requirements of birds of prey are a bit of a blind spot in my general knowledge).

As the mighty eagle plummeted from the skies, Bumscruff looked up and waved. I realized that this was the bird we'd seen overhead on the mountain road, the one I'd thought was a vulture. The giant bird pulled out of its dive, so that its immense talons dangled down. It let out another ear-splitting call and then swept Bumscruff aloft, latching onto the lad's upper arms. He didn't struggle or complain. I'm not sure it would have done him much good anyway.

Those who hadn't dropped to the floor in terror watched the bird and its cargo fly up toward the peak of Mount Parnassus. Sibyl followed its flight with a look of weary disbelief. She let the marble arm fall from her hands. The fight had gone out of her. She sagged back like Saggy the rag doll.

And what about me? I had done nothing! Not moved one iota from my hiding spot. I edged guiltily back into the shadows . . . and bumped right into another follower of Thanatos.

"The pig's here!" she shouted.

A man joined her from inside the temple. "I don't think Thanatos wanted the pig, just the people," he said.

"Shall we let it go, then?" asked the woman.

And for a moment I really thought they might do it, actually let me go. But then—

"You will do no such thing! That is no ordinary pig," a commandingly aristocratic voice called. "We have to tell the Dark One about this. Thanatos will decide what to do."

A very tall, very thin man swept into view. You could tell instantly that his black robes were of superior cut and cloth. In comparison, the others looked as if they were wearing hooded black potato-sacks.

The tall man hardly glanced at Sibyl, but his lips drew back in a wolfish smile of recognition when he saw me. I could only return that look of recognition, though I found myself unable to accompany mine with even a swinish simper.

It was the tall man, the one who had come to see me in Stavros and Gorgina's restaurant.

BOOK XXIII

A brave hero sees fit to unearth a few hidden secrets.

The tall man ordered that we be held in the temple while he consulted the Dark One.

I'm not sure how long we waited in there, but the followers of Thanatos didn't make any attempt at small talk, and no one offered us a beverage or a snack. That temple wasn't fit for a pig—*any* pig, I mean. Everything in it had been smashed, and all representations of the gods sloppily painted over.

Eventually, someone—not the tall man—arrived with instructions for what to do with us. A small black-robed mob led us back out, turning away from the town toward the mountain that loomed over it.

"Where are you taking us?" I demanded.

"Cave," muttered one of our captors from under his cowl.

The very word chilled me. Suddenly the temple didn't look so bad. "Is that entirely necessary?" I asked. "I mean, all that temple needed was a bit of tidying up and we could have stayed there. We wouldn't have tried to escape. Cross my heart and hope to . . . well, we just wouldn't. I really don't think there's much point tramping all the way out here. . . ."

No one replied, and for once Sibyl chose not to add her comments. We slowly made our way toward a craggy outcrop of Mount Parnassus. The cave was a gaping mouth in the rock face, and our captors fed us into it.

"Do you mind!" I sputtered as we were shoved into the darkness. "We can't see a thing in here!"

Thanatos's followers set about blocking off the cave entrance by rolling an enormous boulder in front of it. Sibyl and I could do nothing but listen to the sound of their grunting and straining. When the boulder had almost sealed the entrance, someone passed in a lit candle.

"Here, you can make shadow puppets now if you like," he said.

"Ho, ho," I answered bitterly. "So nice that you've kept a sense of humor in your line of work. I'm sure not all acolytes of Death remain so chipper."

In response they just rolled the boulder the last few inches, and Sibyl and I were alone in our stony prison. We sat on damp rock.

It was Sibyl who broke the long silence. "Where do you think he is now?" she asked with a defeated sigh.

"Who, Bumscruff? Don't know; don't care. I mean, it's all right for some, having an enormous great eagle swoop down and rescue them, isn't it? What about the rest of us? Aren't we pigs good enough to be rescued, is that it? I mean, what about me, what about—"

"You're babbling, Gryllus."

I stopped. Shadows from the candle were dancing across the rock walls in a way that was making me decidedly queasy.

"It's just that . . . caves make me a bit edgy," I explained. "The last time I was in a cave was when I was in Odysseus's crew and . . ."

Sibyl's eyes glittered darkly as she waited for me to go on. I sighed. Why not? Here we were, trapped in a cave, waiting for Thanatos to decide our fates. How much worse did things have to get before I could finally get matters off my chest?

"Listen," I sighed, "a while back you asked why I stayed a pig. Well . . . it all goes back to the time me and some of Odysseus's crew were packed into the Cyclops's cave. It was . . ."

My voice trailed off. I'm not usually at a loss for words, but how could I begin to describe the claustrophobic darkness of that terrible place, the awful stink of the flock of sheep that the one-eyed giant kept indoors? Or the even more dreadful stink of the Cyclops itself?

Finally, I condensed all these feelings into a single phrase: "It was . . . not very nice in there."

Sibyl waited for further explanation.

"Not very nice . . . at all," I clarified.

I looked around at the cave Sibyl and I were trapped

174

in now. The ceiling was lower here, but it wasn't all that different. A cave's a cave, after all. You can hang fancy lace curtains and paint the walls pink with little flowers, if you want, but face facts—it'd still be a cave.

"Things weren't looking too hot," I continued, "but guess what? They got worse." I took a much-needed deep breath. "'Cause the Cyclops, he started . . . he started eating people. . . . He just reached down and picked up the guy next to me as if he were a lollipop. I had to close my eyes, but I could still hear the crunching sounds."

My eyes slid away from Sibyl's.

"Of course, we were all afraid—who wouldn't be?— but somehow it was different for me. I was *petrified*. Even my goose bumps had goose bumps. My brain was scrambled with fear. Even when Odysseus managed to trick our way out of the cave, I was too terrified to move. A couple of the lads had to pick me up and carry me out of there.

"It didn't get any better when we were back on the ship either. I couldn't stop thinking about the whole incident. I was a wreck. I didn't understand why the rest of the crew was able to put the episode behind them. Okay, we'd nar- rowly avoided doom at the hands of the Cyclops, but what was there to say we'd be so lucky next time? What other terrible dangers lurked on the next island or around the next corner?"

I stared into the darkness of the cave as if I might make out the shape of my own dread. After the Cyclops's cave, there hadn't been any room in my head for anything *but* the dread. It crouched in my brain and booted out every other thought like an overachieving cuckoo. I couldn't eat—what if a chicken bone lodged in my throat? I couldn't drink—what if my mug of hot chocolate turned out to have an extra spoonful of deadly hemlock? Getting dressed in the morning involved endless speculation as to which of my sandals might be housing a lethal scorpion. At night I couldn't sleep a wink—what if I dreamed that I was eating a giant marshmallow and I actually choked on my pillow? My every waking moment was consumed by one horrible thought: *You are going to die. Precise details to follow—you might get eaten by a sea serpent, or you might be run through by a brigand's sword, or you might just succumb to the world's worst head cold— but these are no more than alternative routes to the same final destination. All roads lead to this place and I'm not talking about Athens.*

Face it—one way or another, you ARE going to die.

Check out.

Croak.

Kick the Athenian urn.

It wasn't easy to summarize all that, but I took a shot at it.

"I was in a bad way," I told Sibyl, "and it didn't help that everyone else was in the same boat. They just didn't realize it! They still don't! I mean, you heard it. Thanatos is stalking the land, the gods themselves are on the run, and people *still* don't get it! They think they can run or hide. Or just switch, start worshiping Thanatos, and everything will be okay."

"There's a medical term for what you've got," said Sibyl.

"It's called *cowardice*." But for once her face wasn't entirely lacking in sympathy.

"No!" I cried. I mean, okay, she was right about me being a coward, but being a coward was a natural response to this hostile world of rampaging monsters and uncaring gods. "The term for what I've got is *the human condition*. You're born, you have next to no time for a look around and a bite to eat, and then you die. What sort of life is that?"

Sibyl just shook her head. "So where does turning into a pig figure in all this?"

I sighed. "Things only changed when we arrived on Circe's island, that day our scouting party got turned into oinkers. That's when I got a glimpse of another way. The rest of the lads were a bit upset, but it was different for me. At first I wasn't sure why, I just felt calmer somehow. The obol finally dropped not long after I'd skipped out of the sty, looking for some more grub. I was deep in the woods, see, snuffling for roots, and the sun was on my back, and I wasn't thinking of much at all."

I paused, basking in the warmth of the memory.

"And?" Sibyl prompted.

"And that's it! That's the whole point! For just a few glorious minutes, *I forgot and the fear went away*."

In my mind's eye that brief feeling flickered like a birthday-cake candle against the gale-force wind of my dread.

"Of course, the terror didn't leave for good, but I'd had a taste of how things could be, hadn't I? Humans just think too much—we can't help it! Thought and language and all that junk. . . . But there's a better way! Animals don't spend all their time agonizing about how they'll wind up. They just *are*. They don't dredge up past nightmares or fret about future ones. They just get on with life; they exist in the here and now, and that struck me as a much nicer place to be. That's all I want, to find my way back to that place. . . ."

"So, that's why . . . ?" Sibyl's voice trailed off.

"That's why I hid in the shrubbery when Odysseus showed up and got Circe to turn the crewmen back into their old selves. It was my only chance. I knew I could be happier like this, happier as a pig. I mean, why would I want to go back to *my* old self?"

I expected Sibyl to have her arguments all lined up in neat rows, ready to fire. Instead, she just shrugged, her eyes shining with sadness. I could see my reflection in them: two tiny fat pigs in the dark mirrors of her pupils.

"Beats me," she said.

BOOK XXIV

Death pays a social call.

While the candle remained lit, we could roughly measure time by how much wax was left. But then the candle burned down completely, and we were in a place without light or time. Hours passed, maybe days. Who could tell?

I drifted in and out of dreams. The good ones featured tables heaving with fresh pies. In the bad ones I found myself back in a different cave, the nightmarish lair of the Cyclops, listening to the terrible snores of the man-eating giant, feeling the elbows of my crewmates as we huddled together and . . .

My eyes opened to complete darkness. There *was* an elbow nudging me in the ribs, and there *was* a ghastly rumbling, scraping noise.

"Sorry," I murmured sleepily. "It's just, I'd give anything for a pie right about now."

"Your stomach didn't make that noise," said Sibyl urgently. "It's the rock at the mouth of the cave. It's moving!"

That woke me up fast enough. It was true! The rumble sounded again, and there was a sliver of light at the mouth's entrance. Its dazzle was brutal after the complete darkness. The harsh slice of sunlight widened as a dark figure pushed the boulder farther aside. A tiny bud of hope sprouted in my heart.

Then the dark figure stepped inside the cave, and in my heart a size-fourteen hobnail boot stamped on that tiny bud of hope.

In came Thanatos, embodiment of Death. He was impossibly big, almost brushing the roof. Thankfully, it didn't knock his cowl back to reveal the face that hid in that dark place.

Thanatos spoke, and it was the same voice we had heard rising from the rubble of shattered statues.

"I seek the boy," that dreadful, scrapy voice said. "You will tell me where he is."

"We don't know," said Sibyl defiantly. "And even if we did, we wouldn't tell you!" The prophetess had positioned herself squarely between me and the hooded figure. She was too skinny for me to hide completely behind her, but I did my best. (You'll find it hard to believe, I know, but fortitude in the face of impending doom is *not* one of my strong points.)

"Shhh!" I hissed from behind her. "It isn't a very good idea to be rude to Thanatos, IS IT?" (I may not work in a temple, but I felt on safe theological ground here.)

The giant hooded figure took a step forward. Its echoing footfall sounded like the executioner's ax connecting with bone. Or . . . well, I don't know what it sounded like, do I? Like NOT GOOD NEWS.

Only my steely nerve kept me from fleeing—that and the solid-stone cave wall pressing into my back.

"So you might as well buzz off," Sibyl said.

I could hear the wobble in her voice, see the tremble in her legs. Even so, she pulled herself up to her full height and looked Thanatos right in the eye. (Well, she looked in the general direction of where eyes probably lurked in the darkness of that cowl.)

"I must find the boy," said Thanatos. "The Underworld awaits him."

Sibyl paid no attention to the grim threat wrapped in that voice. "Tough! You can always try and send *me* to the Underworld." She let out a deep sigh, and with it she expelled all sense of caution, because then she added, "If you think you're tough enough, that is."

There's a fine line between heroism and foolhardiness. Sibyl had just crossed it and then kept on hiking for several hours.

A lengthy pause followed. "I have dispatched proud kings and mighty warriors to the Underworld," said Thanatos. "I have engulfed towns in volcanic lava before breakfast. I have ravaged whole countries with plague and pestilence. I dragged down the entire city of Atlantis to a briny grave. I think it fair to say that I *am* probably . . . *tough enough*."

"Oh yeah? That's funny," Sibyl continued breathlessly. " 'Cause I heard you were a chicken."

Another ominous silence, broken finally by Sibyl's chicken impersonation: "Bwawk, buk buk bukaw!" In accordance with the ironclad rules of chicken impressions, she accompanied this by flapping her elbows.

Obviously our dire predicament had nudged Sibyl—already a highly strung youth—into the seething waters of madness.

But then suddenly she dug her heel into my flank. "The entrance!" she hissed over her shoulder.

"What?" demanded Thanatos.

Sibyl took another deep breath. "I said, I hope you know Asclepius well."

"Oh?" sounded that dreadful voice.

"Because you'll be needing the god of medicine by the time we're done with you," answered Sibyl.

Again the prophetess's foot gave me a whack, and I understood. Sibyl hadn't gone mad! Well, not completely. No, she was trying to buy me enough time to make my escape. I peered out from behind her skirt. The boulder blocked only part of the entrance now. If I made a dash for it, running for all I was worth, I might just be able to make it while Thanatos was busy listening to Sibyl's bravado.

If I was going to go, I had to go now.

Yeah, but even if you did get out, what could you do? whispered the secret voice of my inner self.

Um, try and find help? I told myself.

Yeah, right! I scoffed right back. *Who from? Apollo? The last time you saw him, he was scared almost out of his toga.*

Um . . .

There's nothing you can do—face it.

As the debate raged within my brain, my body froze in indecision.

Meanwhile, Thanatos was coming closer. Sibyl clenched her fists tight. Oh gods, was she planning on having a fistfight with Death?

I never found out, because suddenly a hearty, booming voice sounded from the cave entrance.

"Hello, in there! Anybody home?"

The enormous rock rolled completely aside to reveal an archway of bright sunlight. And in toddled Bumscruff.

"Sorry I'm late," he said with a grin. "I didn't miss anything, did I?"

BOOK XXV

A mystery is solved, an identity is revealed, a pig is flabbergasted.

Well, it was *sort of* Bumscruff.

Since we'd last seen him, he'd continued to grow and age at an even more rapid rate. I don't know what that eagle had been feeding him, but he was a young man now, tall and broad across the shoulders and with the fluffy beginnings of a beard on his square chin. Thankfully, he'd managed to find himself a longer tunic (just as well, as it was quite chilly in that cave).

I looked at this young adult Bumscruff and knew I'd seen that face somewhere before. Now where was it? I rifled through the sock drawer of my memory but couldn't place it.

Sibyl had less difficulty. She just couldn't believe it.

"It . . . it's YOU!" she gasped.

"I suppose so," replied the goatherd.

I pride myself on my quick intellect, but this I didn't follow. "What's going on, Bumscruff?" I demanded.

The goatherd's smile shrank a touch. "I believe I'd rather not go by that name." His voice was much more authoritative than it had been back in the days when his working vocabulary consisted exclusively of *Bek!*

"The time has come for my true name once again."

"And what's that?" I asked.

Sibyl and Thanatos both answered at the same time, and what they said was:

"Zeus."

Come again! Zeus? As in, Zeus, King of the Immortals? Zeus, the creator and enforcer of laws and justice? The father of the gods? The master of thunder and lightning? Zeus, the big cheese of the mighty Olympians?

I gave a snort of disbelief. "Sorry, for a moment I thought you said . . ."

I turned my incredulous gaze back on the former goatherd. Oh gods, it was true!

". . . Zeus!"

My mouth fell open, and I spoke the entire contents of my mind: ". . ."

That was where I'd seen that face before, or at least an older version of it—on countless statues, getting ready to chuck a thunderbolt at a Titan or something. Now I knew where Bumscruff had gotten that scar on his head—it must have been from when the newborn Athena sprang from Zeus's skull!

This was him all right, the most powerful deity going.

Well now, *this* changed everything, didn't it? I turned toward Thanatos and grinned. "Looks like you're in a bit of trouble now, buddy boy." I had that feeling you get when a schoolyard bully is about to beat you up, and then, at the very last minute, your big brother rolls up to save the day. (Well, I'm only *guessing* how that feels, actually. *My* big brother used to lead the local bullies to my secret hiding place.)

"Go on, Bumscr—Zeus," I urged. "See how he likes a

quick thunderbolt up the back flap of his robes. Bet that'll liven him up, eh?"

But this youthful Zeus did nothing—no smiting with his mighty forearms, no hurling thunderbolts through the air. Nothing. He just sort of shuffled toward Thanatos and nodded.

"Forgive me for the delay," said Zeus. "I wasn't myself for a while."

With a dry creak of bone, Thanatos returned the nod. Then he pointed an impossibly long, skinny arm toward the exit.

"Of course," said Zeus. "It is time to go to the Omphalos, Navel of the World."

As the two deities set off for the light, Zeus looked back at Sibyl. "We can take it from here," he said with a distant smile. "Er . . . thanks for all your help. I'll put in a good word, tell Apollo you did everything he asked."

He had already turned away when Sibyl's shout halted him. "Wait!"

Once she had the god's attention, the prophetess said, "That can't be it. You *have* to explain."

Zeus's face darkened. I think it was the "have to" that did it. But then he gave one of those enigmatic smiles. "But you *do* understand," he replied. "That's the whole point. You understand more than I ever could." Thanatos waited impatiently by the entrance to the cave as Zeus continued. "Since the world was young, I have wandered the Cosmos, from the snow-capped peak of Olympus to the Elysian Fields of fallen heroes. I was present when life was breathed into the first mortals. I have transformed myself into bull and swan, rock and star. The elements themselves are subject to my whims. I am Zeus, all-powerful King of the Gods.

"But my knowledge is not complete, as Thanatos so kindly pointed out to me. There remains a branch of knowledge closed to me. Something that every mortal creature must face, and that all humans must contemplate."

"Dying," said Sibyl flatly. "Right? As an immortal, the only thing you could never know—by definition—is mortality. . . . Someone who will never die can't begin to understand the shadow we live our lives under." Sibyl's gaze never moved from the god. "So you decided—"

"To become mortal," Zeus finished for her.

This was the straw that broke the talking pig's back.

"You didn't do a very good job of it then, did you?" I exclaimed. "What about that explosion back at Thales' place? Most mortals would have needed a bit more than a neck rub and an aspirin after that!"

Zeus gave me an untroubled smile.

"So you made an agreement with Thanatos," Sibyl was saying, carefully piecing the story together as if it were a five-hundred-piece jigsaw puzzle of nothing but sky. "You were reborn as a simple mortal goatherd. But you weren't exactly a normal mortal, were you?"

Zeus shrugged. "Close enough. I merely wanted to hurry things along. In this form, I am nonetheless mortal."

"So you come to the Navel of the World at Delphi," continued Sibyl, "and die? And then what?"

"And then I shall be reborn a god once more—a *wiser*

god—and return to my throne on Olympus, of course," replied Zeus.

"So we weren't running *from* Thanatos," said the prophetess, a stream of anger now bubbling beneath her voice. "We were coming to meet him. Is that why you made us leave the mountain path and go to Thales' house? You knew Thanatos was going to be there?"

"I didn't *know*," answered Zeus. "I suppose I *sensed* it on some level, yes."

"What about the other gods?" Sibyl continued. "They didn't know about this plan of yours, did they? Why were they involved?"

Zeus threw back his shoulders. "As King of the Gods, I saw fit to teach all the immortals a lesson about mortality. I am not obliged to explain my every decision to them—or to you. The word of Zeus is law!" he boomed. "But as to the destruction of temples . . ."

He scowled at Thanatos, who responded with a bony shrug.

"It's true that mortals will get carried away," continued Zeus with a nod of agreement.

But Sibyl wasn't satisfied yet. "Okay, but what about monsters running free all over the place? Haven't people been dying all over Greece?"

"Regrettable," said Zeus. "But, as you mortals say, you can't make an omelette without . . . um, without a few accidental deaths." Clearly, this didn't seem to trouble Zeus unduly. "And now I must go to the Omphalos and perform the cleansing rituals before the moment of death."

He moved toward the mouth of the cave.

"Hold on a second," said Sibyl. "I'm coming with you! I'm going to see this thing through to the end."

Zeus gave this his regal consideration. "Very well. You deserve that much. You may accompany us to the temple."

Sibyl turned toward me, but I was already backing away. "Erm, I'd love to join you, only I think I've pulled a muscle in my hams or something. It's very sore when I——"

Sibyl cut me off. "Don't worry, Gryllus. You don't have to come. It's over, or at least it will be once Zeus dies, then returns to Olympus. I . . . I just want to see this thing through to the end, for my own sake."

"So the Cosmos isn't going to end then?" I said. "That's nice."

Sibyl gave a brief nod, but she couldn't conceal the dissatisfied scowl on her face. "Good luck, then, Gryllus. I'd get out of Delphi if I were you. You never know what the followers of Thanatos will do while their god is busy." She made a half move as if to give me a hug, then thought better of it and pulled back. She glanced up at the two immortal figures, who were already outside the cave. "And thanks for all your hel—well, thanks anyway."

And with that she marched off after Zeus and Thanatos, leaving this little piggy all alone in the gloom.

The only thought that kept pounding through my head was "Why?"

Zeus could have anything he wanted, so why would he choose to become a helpless goatherd?

Zeus was one of the immortal gods, so why would he choose to experience death?

And while we're at it, why would he allow Thanatos to dispatch the other gods to the Underworld without even telling them what was going on?

The whys were multiplying, hopping around in my skull faster than a burrowful of happy rabbits, until at last I came upon the only words that seemed to keep them at bay:

Who gives a flying fig?

BOOK XXVI

Another mighty hero is brought to ruin by his tragic flaw.

I couldn't quite believe the whole ordeal was over. Or at least, that it was *almost* over. My personal involvement had come to an end, and that was the bit that concerned me the most.

So, I was a free pig once more, free to . . . well, what exactly? Head back to the woods? Try to lose myself in the life of a wild pig again? Somehow, right at the moment when I should have been feeling relief and joy, I was feeling only flat and empty. Or perhaps I was just hungry.

One thing was for sure. Wherever I went next, Sibyl had been right: the followers of Thanatos were an unstable bunch. The first thing I had to do was get out of this dump, and *fast*. Taking care not to go near the town center, I moved quickly through deserted backstreets. Before long, Delphi would lie behind me and the road south to Athens itself would stretch ahead.

Ah, but life isn't always so easy. The scholars among you will know that your typical Greek heroes tend to come with a *tragic flaw*—which is a fancy way of saying a moral failing that leads to ruin and destruction. For some, their tragic flaw is the bitter seed of envy that sprouts in their stony hearts; for others it's an insatiable curiosity that drives them to discover things better left undisturbed. For others still, it's arrogant pride that leads a hero to consider himself equal to the gods themselves.

Naturally, I've got a tragic flaw, too. . . .

Pies.

Gods, I love 'em—rhubarb pies, gooseberry pies, apple-and-fig pies with gallons of ice cream on top. You name a pie, I'll shove it down my throat.

So it was that I didn't leave town quite as quickly as I'd intended. My trusty snout caught a whiff of that telltale sweet-'n'-spicy aroma on the breeze. Somewhere in the vicinity, someone had just taken a fresh batch of pies out of the oven.

Well, one little pie won't hurt, will it? whispered the greedy little pie fiend inside my skull.

But . . . I think I really ought just to get out of town while I can, the sensible rest of me tried to argue.

Yeah, but one little pie won't hurt though, will it? persisted that voice in my skull. How to resist such oratorical skills?

You're not wrong there, little pie fiend, I answered.

And so it was that I failed to escape the shackles of my own tragic flaw. I couldn't resist the glorious siren call of the pie.

The wonderful smell led me to a little café on a side street near the edge of town. Despite all the strange stuff going on in Delphi, the place was open. (I suppose it made sense. After a busy day ransacking temples and destroying statues of the Olympians in the name of unholy Thanatos, people were probably grateful for a place where they could get a snack and a hot drink.)

However, presumably the rampaging mob hadn't called it quits for the day yet, because at the moment, the owner was the only person in the joint. He was standing behind the counter, idly drying goblets with a dirty rag and humming to himself.

"Nice day for it," I said, being careful not to specify what "it" was.

"Praise be to Thanatos," he mumbled without enthusiasm. He was unfazed by the sight of a talking pig. (Well, things *had* been pretty weird around Delphi lately.)

"I couldn't help noticing the enticing aroma of fresh pie," I went on.

"That'll be our fresh pies," the man answered glumly. "Raisin and almond."

"I'll take one!"

His world-weary eyes narrowed. "Got any money?" (The imminent end of the Cosmos is one thing, but business is business.)

My brain was racing. Could I offer to work for pies? Tell him that my money was outside?

Of course not! But all was not lost, because that's when I realized that Sibyl had forgotten something. She hadn't taken the clay jar containing the Erinys from around my neck. (Even then, I knew I would have to give this my due consideration. Why had the Erinys remained silent since that time when Athena showed up? But now was not the time. There were pies to be eaten.)

"All my money's here in this jar," I said hurriedly.

The man nodded and called my order through to the kitchen. A couple of minutes later, he brought out the pie.

"Twelve obols!" I gasped when he muttered the price. "That's a bit steep!"

The man shrugged and began to take the pie back.

"Okay, okay," I grunted. "Twelve obols!" It didn't matter too much anyway, as in fact I did not possess even two obols to rub together.

He set the pie on the floor, and I dived in. The pastry-to-filling ratio left something to be desired, but I still demolished that pie in about three seconds.

"Another!" I called with an appreciative burp.

While the second pie was being heated, the man behind the bar felt obliged to have a stab at conversation.

"So," he began, "we don't get many talking pigs in here."

I was *going* to say it, I really was. I was going to say, "I'm not surprised, with the prices you charge." But before I could open my mouth, the door opened behind me.

"Praise be to Thanatos," muttered the café owner. There was no increase in his enthusiasm levels.

"Yes, yes, quite," came the impatient answer.

A cloud of perfume—the expensive stuff, mind you, none of your cheap rubbish that fell off the back of a donkey-cart—wafted across the room. I recognized that scent as easily as I recognized that voice.

It was *him* again—the tall man, the one who had been at Stavros's restaurant, the one who had ordered our incarceration in the cave. He was now accompanied by two squat, muscular types who didn't look as if they'd been brought along for their sparkling conversation.

The tall man's aristocratic eye landed on me. His upper lip rose in an elegant curl.

"There it is," he drawled. "Apprehend it."

The hired muscle looked up in momentary incomprehension until the tall man rolled his eyes and barked, "It means, GET the pig!"

With a preparatory crack of their knuckles, the two henchmen headed my way. They looked as if they meant business, and I'm not talking about olive exports.

I did the only sensible thing open to me. I charged past the counter and toward the kitchen.

"Here, wait!" yelled the man behind the counter. It was the most animated I'd seen him. "You haven't paid for them pies!"

But I was already charging through the kitchen. A woman was taking another pie out of the oven. She let out a scream at the sight of a panicked pig fleeing through her kitchen. She hopped backward and dropped the piping-hot pie. A spilled pie is a sorry sight indeed, and I almost stopped to take a slurp, but the cowardly portion of my brain pulled rank on the greedy part. I bolted for the back door and shouldered it open.

I heard a crash behind me as one of my pursuers skidded on the pie and careened into a rack of kitchen utensils. Sadly, there wasn't time to look back and enjoy the moment.

Once outside, I faced the question of where to go. Picking a direction at random, I crossed a mud lane and whizzed around the corner. Here, on the edge of town, the ramshackle buildings were spaced wider apart for farming use. I searched frantically for a hiding spot.

And then I saw it.

There, across the way, a kid was cradling a piglet in his arms! He was carrying it toward a pigpen, where a throng of noisy pigs went noisily about their piggy business. Yes!

A philosopher once said, "What better place to hide a stone than on a pebble beach?" Yes, well I imagine he'd be flat out of luck if he wanted to find the same stone again. And anyway, when's the last time you needed to hide a stone? BUT. . . there was still a thimbleful of sense in the basic idea.

No, I wasn't going to hide on a pebble beach! I would hide in plain sight by mingling with the rest of the pigs. My pursuers would never be able to pick me out!

Even in my haste, I took a moment to congratulate myself on the sheer genius of my sneaky plan.

BOOK XXVII

Our hero ponders the difference between beast and man.

The job of swineherd is not traditionally considered a springboard for a high-powered career as tyrant of a city-state or some such.

This lad was no exception. When I trotted over, he didn't waste mental energy questioning how I had escaped from the pen. He just tucked the piglet under one arm and drove me toward the gate with the switch in his other hand. He wasn't the least bit curious as to why I waited patiently for the gate to swing open. The swineherd let me in and then wandered off to take care of his other duties (whatever they were—funnily enough, detailed knowledge of the farming life is not one of my strong points).

And then I was in there, just another pig in the herd. At first I tried staying near the outer perimeter of the group, but it was hard to hold your ground in that mass of pigs, and I soon found myself pushed and shoved toward the middle.

The pigs around me were making a right old din, snorting and grunting and belching and squealing and oinking all over the place. Every last one of them had a poorly defined sense of personal space. None of them thought twice about bumping and jostling and barging you aside as they snuffled and rooted and gobbled down their swill. It was like being tossed about in a pink sea (only the smell in the air was no refreshing ocean breeze, if you catch my meaning).

I managed to lift my head just in time to see the two henchmen arrive at the enclosure fence. They stared crossly into the pen, trying to spot me.

I was feeling pretty proud of my brilliant ruse—how would they ever find me in the middle of this lot?—when I suddenly remembered that stinking clay jar around my neck. Quickly I tucked my head down and cunningly hid the jar within two folds of my pig neck.

By the time I sneaked another peek, my pursuers had turned and were heading back toward the café. I noticed that one of them had an enormous pie smear down the back of his ceremonial robes.

Brilliant! I patted myself on the back. *Now I just have to get out of here before they come back.*

Something gave my tail a bite. I yelped and whirled around.

"Excuse me! Do you mind?"

It was a pig—although that's like saying King Croesus wasn't short of the odd obol or two. It was the pig to end all pigs: an enormous hog, and it was glaring at me in a manner that even the sunniest of optimists couldn't call friendly. All I could see were those yellow-lashed piggy eyes and that big, wet, snuffling snout with its ghastly grunting mouth hanging open to show all those unpleasant-looking teeth. (People don't often think of pigs as having sharp teeth, but we do. Any animal that will eat more or less anything has got to come equipped with the choppers for the job.)

The animal's grunt was the Gurgle of Doom. The monstrous beast clearly hadn't taken a shine to me, that's what that grunt said, and there was nothing I could do to change its bestial mind. No, there was no reasoning with a creature like this, no persuading, no outscoring it in an argument. All I could think about was the out-and-out, straight-up ANIMALNESS of the beast in front of me. This was a real pig, a pig's pig. It was a big, fat, raw, piggy hunk of PIG, pigness incarnate. It was everything piggy in the world rolled into one gargantuan hog. It was a bit on the smelly side, too.

A thought hit me with the force of a two-ton Hydra landing on my head. Who was I trying to fool? I could never be *this*. I might walk the piggy walk and sport the corkscrew tail, but I could never truly grunt the grunt like this unknowable beast. The gulf between us was vast and uncrossable.

Did this creature's animal instincts also sense this unbridgeable gap? Perhaps so, because suddenly the hog let out an explosive grunt and lunged, snapping at one of my ears.

"WAAAH!" I commented. I didn't wait for a response, opting instead to duck under the attack and make a dash for a gap between two young porkers. It took a bit of wriggling, but I squeezed my way through. With a fearsome bellow, the enormous hog tried to follow, but its immense bulk slowed it down. I made my getaway with just one more bite to the tail.

I was safe again for the moment, but, as a great philosopher once said, "Safety is like a nice pie—it doesn't last long." It didn't last long at all, because moments later I saw the tall man approaching the pigpen with his long, unhurried stride. He set a black canvas bag on the ground.

Afraid that he might spot me staring, I pretended to sniff at the mud, once again concealing the jar. I needn't have bothered. The tall man didn't even look my way as he slowly pulled out two long butcher's knives. With a tranquil smile he began to sharpen the blades, one against the other. The sound of knife on knife is not a pleasant one, frankly, and even the chorus of grunts around me could not cloak it.

I couldn't take my eyes off those blades. It was as if they, not the Omphalos at Apollo's temple, had become the true center of the world. The entire Cosmos seemed balanced on the glinting edge of one of those butcher's knives.

What was he going to do? Surely he didn't mean to slaughter every pig here, just to make sure he got me? Fear swept through me like a tiptop cleaning service.

But here's the thing: none of the other pigs around me even noticed! The ignorant swine were quite content in their ignorance! They just went on shoveling food into their fat faces and grunting and biting and bumping into each other. They were completely unaware of what the tall man was up to, right there in plain view.

Not me! I was denied the animal luxury of their innocence. I knew what a pork pie was, and I didn't want to be one.

There was nothing else to do. I would have to escape *now*. Willing myself not to picture the sight of those butcher's knives, and not making a very good job of it, I began to battle my way through to the other side of the sty. Pigs all around jostled and shoved and pushed, but I didn't give up.

Finally, bruised and alone, I reached the far barrier. The wooden fence was designed to keep us in, of course, but its makers hadn't taken into account the possibility of so intelligent a pig. If I could just dig a bit of a hole, I figured I would be able to squeeze my way under the bottom of the fence.

My hooves scrabbled quickly at the earth. It was soft, and the job wasn't hard, despite all the bumps and shoves I had to endure from the pigs behind me.

I eased my snout under the bottom bar of the fence, then began to wriggle the rest of my body through. Everything went okay . . . until my midsection hit the fence.

That's when all forward movement came to an end. I was stuck. However much I wriggled, I was stuck fast. I cursed myself for never once skipping dessert. Defeated, I tried to pull back into the pigpen, only to find that I couldn't even do that now.

Suddenly a pair of sandals appeared in front of me, and I found myself staring at ten slender, beautifully pedicured toes.

"Well, hello, Gryllus," purred a silky voice from above. "How simply delightful to see you again!"

BOOK XXVIII

A lovely spread is no guarantee of a pleasant afternoon.

Another grape? I asked myself. *Why not? But save space for dessert!*

I'd been feeding my face for hours. Seems I had fallen on my pig's feet! There had been no reason for fear whatsoever! Here I was, lying back on a luxurious couch. The couch was in a high-ceilinged room, and the room was inside the swanky villa that the tall man's employees had led me to (once they'd extracted me from the fence, that is).

I hadn't known what to expect—certainly not a feast. Even before we reached the room, an onslaught of delicious smells attacked my snout.

Better yet, the banquet was all spread out on a long table low enough for me to eat from. There was plate after plate of it, all kinds of food and as much as even I wanted: cheeses, breads, pastries, olives, fruit, white fish sliced into delicate fingers, then coated in breadcrumbs and lightly fried. (This rare and exotic delicacy is served with sliced, fried root vegetable. The dish is called Sticks of Fish and Phraxian Fries.)

And it was all for me! I chuckled contentedly at the strange turns the threads of Fate can take, and then I got down to some serious eating. I ate until I couldn't comfortably eat any more, and then I ate some more.

I was just deciding whether a quick nap was in order when the door opened again. In came the immaculately groomed tall man.

"At long last, we have an opportunity to talk," he said, using his long, slender nose to deliver a whistling laugh as he looked me over. "My name is Epicurus."

I wasn't born in a sty—I knew this was a classy guy. Expensive clothes, jewelry all over the place, hands that considered anything more than holding a knife and fork to be hard labor.

His mouth twisted up into something like a smile. "I suppose you must be wondering what's going on," he said.

"Now that you mention it, yes," I answered. "I mean, I know you work for Thanatos and all, so I'm not quite sure why . . ."

Epicurus's smile thinned to a crack. "I have—how shall I put it?—adjusted to the current situation here in Delphi, that is true," he said. "But at present I am acting on my own authority."

"Oh," I said, giving this a suitably thoughtful quality. "So . . . you weren't following Thanatos's orders when you came to see me at the restaurant?"

Epicurus gave an elegant shake of his aristocratic head.

"I knew it!" I exclaimed. "You *are* a theatrical agent, aren't you? I knew Sibyl was wrong!"

"That isn't *exactly* correct either," said Epicurus. "However, I was in the north country on personal business, and I *was* looking for a fabulous creature of some kind. I had heard rumors that chimeras had been sighted in the area.

I was searching for one when I heard about something even better . . . you."

A warm glow of pride settled into my heart—it's always nice to feel wanted—right next to the shiver of confusion.

"I can't tell you how annoyed I was to lose you," Epicurus continued, a dusting of frost in his voice now. "I was due in Delphi for an important meeting and here I was, empty-handed." Epicurus displayed two empty hands to illustrate the point. "Imagine my surprise when I arrived here and found the temples of the gods in disarray and the Dark One, Thanatos, taking up residence in the place."

"Bit of a shocker, I expect."

"Indeed, and a quite delightful one," Epicurus simpered. "It's so refreshing to have a deity who doesn't make a song and dance about morality, I find. Even though our meeting was postponed, the situation was interesting enough for me and many of my colleagues to stay."

His lips quivered in another shot at a smile. "And then you turn up, right here on our doorstep! Who'd have thought that Thanatos's order to capture the boy would lead to such a happy reunion? It's almost enough to make one a follower of the Fates after all!"

"Wait, you don't know the half of it!" I exclaimed. "You won't believe who that lad actually is! He's—"

"The dealings of the old gods are of no concern to me," Epicurus snapped, his lips thinning to angry lines. "All I desired was that Thanatos let me see you when he was done. Alas, I found the cave deserted." His lips had almost disappeared now, then suddenly they re-emerged in a smile. "However, no harm done! You're here now, which means that our meeting can go ahead as planned. My friends and I will be able to have our cake and eat, as it were."

"You can't beat a bit of cake," I agreed. "Except for pie, that is."

Epicurus's aristocratic nose twitched with noble disdain. "And now tell me. Was the food to your . . . satisfaction?"

I was happy to be back on a more pleasant topic of conversation. "It was a very tasty spread," I pronounced.

"Ah," sniffed Epicurus as he looked at the remains of my food. "But I see that you have neglected to eat your apples?"

"That's right," I declared proudly. "Apples give me gas. I'm a little like the goddess of wisdom in that respect. Just one apple and I could blast—"

Epicurus's hand flew up like an alarmed dove. "Yes, yes, quite!"

He did seem unusually put out by the sight of those uneaten apples. Sulky, almost.

"Look, if it means so much to you, I'll eat 'em," I said. "I mean, I don't mind if you don't. Better out than in, right?"

His face brightened. "Really? Could you? That would be awfully decent. They do flavor the flesh so wonderfully. You know, pork and apples are a classic combination."

I'd already chomped the first apple when the meaning of his words hit me with the force of Atlas dropping the vault of the heavens right on my skull. The whole world seemed to reel under the impact.

"Pork? You mean . . ."

Epicurus smiled patiently, a kindly teacher waiting for a slow pupil.

"You mean, you're going to . . ."

"Ye-es . . ."

"Eat me? You're going to EAT ME!"

"Bingo!" Epicurus declared, suddenly looking not quite so classy. "Naturally, we're going to eat you!"

"But . . . but that's cannibalism, that is!" I exclaimed.

I could see the butcher's twinkle in his beady eyes now. "Ah well, strictly speaking, cannibalism involves eating within one's own species," he explained calmly. "Whereas you, my fine fat friend, are what we would call . . . a pig."

"Well, number one, less of the 'fat,' thank you very much—I'm just big-boned. And number two, I'm not exactly your average pig, am I?" I yelled. "I'm a sentient creature, I am! I can talk! I can think! I can feel pain—and I don't like it very much!"

Epicurus let out a long, whistling sigh through his long, aristocratic nose. "I think you'll find that is the whole point," he explained coldly.

His impatience was beginning to show through like a pair of bright-red underpants under a thin white toga. He wasn't coming across much like a kindly teacher now. More like a *nasty* teacher—a nasty teacher who wanted to eat me for dinner.

"Your awareness of the situation will lend a certain extra *something* to the dinner," he said airily.

"That's sick!" I cried.

Epicurus gave a little nod as if I'd just complimented him on his taste in bracelets. My heart sank faster than Narcissus changing into a new outfit.

"But . . . I'd be chewy," I moaned. "And fatty. Too much fatty food isn't good for you—that's what they say on the islands. You want to have yourself some grilled fish and a bowl of bran flakes, not a big fat pig like . . ."

The end of this sentence shouldn't have been so hard to find—in case you're wondering, the missing word is "me"—but my brain was suddenly scrambled mush. The insides of my skull felt like the whirlpool Charybdis (all swirling around, I mean, not full of thousands of gallons of salt water).

I tried to get up on all fours and immediately collapsed. I lay there, watching the violent spin of the room for a while.

Epicurus was leaning over me. "Congratulations," he said with a leer. "You have the honor of being the next meal of the Epicurean Supper Club. You see, our exclusive dining group has eaten simply everything the finest tables in Hellas have to offer. Our palates are bored, jaded. And yet, and yet . . . just occasionally something comes along that is a truly different dining experience. A couple of years back, for example, we had Hydra Hotpot. Exquisite! Last year, it was roast phoenix. It was quite superb—firm white meat not entirely unlike chicken, but with a smoky aftertaste." Epicurus smacked his lips at the memory. "But we have high hopes that you, my friend, will top them all. Prepare to become a culinary legend!"

I wanted to say what anyone in my position would: "Why, you—you rotten, stinkin'—!!"*

At least, that's what I tried to say. What I *did* say was, "BOH!"—mainly because this was all my brain and tongue could come up with between the pair of them.

"That's the ticket," said Epicurus encouragingly. "The poison's working already." Seeing the look in my eye, he added, "Oh, I know what you're thinking, but not to worry! The poison is my own recipe. After it's done its job and the carcass has sat for a few hours, all traces will be gone. You'll be perfectly safe to cook and eat."

I would have replied "BOH" to this also, but my mind had started its long slide down into a murky domain. I rallied my brain and vocal cords for one last attempt at language, one final comment, which I spat out with the dregs of my swiftly ebbing vital force.

Part of me still couldn't believe it. After all I'd been through, this couldn't be the end for poor old Gryllus, could it?

But it could.

And it was.

'Cause that's when I died.

*Translator's note: The words in this passage appear to be unknown—at least, I can't find them anywhere in my Greek-English Lexicon. The closest approximations I can find are "cheeky fellow" and "mischievous young scamp."

BOOK XXIX

The dead live up to their reputation as poor conversationalists.

If you have to go and die, let's hope you don't mind a bit of fog. There was nothing else all around me, nothing but billowing white and gray fog all over the place.

I couldn't see a thing, but somehow I knew which way to go. The ground beneath my feet felt scorched and barren and clearly hadn't needed mowing in ages.

A question drifted into my mind. Where was Thanatos, then? Wasn't Death supposed to dispatch me to this dreadful place? Admittedly, he certainly had his mind on other things lately, what with Zeus and all. Or maybe I just wasn't important enough? Rumor had it that Thanatos showed up in person only for the more important deaths. (Even in death, your average Joe not blessed with pots of gold or royal parents gets a raw deal.)

As I felt my way forward through the fog, a jumble of voices echoed around me. Most of it was meaningless babble, but I could make out a few of them:

"It's only a head cold. Right, Doc?" said one.

"Hey, look at me! I'm up here on the roof!" called another.

And another still: "That log looks a bit like a crocodile, doesn't it?"

Don't ask how, but I knew what I was hearing—they

were dying words, the final words spoken by mortals before they passed into the Underworld. Hundreds and hundreds of them reverberated in the gloomy gray, though I set eyes on no speakers. The disembodied voices continued:

"I think the cliff edge is somewhere around heeeeeeeeeeeeeeeeere!"

"Bubonic plague? I'm never coming *here* on vacation again!"

"Tell Memnon that the gold is hidden under the . . . er . . . the . . . what was I saying?"

And among them all I heard a voice that was familiar to me, familiar because it was my own. I heard the final words I myself had uttered: "I *thought* those mushrooms tasted funny."

(Okay, these might not be the most profound dying words ever uttered—not likely to get engraved on too many sarcophagi—but you can't deny their poignant charm.)

My senses were numbed, as if they had been wrapped in extra-fluffy wool, but I slowly became aware of a change in my surroundings. I looked down and saw the black water of a slow-moving river. It didn't look too inviting, which probably accounted for the lack of people paddling or bodysurfing.

So this was the River Styx. The thought floated through my mind with the treacly slowness of the water itself. The river was an ever-changing black mirror. I looked at its oily surface and saw my face reflected back at me. . . . Not a pig, but a human. It was my real face.

My human face.

But even this had changed. The person who stared back at me was not the husky-but-handsome devil of my memory. My reflection looked scared and tired and lonely.

A little farther along the bank, a wooden boat was moored to the shore. This must be the boat of Charon, the immortal ferryman of dead souls. The only thing was, the boat was empty. No Charon anywhere. The whole death process had become a bit too self-service for my liking.

There was a little note propped up on the ground. It might have said PLEASE OPERATE BOAT YOURSELF, or it might have said BACK IN FIVE MINUTES. (As you know, reading wasn't one of my strong points—and I had the distinct feeling that it was a bit late to start learning now.)

Next to the boat sat a bowl. I peered in and saw a few obols at the bottom. Was there an honor system in place— were you supposed to leave the traditional obol in the jar as fare?

Well, forget that. It was bad enough being dead—I wasn't going to pay for the privilege of ferrying myself across.

I stepped into the boat, unhooked the rope, and sat at the oars. Even in death, my rowing skills had not improved, and a fair bit of Styx water sloshed into the boat. But eventually I made my way across and managed to exit the boat without falling into the black waters.

And so I entered the wide-gated house of Pluto, Lord of the Underworld.

Well, I say "house," but it wasn't exactly homey—

enormous underground caverns rarely are. I could make out craggy rock faces here and there, rising out of the fog.

The souls of the perished were all over the place. They looked as pale as blanched vegetables, and almost as peppy. Most just shuffled about aimlessly. Some, apparently fed up with shuffling about, opted instead to sit around and stare vacantly. The whole place was less lively than a wet weekend in Samothrace.

Just then I recognized one of the shades. He was one of my old crewmates. I wandered over and said, "I know you!"

The shade's smoky eyes showed no flicker of reaction.

"It's Ichthyos, right?" I continued. "You look, er, great . . . all things considered."

The last time I'd see him had been on Odysseus's ship, not long into our epic voyage home from Troy to Ithaca. I had been on laundry duty that week. (I usually requested that shift because rowing the ship's big wooden oars gave me terrible blisters.) I was just going to hang up a load of whites to dry in the rigging when I tripped on a cable and dropped Odysseus's favorite undertunic overboard. Of course, I would have hopped over and retrieved it, but swimming was never one of my strengths. All that salt water gave me a sinus headache when it went up my nostrils. Ichthyos, on the other hand . . . that lad had set his sights on swimming in the Olympics. He was like a fish (well, minus the scales and gills). So, all I did was ask him to dive over and fetch the tunic. How was I to know how it would turn out?

"Yeah, I'm really sorry about that whole business," I told

the ghost of my former crewmate. "Who'd have thought there'd be a tiger shark in the water, right there of all places? The way you fought it off with just a butter knife and a dishcloth, that was incredible . . . the stuff of legends. And then, after all that, for there to be a giant man-eating squid in the vicinity, too. I expect all that thrashing about with the shark caught its attention. I mean, of all the rotten luck!"

"I've forgotten all about it," Ichthyos said in a voice like a whisper of damp sea air through a cave.

"Well, that's very decent of you, Ichy," I said.

"No, I've *really* forgotten all about it." His eyes drifted out of focus.

"What, you can't remember any of it?" I asked.

"Any of what?" The shade gazed around in a bemused fashion. "What were we talking about?" he asked.

"When we were on Odysseus's ship together."

A long pause, and then: "Whose ship?"

"Odysseus's."

"Oh . . . who's that?"

"He was our captain, yours and mine."

"Oh . . . and you're . . . ?"

"Gryllus."

"Oh . . . and I'm . . . ?"

"Ichthyos."

Ichthyos had never been the most gifted talker—not unless you were set on debating the merits of breaststroke versus front crawl—but death had really had a negative effect on his conversational skills.

I edged sideways. "Well, it's been great catching up with you."

Ichthyos's gray face was as blank as fog across the ocean.

"We must do this again sometime," I continued. *Yeah, perhaps when the residents of the Underworld decide to get together and organize an all-dead five-a-side soccer tournament,* I thought—which was to say, NEVER.

Thing is, I didn't really care. The fog in that place wasn't just on the outside. It seeped into your brain as well. I suppose that's how it went in the Underworld. I mean, I was still enough of a newcomer to remember stuff, to feel a certain amount of regret about all the things I hadn't gotten around to doing in my life as man and pig. But there was already some strange comfort in the notion that the hefty load of regret would slowly dissolve and fade, as your mind just sank into the damp numbness of the place, like a hog easing into cool mud. Before you knew it, the Overworld wouldn't be even a half-forgotten memory, and the fog would be all.

But then the steady mumbling of the shades suddenly became a wail, and my attention was drawn back to the halls of the Underworld. The souls of the dead were parting like nervous sheep to let someone through.

Or some*thing.*

A towering figure in tattered black robes emerged though the mist. A hint of gray skull glistened beneath the cowl.

It was Thanatos.

BOOK XXX

The primordial soup is none too appetizing.

The sight ignited a tiny spark in my no-longer-beating heart. What was it? Curiosity? Anger? Suspicion? Whatever, it was hard for that spark to remain lit in the face of the numbness steadily creeping over me.

The majority of my brain voted in favor of simply not caring, doing nothing. This, after all, seemed to be the done thing here in the Underworld, and I have always had a hard time resisting peer pressure. (That's how I ended up in the Greek army in the first place. I never believed all that "Visit exotic cities and lay siege to them" stuff. But all my buddies were signing up, so I did too.)

Suddenly a small voice piped up from nearby.

"Well? What are you waiting for?"

It sounded like a little old lady—a *cross* little old lady. I knew that this voice did not come from one of the shades around me.

"Who said that?" I asked.

"Me! We're finally in a place where you can hear me! I've been dying to give you a piece of my mind."

The voice was coming from the clay jar that still hung around my neck and now glowed a dull orange that looked out of place in this world of gray.

It was the Erinys, the spirit of divine vengeance.

"Follow him, laddie!" she said.

She could only be talking about Thanatos, who had begun to climb a flight of steps carved into the rock wall. I took a couple of listless steps in that direction.

"You'll not catch up at this rate!" The Erinys's nagging fanned the spark in my heart. I stumbled forward, picking up speed until I was dodging in and out of the assembled shades of the departed.

"Excuse me, sorry, 'scuse me. . . ."

"This is no time to be polite!" cried the Erinys. "He's getting away!"

I switched tactics from dodging to barging through. A couple of shades fell over as I elbowed them aside, but they didn't seem too troubled. (I'm not sure they even noticed.)

The very sight of the rocky steps filled me with weariness, but the Erinys wouldn't let up until I began climbing. Almost immediately, my weariness lessened. The higher I got, the farther from the rolling fog below, the more clear-headed I became. Soon I was taking the steps two at a time, though this still wasn't quick enough for the Erinys.

"Get a move on!" she urged.

"Thanatos has got longer legs," I replied. "AND he hasn't got any flesh or organs to carry around and slow him down."

By the time I reached the narrow ledge at the top of the steps, Thanatos had disappeared.

"That way," said the Erinys. "Second cavern on the left."

I made my way along the ledge. We were high above the main chamber of the Underworld, but all I could see below was a blanket of fog.

As I neared the cave entrance, fear weighed me down like an anvil around my neck.

"What are you waiting for?" said the Erinys. "What's the worst that could happen? You're DEAD, aren't you? Are you afraid you're going to get DEADER?"

She had a point there, but it's not easy to break the habit of a lifetime—even though my digestive system was no longer working, a ball of anxiety managed to settle in my stomach as I edged closer to the gloomy entrance.

It took my eyes a moment to adjust to the deeper darkness of this inner cave. I could make out a figure at the far end of the cavern. It was Thanatos.

He rested one bony hand on something and, to my amazement, I recognized what the object was. It was exactly like that toaster Thales had shown us, only this was much, much bigger—the size of a wagon. Of course, they might just like *really* big toast for breakfast down here, but I didn't think that was the explanation. Insofar as a kitchen appliance can, this toaster exuded a sense of undeniable menace. What's more, it was placed right on top of a thick vein of the silvery substance Thales had told us about. What was it called? Pluto's Iron.

Plutonium.

Thanatos was looking up at the sheer rock wall at the back of the cavern. "The plan is working!" he rasped. "I told you it was unnecessary to send monsters to bring him to us. Zeus gave his word that he would come."

At first I couldn't figure out who he was talking to. But then I realized that there was a wide crack of even blacker black that ran vertically up the rock face. When Thanatos spoke, the contents of this huge crack seemed to light up. It looked like a portal into another realm, a place where things like shape and color and pattern were meaningless. It was a formless jumble, a never-ending swirl that seemed to go on forever.

As we watched, something began to emerge in the whirl-pool through the crack. The swirling shapes merged into a form of some sort. At first it didn't look like much of anything, but if you stared long enough, you could make out what it was—a face. An immense face made of a million pieces that seemed ready to fly apart at any moment.

"Wh-What's that?" I whispered.

"Chaos," said the Erinys in the jar. She no longer sounded like a cross little old lady—more like a little old lady who's worried sick because she's just spotted the cosmic nothing-ness that existed before the universe as we know it was born.

Chaos? My brain struggled to get around this like an Olympic shot-putter trying on a petite toga. Chaos was the unshaped material from which the universe had arisen, right? That's how Thales had described it. The scientist had failed to mention that Chaos was a supernatural entity—what's more, a supernatural entity *with a bad attitude,* judging from the conversation that followed.

"When?" shrieked Chaos, and its voice was like a thou-sand voices all trying to speak as one and doing a crummy job of it.

"Soon," answered Thanatos (who suddenly wasn't

sounding so bad). "I left Zeus at the Omphalos. He is making his final preparations."

The giant face of Chaos trembled under the strain of maintaining something as unnatural as a form. It stretched and wobbled as it unleashed a truly crazy laugh. It sounded like a billion cawing seagulls—all in all, not the kind of laugh that makes you want to join in.

"That wasn't a joke," Thanatos explained without emotion. "When Zeus has completed the cleansing ceremony, it will be time."

The face of Chaos danced. "The fool is delivering himself to his own doom!" it crowed. "Soon the Cosmos will be all mine again!" It went off into another of those nutty laughs, and Thanatos nodded slowly to acknowledge that it was more appropriate this time.

The crazy laughter continued until the face of Chaos could stand the strain no longer and it shattered into its earlier formlessness. Thanatos was alone in the darkness.

"Let's get out of here," I said to the Erinys. I tried to say it quietly, but my voice echoed in the confines of that cavern. (Well, how was I to know? Was I Professor of Physics at the Athenian Academy? Did I ever *say* I was an expert in acoustics?)

Thanatos slowly began to turn, but I was already dashing through an archway into an adjoining cave. It led into a narrow tunnel. For a stretch it was so dark that I had to feel my way along the rocky walls. They felt real enough—it was my own continued reality I was worried about.

"Don't stop now, boy," said the Erinys fearfully.

"I hit my head on a stalactite," I explained. "Or is it stalagmite?" I didn't suppose this would matter soon, not if the conversation between Thanatos and Chaos was anything to go by.

Suddenly my hand ran out of wall as the tunnel opened into another, smaller cave. It was still gloomy, but an entrance back to the main chamber lit it with faint, pale light.

I moved toward the light. Part of me just wanted to get back to the welcome nothingness of that fog. That way, whatever was going to happen, at least I'd be unaware of it. We were halfway to the exit when a desperate voice called out from one side of the cavern.

"Are you here to help?"

"Er, not really," I answered. "Sorry."

I was all for continuing on, but the Erinys told me to go to where the voice had come from: a wall of stalactites and stalagmites that had joined to form a row of bars.

A little face was pressed against one of the thin openings between the bars. An owl's face.

Athena!

"Not you again," groaned the owl. "I thought it might be a hero."

"He may not be a hero, but he's a good boy," said the Erinys from the clay jar around my neck.

"How did you recognize me?" I asked.

The owl hooted miserably. "Even in this form, your pigginess shines through, Gryllus."

Someone let out a heavy sigh behind her, and I realized

that Athena was not alone in this prison. (I thought I glimpsed a giant lobster back there, but the poor lighting was probably playing tricks on my eyes.)

"Er, who else is in there?" I asked.

"Some of the other gods," said Athena, casting a worried glance behind her. "But they are without hope. When they saw that even Ares couldn't escape from this place using his head as a battering ram, they just gave up. But I'm not going to." Her yellow-gray eyes locked onto mine. "You have to do something. You can't let Zeus die at the Omphalos!"

"Er . . . why?"

"Because he's the only one powerful enough to stop Chaos! But he has to be in the Overworld and in his true form to do that!" the owl explained. "Of course, he's also the one who let this whole dreadful mess develop in the first place," she added bitterly.

"Er . . . what?"

The owl sighed. "Before there was anything else in existence, there was Chaos. And it wasn't very happy when the Cosmos came along. It's been waiting ever since. For everyone else, it's been eons, but time is irrelevant to Chaos. It sat outside our universe and waited."

"Er . . . what for?"

"Well, it wasn't waiting for a Number 7 bus!" exploded the goddess of wisdom. (Under other circumstances I might have asked what a "bus" was, but this was not the moment to unravel the arcane knowledge of the Olympians.) Athena went on, "It was waiting for a chance to destroy this

Cosmos and bring everything back to itself. And the chance came when Thales invented his Atomos Device."

"You mean his toaster?"

The owl nodded. "Chaos saw it and he knew—if detonated in the right spot and with sufficient amounts of plutonium, this machine could destroy the entire Cosmos."

This was getting as hard to follow as a Minoan underground maze.

"Er, what about Zeus?" I asked.

Athena shook her head in dismay. "Chaos knew that only Zeus might be powerful enough to ruin the plan. So he enlisted the willing help of Thanatos, who persuaded the father of the gods that he needed to become mortal. Zeus fell for it, of course. It appealed to his vanity. And while he was playing at being human, he even gave Thanatos the go-ahead to round the rest of us up as well."

"So, once he dies and visits the Underworld, Zeus *isn't* going to be reborn and then return to Olympus?"

The owl leaned backward in an attempt to roll her eyes.

"Once Zeus is here, Chaos and Thanatos will detonate Thales' toaster. It's positioned directly below the Navel of the World—the Cosmos will be ripped apart. The earth, the heavens, gods and monsters, humans and beasts . . . everything will be returned to the primordial state. Chaos. Everything will be destroyed."

I let these words sink in. "It doesn't sound very good when you put it that way," I said.

"Avert your eyes!" said Athena.

"What?"

"Oh, forget it." The owl began to bob her head back and forth. Suddenly her beak opened and another owl pellet shot out. This one glowed a mysterious gold.

"Take this pellet to the banks of the Styx, near the main entrance of Hades, and eat it," said the goddess. "It will help you return to the Overworld . . . but only if you truly wish it. The pellet alone is not enough. . . ."

I looked down at the pellet. It might be glowing with magical power, but it had still been barfed up, hadn't it?

"Haven't you got anything I could drink instead? Some magic juice?"

"No!" the owl snapped. Reluctantly I picked up the gold pellet.

"Oh dear," the Erinys piped up. "Remember how I said you had nothing to worry about because you're already dead?"

"Yes?"

"I'm not sure that's really true."

"Of course it isn't true!" wailed the owl. "If the Cosmos returns to Chaos, there won't be an Underworld either, or anyone to populate it. There'll be nothing but Chaos and the Void."

"There's something else, too," persisted the Erinys.

"Okay, okay, I get it!" I huffed. "There IS something worse than being dead."

"Not just that," said the Erinys. "Something is coming, and I think it's Thanatos."

It was true! The scrape of bone on rock echoed along the tunnel we had just come through. Thanatos was coming.

"Go now!" chimed in Athena. "Try to stop Zeus! Go!"

I whirled around and charged for the exit. I didn't have much idea which way to go on the ledge. As it turned out, I didn't have to choose (a good thing, because I can never make my mind up in stressful situations—and, let's face it, being chased through the Underworld by Death ranks pretty high on the old Stress-o-meter).

No, the ledge was especially narrow here, which was why I raced out of the cavern and went straight off the edge. There wasn't even time to say "Oops!" before I was free-falling.

For a couple of seconds I could see nothing but cotton-ball whiteness all around. Looking into that numbing fog, you could almost believe that everything else was just a bad dream, that there was nothing but the cold comfort of the fog. Reality struck in the form of the rock floor, which I hit with a crumpled thud.

"Ow!" I moaned.

It shouldn't really have hurt, only, even as a dead man, I had a low pain threshold.

BOOK XXXI

Our hero books the return trip.

"It's just a scratch," said the Erinys, sounding like an especially tough school nurse. "On your feet now! You've got lots to do. Where's that pellet?"

"I don't know," I whined.

"Find it!"

I knelt down and felt around for the owl pellet. All the while the fog billowed around me, and I could feel it oozing back into my soul. Maybe none of this did really matter. Thanatos, Chaos, Athena . . . they were already starting to seem like half-remembered dreams.

"Don't give up now!" cried the Erinys.

My hand hit something: the pellet. I looked at it dubiously.

"Go on, then," urged my companion. "Count to three and hold your nose if you have to."

I counted to three.

Then I counted to three again.

Next time I lost track of what I was doing, what with the fog wrapping itself around me, and I had reached sixteen before the Erinys yelled, "EAT IT!"

I popped the pellet in my mouth and swallowed.

There was no magical transformation, no starbursts of light.

Nothing.

"It didn't work."

Oh well, never mind. I just stood there and let the fog wash over me.

"The goddess said the pellet alone is not enough," cried the Erinys. "YOU have to do it, too. You have to force yourself back to the Overworld. Try and picture it in your mind!"

That was all well and good, but how? The memories of

my life up in the sun were becoming as hard to grasp as the mist around me. I hadn't been much use saving Bumscruff or Zeus, or whatever his name was, back when I was alive. Now that I was dead, how could I help . . . oh, what was her name, it began with a sigma . . . or was it a beta?

"It was a sigma—her name is Sibyl!" said the Erinys. "Try harder!"

"But . . ."

"Think of Sibyl. THINK OF HER! She saved your life. Now try and picture her face!"

At first I could see nothing except formless gray, but finally an image of a girl's face did swim into my mind. She had one eyebrow arched in a look of disbelief, and she was laughing at something. Her face wasn't like the blank and ashen ones all around me now. It was full of energy and interest and feeling and LIFE, not just a dull echo of life.

I shook my head. "I . . . can't." Most of my brain knew that it was all just too much effort. So much easier not to try, to give in and simply let the fog sweep over and around and through my mind.

And yet . . .

"If you truly can't, then all is lost," said the Erinys sadly.

Something flickered in the damp and cold of my heart.

I shut my eyes so that I couldn't see the shifting fog of Hades. Instead I tried to picture everything I had left behind, all the things back in the land of the living.

"I'm not supposed to be here," I said aloud, "not yet." My voice sounded hollow and unconvincing, so I said it again, louder. Several shades gave low moans of surprise, as if I'd breached some rule of Underworld etiquette. I ignored them and went on.

"I'm not finished on earth, am I? So send me back 'cause I'm not done living!"

"I can't hear you," hissed the Erinys.

"I SAID I'M NOT DONE LIVING!"

"That's better!" she said encouragingly. "Let it all out, boy. . . . It's the only chance."

"I . . . I WANT TO FEEL THE SUN ON MY BACK AGAIN. I WANT TO FEEL THE WIND ON MY FACE! I WANT TO WAKE UP AND SMELL THE ROSES, *AND* THE TULIPS AND THE DAFFODILS AND THE . . . THE . . . I WANT TO *LEARN* THE NAMES OF ALL THE FLOWERS! I WANT TO COUGH AND FART AND BURP AND SNEEZE, BECAUSE IT'S TRUE, OUT REALLY *IS* BETTER THAN IN! I WANT TO GET PINS AND NEEDLES IN MY FEET SO I HAVE TO LEAP UP AND HOP AROUND TILL THEY GO. I WANT TO STUFF MY FACE WITH TOO MUCH PIE AND THEN GO BACK FOR SECONDS. . . . OKAY, YOU TWISTED MY ARM, I'LL HAVE THIRDS! I WANT TO PICK MY NOSE AND YAWN AND WIGGLE MY TOES AND SCRATCH MY BIG FAT BELLY. I WANT TO ROLL OVER FOR TEN MINUTES' EXTRA SLEEP ON A FROSTY MORNING. I WANT TO GET HUGS AND TICKLES AND PATS ON THE BACK. I WANT TO PLOP MYSELF DOWN IN A TAVERNA

AND DRINK ALL NIGHT AND START SINGING THE OLD SONGS, THE SORT THAT BARDS DON'T SEEM TO WRITE THESE DAYS. OH YEAH, AND I WANT TO LAUGH AGAIN, AND NOT A POLITE LITTLE TITTER EITHER, BUT A GREAT BIG GUFFAW OF A BELLY LAUGH! I WANT TO GO FOR A PADDLE IN THE WINE-DARK SEA — I WON'T EVEN COMPLAIN IF THE WATER'S TOO COLD, HONEST I WON'T! AND, AND . . . I WANT TO SEE MY OLD PALS AGAIN — I DO, REALLY I DO, EVEN THE ONES I OWE MONEY TO — AND I WANT TO SEE MY FAMILY — well, except maybe Uncle Xerxes, who does tend to ramble on a bit about his bad knees — OKAY, OKAY, I'LL EVEN SEE UNCLE XERXES . . . SO LONG AS WE CAN KEEP IT QUICK. AND I WANT TO DANCE! I'LL JIG AND PIROUETTE AND FOX-TROT AROUND UNTIL I CAN'T MANAGE ANOTHER STEP. JUST GIVE ME A CHANCE!

"I WANT TO BE ALIVE AGAIN!

"I

   WANT

      TO

        BE

          ALIVE!"

I became aware of a warmth that had been folding itself around me. It wasn't only the physical warmth of the air, it was a warmth in my soul, if that makes sense. Even before I opened my eyes, I knew I was back, back in the land of the living. I knew I was a pig again.

I would have cried out for joy, but there was just one problem.

Actually, a couple of related problems—first, I couldn't move. And second, my mouth was propped open . . .

. . . with an apple.

BOOK XXXII

The Epicureans get their just desserts (and we're not talking rhubarb crumble).

There was something else. When I opened my eyes, you'll never guess who was standing there, right in front of me.

Go on. Take a guess.

Go on.

I can wait, you know, I've got all day.

Go on, then.

It was Homer!

Remember him? That weird kid from the kebab house? The one who was always plinking away at the lyre and wanted to know every last detail about the stories of gods and monsters?

Naturally I wasn't expecting to return from the dead and see him. Then again, if anything, he was even more surprised when he saw me looking up at him. The poor, sensitive lad emitted a strangled cry and hopped back in terror.

"Y-You were dead," he managed to say.

Luckily I was able to take the initiative. "Geh gih ackuh ow o' ai owf!" I said.

A look of confusion joined the look of astonished fear on Homer's face.

"Erm . . . pardon?"

"GEH . . . GIH . . . ACKUH . . . OW . . . O' . . . AI . . . OWF!"

Homer shook his head apologetically. "No, I still don't follow you. I think it's because you've got that apple in your mouth."

He reached out and gingerly freed the offending Red Delicious.

"Sorry, what were you saying?"

"I said, 'Get this apple out of my mouth!' you . . ."

As my mind scanned all the possible names to call Homer, another deep-down part of my brain reminded me that I probably shouldn't insult the best chance I had of avoiding a return trip to the Underworld.

There was a sudden hammering from the pantry door. "Let me out!" shouted a muffled voice.

"That's the cook," explained Homer, in the manner of someone who half suspects he'll wake up from the nightmare in a minute and maybe even chuckle about it over a bowl of corn flakes. "I shut him in there when he was getting the herbs ready for the . . . you-know-what. Can you get up?"

"No! I don't think the poison has worn off. You'll have to carry me. . . ."

Even as I said it, I realized that the pasty-faced poet had as much chance of picking me up as a miniature poodle would of plucking a squeaky toy from the jaws of Cerberus, hound of Hades. Nevertheless, he gave it a try.

At least he displayed all the customary signs of lifting a heavy weight—red face, eyes scrunched up in pain, tendons and veins standing out all over the place—everything, in fact, apart from the actual lifting.

"How much do you weigh exactly?" he groaned.

Before I could answer, we heard the mumble of voices from outside. One deep voice muttered something about getting a bite to eat before starting the night shift.

Desperately, Homer tried again to pick me up. With the extra boost of adrenalin, he even managed to get me off the table. Now all he had to do was carry me a few steps and out the side door.

The lad staggered forward, but the voices outside were growing louder. It was time for a cooler head to take control here. "OH GODS, QUICK!" I wailed.

With an enormous exhalation of breath, Homer plopped me back down on the table.

"I can't do it," he gasped. His eyes darted around in panic like small, darting-around things that were, um . . . panicking.

"What can I do?" he gasped.

Now my eyes darted around the room like small, darting-around things that were *desperate*.

"Pan!" I shouted.

"Pan?" Homer was baffled. "I don't see how invoking the woodland god can help at a time like this. . . ."

"The frying pan, you nitwit! Pick it up and start hitting people with it!"

An instant later, several armed thugs appeared at the doorway. They immediately figured that things weren't as they were supposed to be in this kitchen. I took a look at them with their big muscles and deadly assortment of swords, daggers, and axes. Then I looked at Homer, with his little pipe-cleaner arms and his big frying pan at the ready. Unless the poet was a master of a little-known martial art involving kitchenware—and let's face it, this didn't seem likely—we were in big trouble.

To his credit, Homer did his best, he really did. He brandished the pan and warbled, "Don't come any closer!"

"Please don't!" one of the thugs smirked. "Watch out, lads—he'll fry up some eggs if we're not careful!" (Get any group of hired thugs together and you'll always find one comedian.)

They began to close in on Homer like a pack of wolves at a roast-lamb dinner with all the trimmings.

Then I noticed it: the clay jar of the Erinys. The leather cord had been untied, and the jar set on the kitchen table-top. Homer had set me closer to it. It was just about within my reach, if only I could get my body to override the numbing effects of the poison and actually do something.

I stretched out a front hoof. It felt as if it didn't belong to me and I had to ask it politely to do my bidding. Like an ancient, impertinent butler, it agreed, but slowly. It wobbled toward the clay jar. Epicurus's hired thugs didn't notice; they were too busy chuckling away as Homer swung his pan.

"Watch out, lads!" quipped the would-be comedian. "It's nonstick and he's not afraid to use it!"

My hoof made its unsteady way to the jar and finally gave it a poke. The clay holder rocked slightly, then righted itself. I summoned all my energy and jabbed it one more time. The jar disappeared off the table and landed with a sharp crack. I let my leg fall dead. I had done all I could do.

I just lay there and watched . . . as a little old lady stood up.

"That's more like it," she said, rubbing the back of her neck. "Remind me to tell that prophetess girl not to put the stopper in so tight next time if she's going to summon a spirit of vengeance. Defeats the whole purpose if I can't even get out!"

She shuffled toward the gang of ruffians.

"Excuse me, boys."

The thugs turned to see a little gray-haired old lady in a long toga and a beige woolen overgarment known as a *cardigan*.

"You're in the wrong place, lady," growled one.

The old dear's mouth made a little bowlike smile of almost grandmotherly sweetness. ALMOST . . . there was something else behind that smile, something a touch more unnerving than your average granny. Something that would send a chill of terror down the spine of your average grandchild.

They might not have been able to put their stubby fingers on it, but even these thugs sensed that something was wrong here.

"You seem like nice boys," said the little old lady, "but you've gone and let your youthful high spirits carry you away, haven't you?"

One of the thugs attempted to hide a short-handled ax behind his back.

"I don't think you young boys should be doing this," said the little old lady. Then, with just a hint of menace. "*Should* you?"

Several close-cropped heads shook.

"Well then, I think you should probably just be on your way now, don't you?"

The shakes changed direction and became frantic nods.

"Off you go, then."

The thugs dashed for the door.

"Not you with the pan," said the little old lady.

Homer reluctantly turned back.

234

"And close the door behind you," shouted the old lady, but the thugs were already out and fleeing into the night.

Homer still held up the pan like a shield. "Wh-Who are you?" he stuttered.

"Well now, I am the wrath-bringer, the scourge of wrongdoers," replied the little old lady. "I am the Erinys, sprung with my sisters from the blood of Uranus. I am the spirit of divine retribution, the pitiless avenger of all that violates cosmic law, and I am relentless." She buttoned up her cardigan. "You'd best just call me Gladys."

You're probably wondering what Homer was doing there in the kitchen, anyway. I was, I can tell you.

It turned out that, back on that fateful night when I'd made my escape from his aunt's restaurant, the young poet had run out after me. He was too late to see Sibyl rolling me off to the woods, but he did hear Epicurus ordering his coachmen to wake up that instant or else he'd fire them. The more he overheard, the more Homer realized that there was something suspicious about the tall aristocrat and his interest in me. Making a snap decision, Homer had rushed forward and asked Epicurus for a job, seeing as how his other employees were temporarily indisposed.

In this way, Homer had traveled as part of the aristocrat's staff to Delphi. Here, his official duties entailed doing the dishes and peeling grapes for feast evenings. He had followed the events in the town with mounting horror. But what could he do? And then my carcass had been hauled into the kitchens, with instructions to let it sit for a few hours before the butchering could begin . . . well, it was almost too much for a sensitive lad like Homer.

Of course, I found out all this much later. Right now we had more than enough on our plates, what with having to save the Cosmos and so on. We had to try and stop Zeus before he went and sacrificed himself. I mean, that's what any legendary hero would do, right? The only thing is, when you hear epic tales about these heroic types, the bards tend to leave out the bits where the trusty hero has to ask for directions, don't they?

"I'm all turned around," said Gladys. "Where is the temple of Apollo, anyway?"

I tried to shrug, but my body was still not obeying. The Erinys took hold of my head in her clawlike hands.

"Just relax and you won't feel a thing, laddie," she said.

"YEEEARRGH!" I replied as she twisted. The bones in my neck protested with a burst of clicks and pops. Then I realized something: I could feel my limbs again. Whatever Gladys had done, it had counteracted the effects of Epicurus's poison. I still felt woozy, but I could move again.

"That feels terrific," I said, rolling my neck this way and that.

"The temple?" Gladys repeated.

"Er . . . don't know," I said. "But I know someone who *will*."

The three of us headed toward the main part of the villa, where the members of the Epicurean Supper Club had begun to gather. I could hear the buzz of chatter from the great hall. I peeked around the corner.

The gloomy black robes of Thanatos were gone. The room was filled with fifteen or so people who probably considered themselves "beautiful young things," despite all the evidence to the contrary. They wore robes of the finest silk, gold and jewels glittered and shone, and there was enough hair oil in the hall to fry chicken for the entire Greek army for six months.

I stepped confidently into the room, my hooves clacking on the marble floor. I didn't need to draw anyone's attention—they were all sitting bolt upright on their luxury couches and staring at me with mouths hanging open—but nevertheless I cleared my throat.

"Ahem . . . evening, all," I said, choosing to ignore the angry whispers that ran around the hall.

"What is the meaning of this?" demanded Epicurus from the top table. His face did its best to arrange itself into a superior smirk, but it ended up all twisted and angry.

"I regret to inform you that honey-glazed ham is no longer on the menu this evening," I announced, "on account of the aforementioned ham not wishing to be eaten."

"This is preposterous!" Epicurus declared haughtily. "Guards! Return the hog to the kitchen this instant!" His gaze swept across the hall. "Fellow members of the society, I trust you can wait a little longer for supper."

"You don't quite get it, do you?" I snarled. "There *are* no guards now. And there's not going to be any dinner, either." I raised my voice over the angry hubbub. "But there *is* someone I'd like you all to meet."

I looked to the doorway and gave the signal. Homer

came in, leading the Erinys. She let go of the poet's arm with a grateful nod and shuffled to the center of the hall. She carefully took off the exotic beige cardigan and placed it on the back of an empty chair. Then she squinted around at the assembled guests. There was a little smile on her face that you could really only describe as sweet and kindly, and so it was quite odd that the guests shuddered whenever that smile happened to be pointing in their direction.

"You've all been very naughty," said the Erinys, sounding regretful. She turned to Homer and me. "Why don't you two boys wait outside?"

"But—" Homer began. Chances are, he was going to rattle on about poets needing to relish new life-experiences to the full, et cetera, et cetera, blah-de-blah, blah. A jab to the side with my snout soon cured him of that, and we got out of there fast, closing the iron gate behind us.

Then we waited. From inside the villa came the kind of thick, heavy silence you get when everyone knows something really, really bad is about to happen—it's only a matter of when. . . .

Almost immediately, as things turned out.

Suddenly there was all this screaming from inside.

"They say just one look at an Erinys's true form can drive a person mad with fear," I explained to Homer.

He nodded. " 'The terror-bringing Erinyes.' That's what the epic poems usually call them."

We spent the next couple of minutes inspecting the flowers in the backyard and trying to ignore the din behind us. After one particularly loud scream I couldn't help glancing around. Just for an instant, before I squeezed my eyes shut, I glimpsed the cause of all the commotion. I couldn't make too much sense of what I saw, but it involved plenty of tentacles, claws, beady eyes on stalks, leathery wings, various scaly and armored parts, snakes and tails waggling all over the place, lots of talons. Oh, and a fair few spearlike teeth, not all of them where you might expect to see them. It was the sort of sight that, if a little kid drew it, his or her parents might consider hiding the crayons.

Anyway, the members of the Epicurean Supper Club were all duly impressed, judging from their screams of abject terror. They began piling out of the gates, which we now helpfully unlocked. One of them stumbled and fell, but that didn't stop the rest from running over him. Wide-eyed with horror, they hitched up their robes and fled for the safety of the woods. Shrieks echoed in the night and gave every impression that the club members would be dining on berries and rainwater puddles for quite some time (assuming there was *any* time left, of course).

A small, round-shouldered figure came shuffling out through the gates—the Erinys in little-old-lady form again. She pulled her mystic cardigan around her shoulders against the cool night air. With her other hand she held the back of Epicurus's tunic in an iron grip. The founding member of the Epicurean Supper Club looked terrified out of his wits.

"You should be ashamed of yourself," Gladys reprimanded the quivering aristocrat. "Smashing up perfectly decent statues, which weren't your property in the first

239

place, and going around worshiping Thanatos, and then trying to eat nice, law-abiding folk who just happen to be pigs. What have you got to say for yourself, mister? Well?"

Epicurus gibbered some stuff, but it wasn't easy to follow.

"I think you'd better just tell us where the Omphalos is, hadn't you, mister?" said Gladys.

Epicurus pointed a wildly trembling finger into the night.

"Good. And now I think you'd better catch up with your little friends, hadn't you?"

Epicurus took off as if his top-of-the-range Athenian-made kid-leather sandals were on fire.

Gladys turned to Homer and me. Her watery eyes betrayed the merest flicker of the dreadful thing that lay behind the sweet old lady's face.

"I expect you boys ought to try and save the Cosmos," she said anxiously.

BOOK XXXIII

The beginning of the end of the world looks like this.

"So . . . what's the plan?" gasped Homer.

"I don't know!" I gasped back. "You're the epic poet. *You* make up a plan!"

240

Homer and I were running toward the temple of Apollo (hence all the gasping). I would have felt much safer with the Erinys, but she had gone to see if Thales was still alive. (It had taken us days to cover the same distance, but Gladys said she'd be back "in a jiffy." Of course, Homer and I weren't able to watch her head off in her true, terrifying form, but we heard the flap of leathery wings and a whooshing sound that suggested high speed.)

The darkness around us seemed unnatural. Ragged clouds dragged across the skies in patterns I'd never seen before. Winds gusted in every direction, often at the same time. It seemed as if the gods normally in charge of this sort of thing had given up and just let the elements get on with it unsupervised.

"Well," wheezed Homer, "I suppose we should just . . . tell Zeus everything . . . and . . . see . . . what he says!"

"That was *my* plan!" I cried.

Extreme shortness of breath brought our conversation to an early end. For the rest of our slog up the lower slopes of Mount Parnassus, we just listened to the dreadful gasping of our own breathing. Finally, a dark shape loomed ahead of us. It was the temple of Apollo.

"We're . . . here," managed Homer.

I looked up at the words carved into the stone lintel over the entrance. "You know what that says?" I asked, remembering what Sibyl had once told me. "'Know thy-self.'"

Homer shook his head. "Not anymore. Someone's smashed up some of the letters," he said.

I looked up at the remaining letters on the lintel:

NOW T**H**Y**SELF**

When Homer read this out, I wondered for the briefest instant if it had some momentous symbolic meaning. Then my head began to hurt, and I flicked the thought aside.

With a trembling hand Homer pushed one of the doors open. The first chamber was lit by a single wall torch. Someone was in there, sitting cross-legged in the corner.

It was Sibyl.

Alone.

She didn't look surprised to see me or curious about Homer's presence. She didn't look much of anything really, except sick and tired of this whole business.

"You missed it," said the prophetess flatly. "The big moment . . . Zeus died, oh, about twenty minutes ago." (We were too late!) "He walked outside, lifted up his arms to the heavens, and shouted, 'Come on, then. I haven't got all day.' And then a bolt of lightning hit him right on the head."

I hopped hastily inside the doorway just in case I was standing on something I'd rather not be standing on.

"So . . . he didn't suffer, then?" asked Homer with concern.

In place of an answer, Sibyl turned her attention back to

the huge stone block of the Omphalos. (So this was the Navel of the World? It didn't look like much of a navel to me—more like a giant stone egg.)

"I'm waiting for him to be reborn," said Sibyl, "so everything can get back to normal and we can all go home."

"You don't understand!" I wailed. "Nothing's going to get back to normal! Zeus was tricked!" I launched into a speedy explanation of everything I'd learned since I last saw Sibyl.

When I was done, she frowned and said, "What? I didn't understand a single word of that."

I launched into a slightly less speedy explanation, with Homer chipping in here and there with the odd poetic flourish. Sibyl's frown deepened.

"Are you sure, Gryllus?" she asked. "I don't want to be rude, but . . . you're not exactly the quickest chariot in the race. . . . Couldn't you have been mistaken?"

I was still trying to think how to convince Sibyl when an unearthly howling shriek sounded from outside, getting louder and louder until Homer and Sibyl had to cover their ears (an option not open to the nonhuman among us). Through the partly open doors we saw a giant fireball trailing a tongue of flame. It landed in front of the temple, sparks flying.

"Uh . . . what's that?" asked Sibyl, doing a good job of maintaining control of her facial expression.

Before I could answer, two elderly figures appeared at the doors. It's fair to say that Thales was looking less confident in the power of science these days. This probably had something to do with being brought here by a fear-some, airborne, supernatural entity.

However, the supernatural entity was once again in the guise of a kindly old lady.

"Hello, dear," Gladys said to Sibyl. "That's a lovely color on you."

The young priestess glanced down at her black robes. "It matches my mood," she said, then turned to Thales. "How did you get away from the Stymphalian birds? You looked as if you could hardly pedal a minute longer."

The world's first scientist ran a finger along the crease of his tattered trousers. "Ah well, I studied the problem in a scientific manner," he said shakily, "before choosing the course of action with the most likelihood of success."

"Which was?"

"I ran at maximum speed and jumped into the well," he answered. "The birds stayed for a while, but they gave up when it started to rain. No doubt concerned about ferrous oxidization." When Thales saw our blank faces, he rephrased it. "They thought they might go rusty. . . . Before they left, they made a terrible mess of my papers. Most were torn to shreds, some gone altogether."

I wondered whether the birds had taken Thales' scroll diagramming his plutonium-powered toaster, so that the forces of Chaos might build it in the Underworld.

"*Now* do you believe me?" I asked Sibyl.

For once the prophetess was at a loss for words. For actions, too. She just sat there.

And that's when the end of the world started.

The first thing was a muffled *BOOM!* It seemed to come from far beneath us, deep under the ground, but the entire world still shook with the impact. I didn't have time to explain that Thales' toaster had probably just detonated in the Underworld. Because then, the Omphalos, the stone that was the Navel of the World, began to glow.

Homer gave voice to all our hopes: "Maybe Zeus *did* know what he was doing. Maybe he's going to return now, as powerful as ever, and set things right."

Yeah, right—and pigs might fly.

Suddenly a vertical crack appeared in the Omphalos. It widened, paused a moment, and then . . . It's not very easy to explain what happened next. It was as if reality itself just sort of ripped, starting at the Omphalos and extending upward. As if the Cosmos itself was nothing more than an enormous piece of soggy cardboard and someone was tearing it in half.

At the same time, there was a deafening blast that threw us all backward. As I crumpled into the stone wall of the temple, I managed to turn to Sibyl.

"NOW do you believe me?"

BOOK XXXIV

The Chariot of the Sun is a bit on the warm side (so no surprises there).

We managed to stagger out through the doors and back down the slope. One of Sibyl's arms hung limply, and she winced with pain. When we turned and looked back, the sight that met our eyes was truly mind-boggling.

Starting from the temple, the rip in the world extended upward into the sky, getting ever wider the farther up it went. And on the other side of the rip we saw the dreadful swirl of Chaos.

A tiny portion of my brain still clung to rational thought like a rubber duck in a tidal wave, as it worked out what must have happened. Once Zeus had reached the Underworld, Thanatos or Chaos had set off the plutonium-driven toaster. What we were watching now was the result.

The wind howled, not quite drowning out the terrified screams from the people in the city below us. Under other circumstances, I might have found some comfort in the fact that their attempts to please Thanatos had proved useless.

We looked on in horror as the very stars in the sky began to move, slowly dragged toward the cosmic rip. It felt as if the whole world were somehow being pulled toward it.

"What happens now?" yelled Sibyl.

Thales couldn't take his eyes from the widening tear that

split the sky. "Let me put it this way," he said. Then he launched into an intricate explanation that featured words like *fission, matter, antimatter,* and *particles.*

"Erm, I lost you there," I said. "Right after 'put it this way' . . ."

You could almost hear Thales' brain straining to simplify. "Okay, let me put it *this* way," he tried again. "Think of everything in our Cosmos as . . . matter. Now think of what's on the other side of that rip as sort of . . . antimatter."

"So what happens when all the matter meets the antimatter?" asked Sibyl.

"That's easy!" I butted in. "Ka-boom! And then nothing will matter."

Thales nodded gravely. "I wouldn't put it quite like that, but that is, in essence, correct." The scientist placed a finger on his lips. "Unless . . ."

"Yes?" gasped Sibyl.

"Unless one were able to effect a power surge of sufficient energy at the point of interface," he continued. "Yes, yes, I suppose it might work."

"WHAT might work?" demanded Sibyl, grabbing the scientist by his tunic with one fist and almost lifting him off his feet.

"I . . . was speaking purely theoretically," Thales stammered. "It would require an energy source no less than the sun itself to create the necessary fusion. . . ."

Sibyl set the scientist down. There was a glint of mad determination in her eye. She was once again the old Sibyl, the one I had come to know through days of nonstop bickering.

"You want the sun?" she growled. "I'll give you the sun. . . ."

Minutes later we were huddled around a small fire, trying to protect it from the hurricane around us. Working with just one hand, Sibyl did not sprinkle any dried herbs delicately over the flames; she threw great handfuls onto it, eventually tipping out the entire contents of the bag.

A fireball spouted upward, and inside of it was the god Apollo, huddled in a corner. He didn't look happy to be there.

In fact, you'd never believe it was the same god. Apollo looked haggard and afraid. His ringlets of hair now hung lifelessly, and his eyes flitted this way and that. He was still gripping his tortoiseshell lyre in one hand, but a couple of the strings were broken and bent. They boinged every time the god tremored, which was often.

"You can't summon me now!" Apollo whined. "This is the end! We're all going to be destroyed!"

"No, we have a plan," began Sibyl.

"Nothing will work!" the god lamented, glancing at the formless Chaos on the other side of the V-shaped rent in the Cosmos. "You can't stop it! You can't—"

"Oh, put a sock in it, you big baby!" said Sibyl.

Temple etiquette is not one of my strong points, I'll grant you, but I was willing to bet that this was not a turn of phrase gods usually expected to hear from their priestesses.

Apollo was so shocked that, despite his terror, he fell

silent. The only sound that issued from his divine lips was "Um."

"Now, listen," Sibyl continued in a voice that brooked no argument. "We need you to fly your chariot. We need the Chariot of the Sun."

The god was shaking his head fearfully. "I . . . I can't," he stammered. "It's too dangerous. You don't understand. . . . You can't see things like I can. You're just a puny mortal. You're—"

"Fine!" Sibyl cut in. "Then one of us will drive it."

"That's impossible!" Apollo blurted. "No mortal could drive my Chariot of the Sun. It's just not—"

Sibyl was drumming the fingers of her good arm impatiently. "Look, we haven't got all day, in case you haven't noticed," she said sternly. "It's a simple choice. You can summon the Chariot of the Sun and let one of us steer it, or you join the rest of existence in waiting around for the utter end of everything."

Terror had reduced Apollo to a quivering lump of Olympian-shaped jelly. He didn't know what to do. That was the secret that his darting eyes gave away. The god of mystic prediction, the patron of the Delphic oracle itself, did not know what to do next!

Sibyl's eyes bored into the deity so fiercely, the god had to look away in shame. Perhaps the annihilation of the Cosmos palled in comparison with the prospect of a strict telling-off by this pushy priestess.

At last the god let out a wimpish "Okay, I'll summon the horses." The flame of the fire dwindled. "But I'm not sticking around!" the god added petulantly as he disappeared from view, leaving us alone in the roaring darkness. I had one of those terrible moments of clear-eyed self-awareness, the sort I have always tried to avoid. Here we were, on the slopes of Mount Parnassus at the center of the earth: a skinny old man in tattered trousers, a priestess who wasn't yet qualified to conduct the sacred ceremonies on her own, a little old spirit of vengeance in a beige cardigan, an ashen-faced poet who couldn't even wield a frying pan in combat, let alone a sword or spear, and yours truly, a talking pig who only ever wanted a quiet life.

The despair in my heart was as black as the air around us.

But then, on the horizon to the east, there was a sudden flash of light, so bright that you had to look away. At first it looked like any other sunrise, but not for long. The light became more and more blinding—the Chariot of the Sun was not following its normal path.

Specifically, the Chariot of the Sun was heading this way.

"Thales, what are the chances of this actually working?" Sibyl asked, her eyes wide with fear.

The scientist's lips worked silently as he did the math. "Approximately one in twenty-seven billion."

"Is that good?" I asked.

It was impossible to see anything in the dazzling light as it neared us, but I could hear the drumming of hooves and the fiery neigh of the stallions that pulled the chariot.

"You can't drive THAT," I shouted to Sibyl at my side. "Apollo's right. No mortal could drive that!"

"I've got to try," she answered in a tiny voice. "What else can I do?"

"But your arm . . ."

Her injured arm hung, useless, by her side. As I looked into Sibyl's eyes, I realized what was going on behind them. She knew that neither Thales nor Homer had the strength to do this. Gladys would have tried, but she'd said that Apollo's horses were too terrified of her to obey instructions. In her mind that left only Sibyl herself, and so she was going to do it, even though she stood almost no chance of success. She was going to try, because there was no one else.

Perhaps that's what it came down to with all the great heroes of the past—Jason and Perseus and Theseus and that entire bunch of pumped-up he-man types. Perhaps they had all been terrified out of their wits, they'd just found themselves in the wrong place at the wrong time, and there was simply no one else to get the job done.

The thundering of the hooves stopped. Now that the chariot had drawn alongside us, we could make out shapes in the dazzling light. Four enormous stallions glowed as if made of light themselves. Their eyes flashed and rolled wildly, their manes were blood-red flames that danced and crackled. The horses of the sun pawed the ground impatiently, and smoke rose all around them. The chariot they were pulling gave off so much shimmering light you could only just make out the shape of the golden vehicle, handiwork of Hephaestus, the smith of the gods.

Sibyl drew a deep breath and stepped forward.

The sight of this released something in my brain. It broke free a feeling so unfamiliar I couldn't even put a name to it. All I knew was that I had to do something—I couldn't just let Sibyl go to her doom like this. For the first time in my entire piggy existence, it was time to act out of something other than total self-interest. I rushed forward.

I wanted to tell Sibyl that she had left someone out, that she didn't have to do this all on her own. But there was no time for lengthy explanations. I just shoulder-charged the prophetess. The blow was unexpected, and she tumbled over.

"Oi!"

"Sorry, Sibyl!" I called over my shoulder. But I didn't look back because I was busy racing toward the blazing Chariot of the Sun. My pig's feet sizzled when I hopped up onto it.

"What are you doing, Gryllus?" Sibyl called from behind me, but I had already taken up the reins in my mouth.

"HAH!" I shouted once, through clenched teeth.

And to my astonishment, once was enough. The giant winged horses began to gallop obediently forward. Behind us, Sibyl was running to catch up, but she didn't stand a chance. Soon the world became a blur. As the chariot sped across the rough terrain, the rumble of its wheels grew louder and louder, and then suddenly there was no rumble at all, only the whistle of air. I looked over the side—there was nothing around us but the ragged skies. We were flying!

I glanced down once. For just a few seconds I could make out the tiny figures on the ground below, and then we had climbed too high. The peaks and valleys of the earth were no more than the folds of a blanket on an unmade bed.

Then suddenly the land ran out and the sea was sparkling, far beneath us. We were so far up it almost seemed as if the earth itself curved as I looked to the horizon. You might think that, from this godlike perspective, the world below looked little and unimportant. I mean, that's probably why the gods feel free to stomp around like spoiled toddlers and use the place as their personal playpen.

But that's not how the world struck me from up there, not that way at all. It looked beautiful, to tell you the truth. Beautiful and fragile—as delicate as the shell of a bird's egg.

The chariot was pulling a bit to the left. I adjusted the reins so that we were heading directly toward the giant rip in the sky. A couple of the fiery horses whinnied their disapproval. They didn't want to go that way—and who could blame them?—but I managed to hold our course. The reins burned and smoked as they dug into my mouth, but I refused to let go.

The heat was getting unbearable, and the sweet smell of roasting pork filled my snout. Not much longer and there'd be nothing left of me but a mound of lard and a pile of barbecued ribs. It was like being roasted on a spit, but I willed myself not to drop the reins. I was a pig on a mission.

To distract myself from the terrible heat and the pain,

I began to sing aloud, forcing the words past the reins and out the side of my mouth:

"There once was a pig in the sky.
So hot he was starting to fry."

Even my voice seemed to crack and bubble in the chariot's blazing fire. But not far to go now. We were so close, I could see nothing but the swirling dance of nothingness looming in front of me. At the last moment I pulled the reins sharply to the left so that the blazing horses were now flying straight across the rip in the world. The turn was so tight that the Chariot of the Sun swung wide, directly toward the Chaos from which the Cosmos had risen. I continued my song:

"He wanted to live.
He had so much to give!"

For just an instant, the pattern of light formed an immense face once again, just as I had seen in the depths of the Underworld. It was the face of Chaos, the primordial being, only now it wasn't grinning. Now it looked angry. Its eyes were no more than gigantic black voids, yet I knew that they were watching the Chariot of the Sun as it careened ever closer.

You lose! I thought, and it hardly even mattered that I was losing also.

"But alas, it was now time to . . ."

I was no more than a curly tail's length from the rip. There could be no turning back.

"... *die!*"

And then there was nothing but white
a white flash that turned existence inside out
and I was tiny
no bigger than one of Thales' fleas on a flea on a flea,
ad infinitum,
and I was riding inside a
      lightning bolt
      and there was nothing
in all existence
      except the blinding
      light
      that went on
      forever and

      ever.

BOOK XXXV

The pantheon of gods finally shows a little respect.

I woke up with a doozy of a headache. It felt as if Hephaestus, smith of the gods, was hammering his way out of my skull.

My eyes opened to clean, white light. It didn't seem to

be coming from any particular source. The air all around me was crisp and bright. I was lying on springy grass. An infinity of gently rolling hills rolled all around me . . . gently.

The sky was sky-blue. Better yet, it was all in one piece, without any cracks through which one might spy the dread nothingness of Chaos. Did that mean we had succeeded?

When I sat up, I realized my body was human once more. That could mean nothing else — I was dead.

Again.

But this time it seemed different. It was hard to put my finger on it (now that I had fingers again), but this time it seemed *right*.

I became aware of a tiny dot in the sky. It grew bigger and bigger until at last it was close enough to recognize.

The great owl that was Athena glided down and landed in front of me. This time she did transform. There was no burst of light or cloud of smoke or any of that flashy stuff. Reality just sort of shimmered, and the next moment I was looking into the noble face of the goddess Athena.

Over her flowing robes she wore a cloak with a pattern of the Gorgon's head in the middle. She smiled at me from under her bronze helmet.

"Hello, Gryllus," she said.

"Wh-Where am I?"

"The Underworld," she answered gently.

"But where's all the fog and the rocks and stuff?"

"That was the Asphodel Fields. You qualify for a differ-ent section now." She indicated our surroundings. "These

256

are the Elysian Fields, the realm reserved for the spirits of fallen heroes. You more than qualify for a spot, Gryllus."

I quite liked the sound of "hero" there, though I wasn't too wild about the "fallen" part. It's just that, having saved the entire Cosmos, it would have been nice to spend some time in it.

Athena seemed to sense the thoughts in my head. "You can remain here if you wish," she said. "But, by Olympian decree, you are free also to return to the Overworld, if that is your desire. . . . No pellets necessary this time!"

"So . . . does this mean we won?" I asked.

"Zeus wishes to tell you everything," Athena replied with a smile. "But yes—we won." The goddess held out her hand. "Well? Are you coming or not?"

"Yes," I said simply.

There was a burst of light, and Athena's chariot appeared. Dozens of silver reins led to a squadron of white-gray owls, which blinked patiently at us.

The ride was a blur in my mind. I closed my eyes and enjoyed the feeling of being a passenger again. Seconds slipped by, but they might have been days (which is a fancy way of saying that I lost track of the time on account of having been dead, twice).

At last I felt the chariot bank, then come in for a nice, smooth landing.

"We're here," said Athena.

It was only when I opened my eyes that I realized that my arms had become forelegs again, and my fingers and toes were hooves once more. I was back in the ranks of livestock. Wherever we were, it wasn't the land of the dead.

"You're on Mount Olympus," said Athena, "the home of the gods."

We had parked in front of the most enormous temple I had ever seen in my life. Its gleaming white columns soared upward into cloud.

"Nice," I managed weakly.

In fact, even the fanciest of temple carvings or vase paintings couldn't prepare you for the sight of Olympus. For one thing, it was way bigger than you'd expect a mountaintop to be. The horizon seemed to extend for stadia and stadia, ending in fluffy white clouds all around. Everything seemed to glow as if lit by some magical inner light. There were a dozen or so immense and grand-looking templelike buildings, separated by spotless wide streets. Each building was enough to make the grandest temple on earth look like a grubby little outhouse.

But none of the grand-looking buildings looked quite as grand as the one we'd parked outside of. The goddess led me up steps so big I had to take a running jump for each one. We passed through the colonnade and into the temple porch. It was big enough to hold a soccer match, though the gleaming marble floors might have made ball control tricky.

But that was only the beginning. At the end of the porch, two enormous golden doors swung open, and we entered the great hall. It was a *really* great hall, and it was packed with minor deities. There were satyrs and nymphs, centaurs and dryads all over the place, and a buzz of conversation as if everyone was waiting for something to happen.

As Athena led me through the hall, I saw Homer. I tried to shout hello, but the lad was deep in an intense conversation with the Muses, goddesses of the arts and inspiration to all artists. He was directing most of his comments to Calliope, Muse of Epic Poetry, who was nodding in a politely bored way. He didn't even notice that a giggling Thalia, Muse of Comedy, had stuck a sign on the back of his tunic. I didn't have to be able to read to know that the sign said KICK ME.

Sibyl *did* see me. She pulled away from her conversation with Thales, Gladys, and some sort of river god and gave me a giant thumbs-up. The assembled deities fell quiet as we made our way to the front of the hall. An excited silence had fallen over the whole place by the time we got there.

This area was dominated by twelve immense golden thrones that formed a semicircle. Eleven of these were occupied, and Athena took her place in the free one. As she did so, she grew to her "normal" size, which is to say, taller than the average tree.

So there I was, standing before the Big Twelve—the pantheon of gods. Of course, Zeus sat in the greatest throne of all, smack-dab in the middle. He looked every bit the king of the gods again.

Zeus stroked his beard and grinned when he saw me. He whispered something to Queen Hera, in the throne on his right. Then he clapped his mighty hands together and the hall of the gods fell even more silent.

"Gryllus," Zeus boomed with thunderous heartiness, "you are the first pig to set foot here in Olympus. Is our humble abode to your liking?"

"Very . . . roomy," I shouted.

"We owe its continued existence to you," said Zeus gravely. The assembled gods nodded agreement.

"Can I ask a question, your . . . er . . . worshipfulness?" I piped up.

"Any," boomed the king of the gods. "Although I make no guarantee that I can answer it." He laughed heartily at that one. No one else seemed to think it was all that hilarious, but everyone made an effort to smile. Here on Olympus, Zeus was boss.

I took a step forward. All the queries in my head had crystallized into a single question. "Well . . . what happened?"

Another laugh erupted from Zeus, and his massive pearly choppers flashed like lightning. "You saved the Cosmos, Gryllus! Chaos is defeated! Somehow or other, the Chariot of the Sun created a blast that sealed the rip in the world. Don't ask me to explain how."

"Excuse me, I can help there," called a reedy voice. Several dozen pairs of immortal eyes turned on Thales, who was looking exceedingly frail and mortal. His Persian-style trousers, though no longer torn, still looked in need of a good ironing. "You see, it was the fusion of hydrogen atoms in the sun that—"

"Shall I decapitate him now, Father?" demanded Ares, clearly unable to hold his tongue any longer. The god of

260

war leaped to his feet and drew a sword that was as long as a canoe, halfway out of its scabbard. His immortal face was purple, and a large vein pulsated on one side of his divine forehead.

"That won't be necessary, thank you, Ares," said Zeus with the no-nonsense tone of a parent telling a toddler not to redecorate the walls with chocolate pudding. "Thales' ingenuity did allow Chaos to imperil the Cosmos, but it also helped us to save it."

"I've got another question," I pressed on. "What about Thanatos? What did you do with him?"

The king of the gods pointed to a table at the back of the great hall. He was here! Thanatos was here in the hall of the gods! Not surprisingly, the cowled figure sat alone.

"No one can be blamed for following their essential nature," Zeus pronounced. "If you have a job to do, there's no shame in trying to get it done in one fell swoop."

The cowl of Thanatos nodded in slow acknowledgment. He was nothing if not committed to his job.

Zeus held up a hand to quell the babble of comments in the hall. He turned to Apollo and nodded. The god of light shifted uneasily on his throne as he looked to Sibyl with a smile as sheepish as a lamb cutlet.

"Well, um, we'll overlook your breach of ceremonial etiquette back there," he said. "Under the circumstances. In fact, I'd like to offer you a promotion at the temple."

Sibyl crossed her arms. "What, to Assistant Assistant Pythia-in-Training?"

Apollo threw a nervous glance at the other gods. "No, no, to Pythia-in-Chief. You'll be the most important person in the temple."

Sibyl's face broke into a huge grin, the most carefree one I'd ever seen on her young face.

"Thanks," she said, "but no thanks."

Several nymphs and satyrs tittered, and a few river gods (known for their conservative outlook) gasped at the sheer impudence of this mortal. Apollo's immortal lips flapped, but no words came out.

"I've decided I want to do more than just predict the future," Sibyl explained. "I want to go out and help *make* the future."

Apollo flushed red, but Athena nodded proudly and murmured, "You go, mortal girl."

Zeus gave me a solemn look. "As to our other hero," he began, "in honor of your bravery, Gryllus, I have decided to make you immortal."

He bent down and swept up a handful of dust in his mighty hand. For just an instant he seemed as eager to please as a little puppy (assuming it was an all-powerful puppy that could smite you with a thunderbolt if you didn't scratch it behind the ear).

He walked to an arched window, blew into his clenched fist, and then hurled the dust up into the nighttime sky. Moments later, a new configuration of stars was twinkling down on us from afar. It didn't look too much like a pig to me, but the assembled deities let out an "ooooh" of appreciation.

"Henceforth this constellation shall be known as the Fat Porker,"* declared Zeus. "In this way, your name will live forever."

It took me a moment to work out what he meant. "So . . . you're not going to actually make ME immortal or anything. Just name a new constellation after me?"

Zeus's face darkened just a bit. "There are rules even we gods must obey," he said. "That *is* okay with you, isn't it, Gryllus?"

And the weird thing is—it was. It really was!

"What are you smiling at?" demanded the king of the Olympians.

It was hard to explain. "It's just . . . it's funny seeing you like this, so high and mighty. I mean, I remember when you were running around a hillside with your little bum on show, shouting 'Bek! Bek!' Well, *you* were doing the shouting, of course, your bum wasn't, but—"

"Enough!" Zeus's eyes flashed angry lightning. Far-off thunder rumbled, though not far off enough for my liking. The entire hall froze and concentrated hard on not bringing themselves to Zeus's attention. They looked as if they'd had a lot of practice.

And then Zeus's face broke into a grin once more. But here's the thing—the warmth of that smile wasn't quite enough to thaw the chill of the glare that came before it.

*The constellation the Fat Porker was later renamed Ursa Major (the Great Bear) by the Romans when Emperor Nero took the celestial presence of an enormous fat pig in the nighttime sky as a personal insult.

263

That icy glare had gone on long enough for me to realize one thing: as far as the king of the gods was concerned, all debts had been repaid. He was done with the world of mortals. He and I would not be meeting up to reminisce fondly about our adventures over a cup of cocoa.

"Let us not dwell on the past," Zeus proclaimed grandly, "when we should be celebrating." He looked at the young bearded god on the throne at the far end. "Dionysus, do the honors, would you?"

The god of wine sat up as if he'd been paying attention all along, honest, and not in fact nursing a hangover. He waved his vine-covered stick and shouted, "Eat, drink, and be merry, for tomorrow we *don't* die!"

EPILOGUE

A battle-scarred hero contemplates an uncertain future.

When the Olympian party was over, it was Athena who took us all back down to the mortal realm. Apparently Zeus was too busy, what with roaming monsters to sort out, temples to rebuild, thunderbolts to hurl, and so on.

I got the picture. We'd served our purpose, saved the entire Cosmos, and now it was back to our old mortal lives. Thank you very much, don't summon us, we'll summon you, and don't let the temple door hit you on the way out.

We said our farewells to Athena overlooking the sea. At

Sibyl's request, the goddess of wisdom had brought us to the coast, near the Gulf of Corinth. Above us, the Chariot of the Sun followed its usual course. The sea sparkled and seagulls wheeled across the blue sky, unaware that all of existence had been on the chopping block.

The goddess of wisdom's eyes followed them as she spoke to us. "You have helped the gods learn a bittersweet lesson," she said sadly.

"How's that?" said Sibyl. "I mean, Zeus didn't really die, did he? None of you did, because you all came back. So how did you learn anything about mortality?"

"The real lesson is one the other gods will only under-stand far from now, and it is this: one day the Cosmos will crumple in on itself like a bad soufflé. On that day, everything will return to Chaos—even we Olympians," said the goddess. She smiled at the expression on my face. "Don't look so glum, Gryllus. *You'll* be long dead by then."

"That cheers me up no end," I said.

"We gods will have fallen silent by then, anyway," con-tinued bright-eyed Athena, glancing at Thales. "Once mortals realize they can do things for themselves, they won't have much time for us Olympians." Disbelief was stamped on Thales' face, but the first scientist looked guiltily at his feet, poking out from the bottom of his flared trousers.

The goddess took off her battle helmet and shook her dark hair free. "In the meantime, we gods will continue to laugh at the foibles of humanity for some time to come," she said.

"That's better than having them clobbered," I observed. "My foibles are very sensitive. I'm well known for it."

The goddess of wisdom sighed like someone with her work cut out for her. "And what of you, Gryllus?" she asked. "What have you learned from your journey?"

I gave the question a bit of the old deep, analytical thought. "Well, you know, for me I'd have to say it was a trip of personal and spiritual discovery."

"Oh yes? And what did you find out?" asked Athena.

"Well, let's see. . . . I don't have the digestive system necessary for too much excitement. . . . I am quite fond of fish sticks. . . . Um, what else? . . . Reading can actually be useful in certain situations . . . and one more thing. . . . I . . ."

"Yes?"

I caught Sibyl's eye. The prophetess (retired) was nodding as if she knew what I was about to say, or at least what I *ought* to say. (Perhaps she did—she had only just retired from the professional prediction business.)

When I finally spoke, my voice was strong and true.

"I . . . don't want to be a pig anymore."

The goddess of wisdom was smiling broadly. "There's hope for you yet, mortal."

And then, in the blink of an eye, she was gone.

Part of me was disappointed that Athena hadn't just snapped her fingers and said, "Hey, presto!" to transform me back into a human there and then. I suppose I knew that it couldn't work that way. Circe was the one who had turned me into a pig. I would have to return to her island to be turned back.

But Athena had done all she could to help. When we wandered down into the port, we discovered a ship being readied for the voyage. Turns out the goddess had materialized in front of the terrified captain and ordered him to sail to wherever we told him.

The ship would be ready in a couple of days, which gave us a chance to bid farewell to Thales. He had decided to return to his native city of Miletus. But he wasn't going alone. Gladys would be going with him.

"I'm getting too old to be a spirit of vengeance," she explained. "Besides, I want to find out about this bright new scientific future of his." The two of them exchanged sideways glances that suggested a growing affection that went beyond scientific matters.

As they left, they looked just like any other elderly couple, except perhaps for their daring choice of clothing (beige cardigan and bell-bottoms, respectively).

That just left Sibyl and Homer, and both decided to sail with me. After all those years cooped up in a temple, Sibyl wanted to see the world, and a trip to Circe's island was as good a place to start as any. As for Homer, he had this idea that he'd sail on to Ithaca and try to find Odysseus so he could interview him for an epic poem he was planning.

The journey took several days. The seas were as calm as a duck pond—courtesy of Poseidon, Lord of the Seas— and we had a perfect following wind the whole way—

courtesy of Boreas the Wind God. (There are some perks to having friends in high places.)

It was Homer's idea that I should use the time to record for posterity the true account you hold in your hands. I just rattled off what happened, and Homer scribbled it all down. He really wanted to spruce it up with fancy poetic language and put the whole lot into hexameters, but I put my hoofed foot down on that one. As far as I was concerned, he could save all those little tricks for his own projects.

It felt good to have set down on paper everything that had happened, but as we neared the end of our voyage, my thoughts became concerned less and less with the past. Finally I worked up the nerve to tell Sibyl what was on my mind. I found her sitting at the ship's prow.

"Sibyl?" I began. "I know you're starting a new life now, but . . . do you still get glimpses of the future? In dreams and that? Because, if so, I was just wondering what you see . . ."

Sibyl turned, and I knew her eyes were looking at the real me. They saw my "inner pig." Then she drew a deep breath and her eyes fluttered shut.

"Let's see. . . . One day in the future, the world will be a place of peace, love, and harmony," she said.

"It will? Honest?"

Sibyl's eyes opened. "I haven't got a clue, to tell you the truth, but it's not such a bad idea, is it? Probably need to bash some sense into an awful lot of heads first." She smiled and looked back out to sea.

At that moment Homer rushed up to us. "Look!" he cried. He struggled to remember the nautical terminology: "Er . . . land ahoy!"

It was true; there was a distant smudge of land out beyond the prow. I recognized the tree-lined ridge that rose from the sea like the spine of a sleeping monster. It was Aeaea, Circe's island (short on consonants, long on magic).

Homer began scribbling notes furiously on a new scroll of papyrus. He muttered something about capturing the image before he forgot it.

"What have you put?" I asked.

Homer read back his notes. *"Aeaea — distant smudge of land; tree-lined ridge like spine of monster."* He crossed a word out and wrote again. "No, make that *sleeping monster.*"

"That's good, that is — very descriptive," I said. "I might put that in my version."

I looked once again at the island, the saltwater wind making my piggy ears flap like sails. For just a second the excitement in my heart stiffened into anxiety. I turned back to Sibyl.

"Seriously, though, you can still make a guess about the future, can't you? What's *really* going to happen, do you think?"

The Junior Assistant Assistant Pythia-in-Training (retired) just grinned toward the tree-covered isle.

"Gryllus, my friend . . . when it comes to the future, who knows?"

Glossary of Terms
for Barbarians Who Can't Even Speak Greek

Achilles: Greek warrior in the **Trojan War**; killed when an arrow struck him in the heel, his only weak spot, after he ignored a prophet's advice to wear protective twelve-eyelet boots in battle

Aphrodite: Goddess of Love and Beauty

Apollo: God of the Arts, Healing, and Prophecy; associated with the sun

Ares: God of War, well known for dreaded battle cry "Who you lookin' at, pal?"

Artemis: Goddess of the Hunt; twin sister of **Apollo**, associated with the moon; usually accompanied by her three hounds, Tigros, Leonas, and Henry

Athena: Goddess of Wisdom; born when she sprang out of **Zeus**'s head; city of Athens named after her

Charon: Minor god who ferries the souls of the dead across the River Styx to the Underworld

Chimera: Monster with the head of a lion, body of a goat, tail of a snake; not recommended as a household pet because of its tendency to try and eat mortals

Circe: Minor goddess who often turned unsuspecting visitors to her island into animals

Cyclopes: Race of disgusting, one-eyed, carnivorous giants

Demeter: Goddess of Harvests and Crops

Dionysus: God of Wine (and Heavy Partying)

Erinyes: Divine spirits who wreak vengeance on wrong-doers; also known as Furies

Gryllus: A noble hero, dashingly handsome; provided invaluable support services during the **Trojan War**; accompanied **Odysseus** on part of his journey home before striking out on his own epic adventures; winner of the Corfu All-Comers Pie-Eating Contest five years running

Hera: Queen of the Gods; wife of **Zeus**

Heracles (Roman name, Hercules): Strongman and demigod who completed twelve legendary tasks

Hermes: Messenger of the Gods; so fast in his winged sandals that he once got home before he'd even left and got into an argument with himself

Homer: Author of epic poems *The Iliad* (about the **Trojan War**) and *The Odyssey* (about **Odysseus**'s long journey home after the war)

Marcus: Okay, not actually a god, hero, or monster; old pal who also served in the **Trojan War**; winner of the Crete All-Comers Pie-Eating Competition six years running; was promised that he could appear some-where in these scrolls

Muses: Nine goddess daughters of **Zeus**, responsible for inspiring creativity

Nymphs: Female nature spirits:

    Dryads: Tree nymphs

    Naiads: Water nymphs

    Triads: Criminal organizations; okay, not, in fact, nymphs at all

Odysseus: Greek warrior in the **Trojan War**; his journey home to Ithaca is recounted in **Homer**'s *The Odyssey;* renowned for his cunning in getting out of tricky situations (His brother Greg was even more cunning—he never went to Troy in the first place, claiming he had "a touch of the sniffles.")

Olympus: The mountaintop home of the gods, located in northern Greece

Omphalos: Giant stone considered to be the Navel of the World; major tourist attraction at Delphi

Pan: Woodland god with goat's legs and horns; might have been a more successful deity but unable to stick to anything (hence Homer's description of him as "nonstick Pan")

Poseidon: God of the Seas, brother of **Zeus**; identified by trident, seaweedy beard, and smell of sardines

Pluto: Lord of the Underworld, **Zeus**'s brother; also known as Hades

Sphinx: Monster with the body of a lion, wings, and a human face; has an annoying habit of asking tricky riddles, then killing those who can't answer

Stymphalian birds: Fearsome birds with razor-sharp metal beaks and wings; not recommended as a household pet for mortals who prefer to keep all their fingers (for example, piano players)

Thanatos: The embodiment of Death; not really one of the gods, who don't like to have him around much (understandably)

Trojan War: Lengthy conflict between the city of Troy

and the assembled armies of Greece; the Greeks wanted to get back Helen, who was married to Menelaus but ran off to Troy with Paris, thereby inventing the soap opera

Wooden Horse: The Greeks ended the **Trojan War** by offering this "gift" to the Trojans, who weren't bright enough to guess that Greek soldiers were hiding inside the horse's belly; Odysseus is usually credited with the idea, although in fact he was greatly influenced by a mentor figure within the ranks of his own troops (see entry on **Gryllus**)

Zeus: Father and King of the Olympian Gods; given to hurling thunderbolts when grouchy

Note from the Translator

I first came across the so-called *Pig Scrolls* in a disused basement room of the British Museum, where they were incorrectly filed as a directory of Ancient Athenian hairdressers. At the time my thoughts weren't entirely on discovering priceless ancient manuscripts—I was looking for the bathroom. However, as soon as I spied the scrolls, the pressing biological urgency of my visit was set aside for a loftier purpose: that of bringing this invaluable document of preclassical Greece to the attention of scholars.

The work was long and arduous, not to mention quite hard. More than once I felt as though I was lost in the very sands of Time, wandering the eternal shores of History without even a pair of flip-flops to protect my feet. One thought alone kept me going: in translating this treasure of antiquity, I would help this unrecognized author take his rightful place among the masters of the Ancient World.

Paul Shipton

ACKNOWLEDGMENTS

The author would like to express his gratitude to Homer, Plutarch, Thales, and Aristotle—thanks, lads!

Every effort was made to ensure the accuracy of the material, though the great library at Alexandria *was* closed on the Tuesday afternoon the author tried to go there.

Short-listed for the Nestlé Children's Book Prize,
the epic adventures of Gryllus the Pig continue in . . .

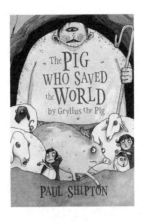

The Pig Who Saved the World

by Paul Shipton

Turn the page for an excerpt. . . .

BOOK I

The past is another country (except the people there still speak Greek and you can drink the water).

"So, what's it like being back, then?"

I placed a tentative hoof onto the rocky ground of Aeaea, unsure how to respond to Sibyl's question. Excitement and nerves were arm wrestling in my heart, and it was a toss-up which would win. It's not easy putting a jumble of feelings like that into words. Luckily the gods have blessed me with an uncanny ability to find the perfect turn of phrase:

"A little freaky."

You could hardly blame me. The island of Aeaea was the only place in the civilized world where I might be turned from a pig back into the fine figure of a man I had once been. It was hard to think about anything else. Throughout the voyage here, I had lovingly built up a mental picture of my new life as a reinstated member of the human race. I'd find myself a nice little island and open up a pie shop, and then I'd lead a nice quiet life with absolutely no dangerous adventures.

Hold on a sec—you *do* know I was a pig, right? When I said that I put a hoof on dry land, that wasn't some fancy-pants poetic metaphor. It was a real hoof on the end of a real pig's leg, namely mine.

Don't go thinking I was just any old pig, either. I was the

An excerpt from *The Pig Who Saved the World*

one-and-only PIG WHO SAVED THE WORLD! (For full details, go and ask your village storyteller to recite the first set of *Pig Scrolls*. Then, if you want to send me a postcard as a thank-you for your continued existence, go right ahead.)

Homer clambered off the ship next. The young poet waded gingerly ashore, holding his sandals in one hand and the hem of his tunic in the other. He gave the wooded interior of the island a wide-eyed stare, no doubt cooking up some la-di-da poetic description of the trees that lined the beach and how foreboding they looked.

Admittedly, there *was* something a bit unnerving about the darkness through those trees.

"So . . . where's Circe's palace?" Homer asked breathlessly.

"Through the dark, creepy forest, then turn right at the nightmarish dead tree stump."

Sibyl was still on board, waiting to confirm plans with Captain Simios, who was currently yelling lots of nautical instructions to the crew. They hopped to it, dropping anchor and tying knots and doing many other things of a technical, maritime nature that I won't describe here, not because I don't understand them; I just don't want to take up valuable scroll-time going into unnecessary detail. So that went well.

While she waited, Sibyl called down to me and Homer: "You should gather some of that plant you told us about, Gryllus. What was it? Moly. We'll need some, and we should leave some with Captain Simios too. Just in case things don't go according to plan."

I responded with the no-nonsense nod of a can-do pig. We *were* on the island of Circe the enchantress, after all, and there's no telling what someone like that will do. Though she wasn't one of the actual Olympians, Circe *was* a divine immortal; she was capable of powerful magic, and she wasn't afraid to use it. A little green plant called moly was the only thing that could protect a person against her powers, so it made sense to stock up.

"Shake a leg, Homer," I said. The pimply teenage epic poet followed me up the beach to the outer edge of the woods. We had to go in a little way past the tree line, but we kept the ship in sight at all times.

"Here's some." I thrust my snout at a clump, and the young poet knelt and pulled the plant up.

"How do you know this stuff works, anyway?" the pale lad asked.

"It was the god Hermes," I explained. "He came and told my old captain, Odysseus, all about it."

The usual spark ignited in Homer's eyes. He got this way whenever there was talk of immortal gods and legendary heroes. If you ask me, that boy needed to get out more.

"Then what?" the epic poet urged me.

I did my best to put him off with a few monosyllabic grunts, but the memories of my first visit to this island came crashing back.

Of course, I had been human when I first trod these shores—a member of Odysseus's crew. We had been on our way back to Ithaca from the Trojan War when we landed here, lost and in need of fresh supplies. Our heroic leader

An excerpt from *The Pig Who Saved the World*

organized a party to explore the island's interior. I could still picture the captain's rugged face as he growled, "Might as well take Gryllus."

I manfully ignored the groans from the rest of the scouting party. (Hurtful as they were, these came as no surprise. I had always been more of a heroic outsider than a team player, more lone wolf than social animal. Or, in the words of my first-grade teacher, I "didn't play well with others.") So that's how I ended up tramping to the middle of the island, even though my military record specifically said that I was excused from such duties on account of flat feet.

It was a long, hard walk. But just as I was urging the group to listen to reason and turn back, the land leveled off and we stepped into a clearing. We found ourselves gazing at a sumptuous palace set back in tastefully maintained grounds, and there were wild animals everywhere—bears, lions, stags, that sort of thing—all just wandering around. The beasts made a lot of noise when they spotted us, but none attacked.

That's when Circe emerged from the front door. She swept back her raven hair and smiled. It wasn't so much a "Come in; why don't I get out some chocolate chip cookies and put the kettle on?" sort of smile. More of a "Looky, looky, here comes fresh meat" sort of smile.

The leader of our group started prattling on, invoking the rites of hospitality observed throughout the civilized world. Circe smiled and nodded, but I don't think she was listening to a word. Then she raised this big wooden staff in her hand and pointed it right at us like a loaded bow.

I tried to dodge, but it was no good. A bolt of light shot out of

An excerpt from *The Pig Who Saved the World*

the staff and wrapped itself around us. I was on fire, as if every last bit of me were being changed and mixed and smushed. It felt like being deep-fried.

It wasn't just me, either. The panicked squeals of my comrades filled my ears—filled my piggy ears, that is. Yes, Circe had turned us all into pigs!

Well, unless Zeus has seen fit to bounce a thunderbolt off your head, you know the rest—how Odysseus, armed with his bag of moly, came to the rescue. How, once she realized that the captain was immune to her spells, Circe agreed to turn the other crew members back into humans. And how, while all this was going on, I hid, having chosen to remain a pig at that time.

"Here's what I don't understand." Homer was cradling enough of the plant in his arms to serve moly salad to a small army. We were making our way back to the ship. "Why? Why did Circe turn you all into pigs?"

"Who knows? Perhaps her mom and dad didn't let her keep a pet when she was little."

Back at the ship, Sibyl had disembarked and was telling Simios that we'd return before darkness. The grizzled captain jerked a thumb back at the crew and said something along the lines of "Oshur de ladz'll len jan, eh?"—which I *think* was an offer to have some of the crewmen accompany us and help. (The captain's thick Corinthian accent was a formidable barrier to communication. When you also threw in his fondness for seafaring lingo, I was left taking random guesses at what he was going on about.)

Sibyl shook her head in apparent understanding.

An excerpt from *The Pig Who Saved the World*

"Thanks, Captain, but I don't think anyone can really help with this."

WHAT? One of my core beliefs in life is *never, EVER turn down an offer of assistance.* But before I could voice my concerns, the captain fixed his salty old sea dog's stare on me.

"Eh, dinna liv tall upta scurra, reet og," he said (possibly).

As usual, I fell back on the same answer I'd used throughout the voyage whenever the captain addressed me: "What's that? Oh, terrific, Captain!"

The seaman's eyes darkened beneath bushy gray eyebrows. I hoped he hadn't just told me that his dear old mother had perished on these very shores.

Sibyl quickly defused any tension by having Homer pass up a bundle of moly to Captain Simios and the rest of the crew.

The priestess turned to me. "Right, then. Are you ready?"

A tremor of anxiety trotted through me, but I reminded myself that anxiety had no place in one to whom the entire Cosmos owed a hearty vote of thanks. I squinted up and in a cool, heroic fashion drawled, "Sibyl . . . I was born ready."

At least that's what I would have said if a gust of wind hadn't blown sand into my eyes. Blinking rapidly, I stepped into a rock pool, where a crab seized the opportunity to nip me on the ham hocks. I had to make do with a startled howl, but it was still sort of cool and heroic—just not in the traditional way—and I think they got the gist.

An excerpt from *The Pig Who Saved the World*

BOOK II

Magical powers are no guarantee of a tidy house.

OK, here's what was supposed to happen:

We'd march at a sprightly pace up to Circe's palace, taking the opportunity to get a little fresh air and exercise along the way. We'd arrive to a warm, completely unmysterious welcome from the enchantress—perhaps something along the lines of "Hello, Gryllus. Back for a little retransformation, are you?" Then she'd add, "Oh and by the way, thanks ever so much for saving the entire Cosmos. Very decent of you."

Cue lots of magical stuff involving mystical staffs and multicolored light shows and open-mouthed gasps of wonder, etc., etc. And then, once I was human again, it'd be time for a bang-up feast, with steaming hot pies all around and several pints of honey wine to wash it all down. Brilliant!

And that's what *would* have happened if there were any fairness in this Cosmos. I mean, is that too much to ask for?

Apparently—and the theologians among you can take note—it *is*. For one thing, the hike to the center of the island was much harder than I'd remembered. Sibyl was the only one who lived up to that whole "marching at a sprightly pace" idea. At least I wasn't the only one struggling. Homer had clearly spent too much time thinking up rhymes and not enough time building up his leg muscles at the local gymnasium.

An excerpt from *The Pig Who Saved the World*

As we trudged along, my mind grappled with weighty matters. This was hardly surprising. After all, had I not looked down on the Earth from the Chariot of the Sun itself? Not a lot of pigs can say that. OK, not a lot of pigs can say anything—but my point is, this sort of experience will get even a pig-of-action like me thinking about the meaning of it all.

Philosophy, that's what they call it. *The love of wisdom.*

Well, I love a lot of things, most of them involving pastry. However, I had decided lately to make room in my ample heart for wisdom as well. Seeing as how I had saved the Cosmos, I was determined also to understand the *point* of the Cosmos.

Sibyl noticed the look of intense philosophical thought on my face.

"What's up, Gryllus?" she asked. "Got indigestion again? I've told you time and again: *breakfast is NOT a competitive event.*"

"No, no. I was just thinking . . ." I cleared my throat. "Life's a bit like this, really. You know, sort of an uphill struggle, through the woods, and . . . and you're not even sure what you'll find when you get to the top, and you try to avoid all the stinging nettles but you still get stung, so there's an itchy rash up the back of your legs and, and . . ."

If I could just focus, I felt I might nudge my brain toward some important truth about this thing we call life. Unfortunately, the brainbox was digging its heels in.

"Know what I mean?" I ended weakly.

As a teenage poet, Homer was no stranger to fumbling

attempts to define life and its meaning. He tried to nod his head in sympathy while at the same time shaking it in confusion. The result was an unusual bobbling motion.

However, a former priestess like Sibyl, more used to the practicalities of temple work, was having none of it.

"Don't think so hard, Gryllus," she advised. "This wouldn't be a good time for your head to go *pop*, now would it?" (Astonishingly, this was Sibyl trying to be friendly. The timetable at the temple in Delphi must not have devoted much time to developing interpersonal skills.)

Still, no time to dwell on such matters, because the unbroken sunlight up ahead told us we had reached the plateau at the island's center. We were almost at the palace of Circe. Within minutes I would be resuming my true human form.

Sibyl entered the clearing first, and right away she let out a gasp. I found out why when I nosed my way past the trees.

When I had been here the last time, Circe's palace looked pretty impressive. Admittedly, not as grand as the marble palaces of Mount Olympus (which I saw not long after *I saved the entire Cosmos,* in case you didn't know), but definitely a nice starter home for the minor deity on the go.

Not anymore. Where once the adjectives *magnificent* and *sumptuous* had jumped to mind, they were now elbowed aside by tougher words like *ruined* and *dilapidated.* One whole wing had collapsed into rubble. The rest of the place looked in need of a lick of paint and several decades' worth of tender loving care. No animals wandered across the unkempt lawn now. As we neared the building, we soon realized there was no Circe in residence either.

"*Not* how you remember it, I assume?" said Sibyl. She spoke softly, but her voice seemed loud in the silence that lay over the entire place, not like a nice warm blanket of silence but more like a funeral shroud or something equally creepy.

"Hell-oooo, Circe!" I shouted. "Are you here, your mystical enchantressness?"

"It's too quiet," said Homer as he stepped carefully over a pile of rocks. "It feels . . . ominous. I don't like it."

"I don't blame you," commented Sibyl. She was already gathering kindling and twigs, which she expertly propped together into a cone shape in the shelter of a low stone wall. She sparked a flame with her flint, and soon we were looking into the yellow-blue flames of a small fire.

"O gray-eyed Athena," Sibyl called in invocation as she sprinkled a secret blend of herbs and spices (all from her trusty backpack) onto the flames, "we humbly ask your assistance."

Sibyl had been a priestess in the temple of Apollo, but recently she had formed a closer bond with his sister, the goddess Athena.

However, the gray-eyed goddess did not appear now. Instead, a rasping, disembodied voice rose from the flames: "The deity you have invoked is not available to take your prayer at the present time," it groaned. "At the sound of the moan, leave a brief message stating the purpose of your

An excerpt from *The Pig Who Saved the World*

entreaty and giving details of the offering you intend to make." This was followed by a ghastly moan and then an expectant hiss.

Sibyl's only response was to kill the flames with a handful of dust.

"Who was *that*?" asked Homer.

"Not a *who*, a *what*," explained Sibyl. "Hephaestus, the Smith of the Gods, created an automaton that would pass on messages to the Olympians when they were otherwise occupied."

I nodded knowledgeably. "Like when they're on the toi—"

"When they're busy doing ANYTHING else," snapped Sibyl. (She had become a lot friendlier of late, but here was a glimpse of the old Sibyl—the one about as friendly as an alligator with an attitude problem and a full set of choppers.)

"Sorry," she muttered.

"Why didn't you leave a message?" Homer asked.

Sibyl's eyes took in the desolate ruins around us. "Because I've got a bad feeling about this place and I would like to talk to one of the Olympians *right now*." The slight wobble in the former priestess's voice didn't do much to set my mind at rest. Sibyl's old temple job had involved predicting the future—when *she* had a bad feeling, it was worth paying attention.

"I'm going to see if there's a temple somewhere in the palace," she said. "That might get a stronger signal through so that I can make contact with the Olympians. In the

An excerpt from *The Pig Who Saved the World*

meantime, why don't the two of you just . . . er, just have a rest. Don't do anything, OK? Don't *touch* anything."

Young Homer nodded sheepishly. Me, I nodded piggily—I don't need to be asked twice to do nothing.

After Sibyl had disappeared inside the palace, I scanned the area for somewhere more comfortable for a bit of a well-earned rest.

"This way," I instructed the young poet. "The moss looks nice and springy over here."

"Shouldn't we wait right here?" Homer cried. "Sibyl said not to do anything. . . ."

I shook my head. "Homer, Homer, Homer," I said, the seasoned hero imparting hard-won wisdom to yet another small-town kid with big dreams. "I think I can be trusted to make a few decisions for myself, don't you?"

An answer was too slow in coming for my liking, so I added, "Look, we're just going to sit down! We can do nothing just as well over there!"

Though not completely convinced, the epic poet followed. I slumped down on the moss. I have always been able to think things through more clearly when horizontal—something to do with the flow of blood to my larger-than-average brain.

"OW!" said a small, muffled voice.

"Er, Gryllus? I think your . . . rear end just said something," said Homer in bewildered alarm.

It was true—the voice *had* come from my other end (the one not traditionally associated with the gift of speech)!

An excerpt from *The Pig Who Saved the World*

This was an odd development, no question, and dozens of thoughts tumbled through my mind about what it might mean in terms of my day-to-day life. I'm well known for looking on the bright side, but I could think of few situations in which having a talking bottom appeared to provide much of an advantage.